I0653710

OFF BOOK

REUTS PUBLICATIONS

OFF BOOK

A LITERARY ADVENTURE

JESSICA DALL

Cover design by Ashley Ruggirello
Cover art Copyright 2015 oghammoon/insan-stock/jurgasan on DeviantArt.com

ISBN: 978-1-942111-13-9

REUTS Publications
www.REUTS.com

To Niles, for his love of all things meta.

Chapter One

THE BELL RANG. STUDENTS POURED OUT OF CLASS-rooms and into the hallway. Eloise ducked through the horde, pushing herself against the far wall to avoid the worst of the human stream.

"Eloise! Eloise! Eloise! Eloise!" The voice echoed over the students and down the long hallway.

Looking over her shoulder, Eloise smiled at the mass of curls barreling toward her as they ducked around the larger students and nearly took down some of the younger ones along their approach.

Columbine slowed, sliding a little on the tile as she came to a stop just in front of Eloise. Her hair continued forward, and she had to push the dark curls out of her face.

Eloise laughed. "What's happened? I haven't seen you this excited since you found out you could get a Johnny Chess album shipped here."

Columbine didn't wait for Eloise's critique of her musical taste. "I got it."

Eloise's smile dropped. "You got it?"

"I got it," Columbine repeated, holding her hand up.

Eloise stared at the envelope. It didn't look any different than any other white, government-issued letter—no confetti or ribbons like there should have been. Eloise looked back up slowly. "When did you get called in?"

"Haven't opened it yet." Columbine turned the letter over in her hands, looking at the pressed wax seal that sat on the back of it, the raised letters "OAT" the only identifying marks to say it came from the Office of Assignment and Transport. "I'm too nervous. I think we should go up to my room, get a lot of chocolate ready just in case, and dissect every word in it."

Eloise just nodded, linking arms with Columbine as they moved toward the doors of the School.

"Have you gotten yours yet?" Columbine tore her eyes away from the letter, forcing her arm to drop nonchalantly to her side.

Eloise frowned. "You know I haven't."

"Well, you're bound to get it soon," Columbine covered, adding a certain nod for good measure.

"I don't know." Eloise shook her head. "I'm starting to think I might just be destined to be Forgotten."

"Oh, don't talk like that." Columbine shoved Eloise lightly. "You're much too pretty to be Forgotten. It's always the average ones that get passed over. You could be, like, a love interest at least. Or some bitchy prep in a bad teen boarding school story. Those are still hot, yeah?"

"A prep school villain pushing twenty?" Eloise raised an eyebrow.

Columbine pursed her lips. "You could still pass for younger. Maybe it will be some twist that you're actually too old to be in high school, but you came back to try to relive your glory days."

Eloise snorted.

"Tell me that doesn't sound like a story."

"Since there's an entire trope called Older Than They Look—"

Columbine waved off the rest of Eloise's analysis. "You see? That just proves it. Prep school novel, population: Eloise."

"Right." Eloise rolled her eyes. "Because Eloise is *such* a popular name these days. We both know the best I could have hoped for was to be in a children's novel.

I mean, the last Eloise picked up was seven. I'm at least a dozen years past my expiration date."

"Oh, you're only looking at the MC list. I'm sure there are plenty of Supporting Character Eloises storied out there."

"Easy for you to say. An interesting name and a birthmark on your neck shaped like a star? Of course you're interesting enough for someone to pick up. Maybe even as a *Main* Character. I'm beyond generic."

"Plenty of people have birthmarks." Columbine brushed her away. "And my name? Some bad associations, I hear, up in the author's world. Nobody wants an MC named Columbine."

"Well, someone obviously picked you." Eloise grabbed the letter from Columbine's hand, nearly pushing them into the doorframe with the momentum. "You never know with the *avant garde*. They like uncommon names. Remember Philomena?"

"That was historical fiction."

"All the same, there's an epidemic of trendy names lately." Eloise held the envelope up to her forehead like a carnival swami. "I see you being cast as the beautiful daughter of some international spy who ends up being caught in a government conspiracy. The *avant garde* are always writing about government conspiracies, you know."

"I hope I'm in a fantasy novel." Columbine took the envelope back, looking at the seal like it would tell her the answer. "I always thought I would be an awesome wizard."

Eloise pursed her lips. "I think girl wizards are called witches."

"Whatever. Same difference. Amandine got picked up in a fantasy novel," Columbine said, words seeming to fall out of her mouth as soon as she thought of them. "She's a nymph now."

"MC?"

"SC," Columbine said. "But I mean, still, she's a goddamn nymph."

"Well, I suppose a children's novel is out." Eloise smiled, opening the door to their dormitory. "What with that kind of language."

"Maybe I'll get to be a vampire." Columbine didn't bother to respond to the comment on her language choices, following Eloise into the new hallway. "Vampires are very in right now. *Trés chic.*"

"Last thing the world needs is another crappy vampire novel." Eloise sighed, then paused to look Columbine over critically. "Though, you've got the coloring for it. Very Anne Rice, you know, the dark hair and pale skin . . ."

"I think I would be a kickass vampire." Columbine dodged an old couch someone had pushed out into the hall again. "And I personally *like* vampire books, thank you very much."

Eloise tried it out. "Columbine, vampiress. I could see it. You think you'd be okay with having to drink blood for the rest of your life though?"

"Eh, I'd survive. As long as the author didn't go full monster on me."

Eloise smiled to herself, letting Columbine's arm go so they could fit through the thin door that led to Columbine's small, poster-covered room.

Sitting on her bed with a dramatic thump, Columbine studied the envelope as an artistic shot of Eleanor Hibbert watched Eloise from the far wall. So, Columbine had finally replaced the old, raggedy one she'd had of Nora Roberts.

Columbine turned the letter over once in her hands, then suddenly held it out with a jerk. "I can't do it. You open it."

Eloise forced her eyes off the young woman in the poster and looked at Columbine. "You sure?"

"I'm too nervous." Columbine shook the letter, urging Eloise to take it.

Eloise sighed and grabbed the envelope, fingers working their way under the flap. A last look to make sure Columbine didn't want to do it herself, and Eloise broke the gold seal on the back, clear across the middle.

"What does it say?" Columbine bounced nervously.

"Give me a second. My crystal ball's at the cleaner's." Eloise unfurled the letter, clearing her throat officially as the writing came into view. *"Dear Columbine, succession number 63: You have been asked to join the assignment panel at the Office of Assignment and Transport on this coming Friday in room 651 at eight in the morning—"*

"Yarg, eight?" Columbine made a face.

Eloise nodded but didn't pause. *"—for assignment* . . . yada-yada-yada, instructions, be sure you are on time, bring ID and all that stuff. *We look forward to meeting you and assigning you to your upcoming manuscript. We do our best to* . . . random quality statement about how they're *really* looking out for our best interests. *We wish you the best of luck in your future, undoubtedly . . ."* Eloise laughed.

"What?" Columbine frowned.

"Just . . ." Eloise looked up with a smile. "Honest to God, it says *'undoubtedly well-written piece of literature'* -*The Assignment Panel.*"

"It could be well-written," Columbine argued.

"It's the 'undoubtedly' I find hilarious." Eloise held the letter out for Columbine to take. "Have you seen some of what they try to pass off—?"

"Room 651." Columbine looked at the paper, ignoring Eloise's critique of modern literature and running her eyes over the page quickly. "That's the Fantasy room, isn't it?"

"Fantasy and Sci-Fi," Eloise agreed, sitting next to Columbine on the bed. "Maybe you will get to be a vampire."

Columbine's brow creased. "God, I hope it isn't Sci-Fi. I don't understand space travel at all. There's always goddamn space travel in Sci-Fi."

"Not always," Eloise said. "Science Fiction means that there is a scientific explanation, rather than a fantastic one, behind any element the author—"

"You lost me at 'scientific.'" Columbine locked her eyes on the paper in front of her.

"Anyway," Eloise let the rest of her explanation go, "you don't have to understand anything. The author does."

Columbine remained silent, lips pressing together tightly. She finally looked back up, face serious. "You'll have to tell me the second you get your letter, Ellie. Even if I'm in-story. Send an email so I can see the timestamp with the exact minute you got it."

Eloise shook her head, resting back on her hands. "I wouldn't worry about that. I'll likely still be here by the time you get back."

"Ellie." Columbine sighed. "You're, like, one of the smartest people to ever come through here. Everybody says so."

"Doesn't make me any more interesting, story-wise."

"Well, it's not up to you to be interesting. The author can just add all that once you're in-story."

Eloise clenched her jaw, looking back at Mrs. Hibbert on the wall. Columbine always did love being surrounded by authors. Daydream fodder, Eloise had to assume. All of those staring eyes, though . . . they made Eloise's shoulders tense. They taunted that whatever author she'd originally appeared for had forgotten her story not long after she'd shown up on the School steps, knowing nothing but the fact that she was "Eloise." That she was Eloise, and that she was waiting for a story. Just like every other student to ever appear from nowhere. She forced her eyes back to Columbine. "Even if I do get a letter, I'll *maybe* be an mSC. And that's if I'm lucky."

"Don't be so morbid." Columbine rolled her eyes. "But even if you are a *minor* Supporting Character, maybe that's for the better. Henry ended up getting to be a Main Character, and his new parents were killed off within, like, three pages. Didn't even get a chance to get to know them."

"Yeah." Eloise nodded slowly. "But as an mSC you run a much higher risk of being a Red Shirt. Remember what happened to Sylvia? Was supposed to be in and out, maybe ten pages on the job, and then she had a motorhome land on her because some author decided they wanted to rip off *The Wizard of Oz*."

"Well, that's a risk all of us run." Columbine shrugged. "Do you think it's better to just be one of the

Forgotten? I mean, you can hardly see half the Teachers here anymore. No one knows their names. Soon, the next wave is going to fade off. Personally, I'd rather be flattened by a motorhome than go through that. At least people will remember you as the motorhome girl."

"True." Eloise nodded, doing her best not to think about the ghosting Teachers. It didn't always start at the same time, but at some point, as the years ticked by, it happened to them all. Thirty or eighty, those Forgotten by their authors began to fade. Ice ran down Eloise's spine as she felt her remaining time ticking away. She did her best to ignore it, mouth moving with the first thing she thought of. "Do you remember our Teacher from when we were seven? I saw him the other day. He's completely see-through now. He can't be more than forty, and I could make out the writing on the poster hanging on the wall behind him. He's about two shades away from ice."

Columbine scrunched up her nose as she tried to think. "I guess I remember him. Like, a little. I don't think he even had a name back when we had him, did he? He was already just 'Teacher.'"

Eloise pressed her lips tightly together.

"You're going to get your letter." Columbine touched Eloise's arm. "Don't worry."

Eloise forced a smile, shaking it off. "But this is your day. No need to have me glooming it up. You have to call me the *minute* you find out where you're going."

"You're my first call," Columbine agreed.

"I'm going to miss you." Eloise's false smile faltered. "You aren't going to be down the hall anymore."

"Oh, it could be weeks before I'm needed." Columbine shook her head. "You're not going to get rid of me that quickly."

"It still means your School days are over."

"Stop it," Columbine said. "You're going to make me cry."

"We can't have that. You're supposed to be the fun one."

Columbine threw her arms around Eloise before Eloise could react. "I'll write whenever I can. I promise."

Eloise nodded, not bothering with what Columbine would no doubt ignore as pessimism.

"Do you want to stay and watch a movie or something?" Columbine asked.

"I have homework." Eloise shook her head. "*I* still have to pretend I give a crap about classes."

Columbine frowned, but nodded.

Eloise smiled, said her goodbyes, and walked down the hall to her door. She and Columbine had lived five doors apart for as long as Eloise could remember, having appeared within days of each other, both approximately age three. Now, Columbine would be moving out while Eloise remained—watching all of the Chosen leave. After all, only the pre-storied lived in the dormitories.

Eloise pushed the door open and dropped her bag on the ugly mottled carpet, not really caring where it landed. Flopping onto her old mattress, she lay back, staring at the gray plaster ceiling as she waited for the bouncing to stop. Brier gone, Columbine nearly out the door . . . Eloise would soon be out of friends. A couple years, and they would move her down with the Teachers. Being assigned after twenty-two was rare, as authors just aged anyone in-story as necessary after that point. Eloise's stomach knotted.

And being assigned after twenty-five, well, that was unprecedented.

Sitting with a huff, Eloise tucked her feet under her small frame, resting her elbows on her knees as her blonde hair shielded her from the rest of the room. She pushed it back, suddenly wishing she could cut it without it growing right back to its place just below her shoulders within the day. Those pale blonde ringlets with her large blue eyes likely hadn't helped her any as far as becoming storied. They made her look like a classic Damsel in Distress. Sadly, those were no longer a literary staple.

Someone knocked, making Eloise start. Snapping halfway out of her pessimistic haze, she pushed herself off the bed with a grunt, the squeaking springs covering it easily.

The man looked down at her from outside the door, scowling for a moment before he held out a plain, butcher-paper-wrapped bundle. "You got a package this morning."

"Thank you." Eloise took it as the man stalked off toward the staircase. Shutting the door again, she peeled the white card off the top and moved back into her room, throwing the package on her bed.

Eloise,

My story finally finished after a couple years of writer's block. I thought you'd like a copy to see what I've been up to. I got a backstory and everything. You should come by and meet my "parents," if you ever get out to the Houses. We're in SC352. Basically, you go into the SC neighborhood and just start walking. We're on the left. We definitely need to catch up.

Hugs and Kisses,
Lil

Eloise sighed and pulled the letter box from under her bed. She folded the paper up to keep it from floating off course and dropped it, barely letting it settle before kicking the box back into place with the heel of her foot. She turned her attention to the brown package. It wasn't large, probably a short novel, maybe even a novella. It had just taken a long time. Author had probably left them sitting around for who knew how long.

She picked the tape off and pulled out the bound white pages. "*The Fall Leaves by Kathy Brown*" sat on the first page in severe, black type, the Recording Office's seal at the top.

Kathy Brown again.

Eloise recognized the name, flipping through the rest of the pages to see the familiar style— short paragraphs and a lot of dialogue. Kathy Brown had been writing a lot lately, and had been doing her best to keep her reputation for killing off her MCs. Apparently, Lil had made it through with her life, but somebody in that story had undoubtedly died. All in all, Lil didn't seem too scarred by the experience.

"*William Blake stared at the leaves outside the window of his Brooklyn brownstone.*"

There it was. Eloise frowned. William Blake: formerly William, succession number 41,059. He had been added to the list of people who died in the line of duty. It seemed getting an MC gig with Kathy Brown truly was about as good as getting a death sentence.

If she got a letter assigning her to a Kathy Brown novel, would that really be better than fading away? Dying in a story couldn't be that awful, unless the author gave you some flesh-eating virus or something sadistic like that, but *knowing* you were going to die? The anticipation would probably be worse than the actual death.

Eloise flipped through the rest of the manuscript before setting it on the shelf with the other ones old friends had sent her. She sat back down on her bed. As much as she wanted to be happy for everyone who had finished their stories, and to properly grieve for those who had died in theirs, she couldn't fight her jealousy that they were past the waiting and worry. The waiting was the worst. And with the way things were going, she'd probably be waiting up until the day she faded away.

Chapter Two

WITH COLUMBINE GONE, THEIR CLASS WAS DOWN to five. Give it another year, and it would likely be two. If that. And more likely than not, Eloise would be sitting in that very last year of classes alone. Spending her time doing a "research project," or whatever useless busywork they gave twenty-two-year-olds in a last-ditch attempt to pretend the School hadn't entirely given up on them. After that came the "student teaching," and then the long descent into nothingness that was being a true, over twenty-five Teacher.

Eloise's eyes drifted back up to the Teacher at the front of the class. Still mostly solid, the woman didn't look up from the book in front of her, voice nearly inaudible as she mumbled about some post-modern author or another. By twenty, the curriculum really was scraping the bottom of the barrel, apparently. The thought hit Eloise's stomach. Hard. Nearly knocked her breath out of her.

She was going to be stuck teaching these same damn stories over and over again. Teach them, while also having to watch new children grow up and leave for their own stories. And all of them would end up calling her "Teacher" until the day she ceased to exist. How that would be anything but a hell of Sisyphean proportions, Eloise couldn't imagine.

"Eloise?"

She snapped out of her thoughts and looked to the Teacher at the front of the room as one of the School runners, who had apparently snuck in silently, retreated.

The Teacher held out the paper, her normal-volumed voice nearly sounding like shouting after the mumble. "The Principal has asked to see you."

That didn't help Eloise's stomach at all. Still, she nodded and slipped her book into her bag. Slinging the bag over her shoulder, she walked slowly into the deserted hallway. Twenty years old, and the walk to the Principal's still felt no different than when she'd been reprimanded for fighting at six. Even if that entire mess really had been Columbine's fault.

The Principal stood up from her mahogany desk and offered her hand as Eloise entered. Eyebrows furrowing at the oddity of it, Eloise still did her best to recover, shaking the Principal's hand quickly. She could only hope the all but dark room, lit only by a few buzzing halogen lights which were long past their heyday, hid her confusion.

The Principal continued to smile, returning to her seat. "Eloise, I hope we're not taking you away from anything."

"Nothing important," Eloise answered, perching herself on the edge of the thread-worn chair closest to the door.

"How are you?"

"Fine, thank you," Eloise said, mentally urging the bland pleasantries past as quickly as possible.

"No letter yet?"

Eloise's hand gripped the fabric of her skirt, bunching it as she forced a tight smile on her face. "No, not yet."

"Well, nothing to worry about." The Principal took a manila folder out of the pile she had on her desk. "Your file has been pulled a couple times by the OAT. I'm sure they'll match you to your story sooner or later."

"Of course." Eloise clipped her words short.

The Principal nodded and pulled a paper out of the folder. "But, on the off chance that they don't, have you ever considered working with the Recording Office?"

Eloise raised her eyebrows, the question not fully registering for a moment. "I'm sorry?"

The Principal turned the paper toward Eloise with a nod.

Eloise read it and frowned, nothing about the situation fully making sense. "They want me to . . . ? I thought they only took MCs and SCs at the Recording Office?"

"Well." The Principal sat back, tenting her fingers. "Some of our past students have found places over there. One has just taken over as the Head of HR and requested to see some of our students' coursework. It seems he was very impressed with yours. He thinks you'd make a wonderful recorder, even without the life experience."

Eloise worried her lip, attempting to not look as skeptical as she surely did. "I didn't know they were even allowed to take pre-storied at the RO."

"It has been cleared with the Council as a special exception. Why don't you take a more thorough look at that and tell me what you think."

Eloise nodded slowly, holding the paper limply. "Thank you."

"Do you have any questions?"

She looked at the letter for a long moment. It wasn't *the* letter, but it would get her out of the School all the same. Even if it most likely was poorly concealed charity. Was she truly that desperate?

Oh, who was she trying to kid?

"If I did take this job," she glanced at the Principal over the top of the paper, "where would I live?"

"You could, of course, keep your room here, if you would like. We could get you some form of transportation back and forth. Some of the Science Fiction storied have brought back hovercrafts, but cars are still big in town. I'm sure we could get you one to bring you back and forth. Or, if you would like, we could look into finding you a room near the offices, but that would have to go through the Council again."

Eloise pressed her lips together and looked back at the letter. "Thank you. I'll be sure to look this over."

"Let me know when you've made your decision. They're expecting to hear from us within the week."

Eloise nodded and returned to the hallway with a mumbled goodbye. Half-turned toward her class, Eloise changed directions at the last second, heading for the dormitory. With the paper currently in her hand, what was one missed class?

The empty, middle-of-the-day halls gave her the privacy to make it up to her room without small talk. She set the letter on her bed and took her cell phone off silent. It woke with a start, beeping at her. *1 missed call.* She flipped it open and the screen flickered to life. *1 Voicemail.*

She glanced at the letter on her bed, then back at her phone. The letter would keep. She pressed the call button and brought the phone to her ear.

"You have, *one*, new message and, *four*, old messages," the electronic voice told her. "*First* new message."

Columbine's voice came over the phone. "Hey, Ellie! Call me when you're out of class."

Eloise smiled at the continuation of the chronically vague messages Columbine had a habit of leaving. It was like the woman was always so excited to get an answering machine, she couldn't stay on the phone long enough to say anything of substance.

Eloise sat on the chair by her desk and pulled a leg under her, pressing the call button, waiting for Columbine to answer. "Hey, it's me."

"Hey!" Columbine said brightly. "Shouldn't you still be in class?"

"Got out early." Eloise pressed the power button on her old computer to give it time to warm up. "What's up?"

"I'm in a sci-fi."

Eloise lifted her eyebrows, but nodded. "Worse gigs, I'm sure."

"Oh, and I'm an alien."

"Yeah, you look like one." Eloise laughed, hitting the side of the clunky monitor as it flickered unhappily. "Your skin isn't turning green or blue or something, is it?"

"Shut up. No, it's not. If anything, I'm, like, getting paler."

"Paler than you already are?"

"Shut up." The rustle of paper crinkling sounded a little too close to the phone as Columbine shuffled something around on her end. "They gave me a back-story. Want to hear it?"

"You know I'm writhing with jealousy, don't you?"

"Yes," Columbine said, the smile evident in her voice, "but do you want to hear?"

"Shoot." Eloise sighed.

"Well, apparently, I was a member of a humanoid race that was wiped out on a not too distant planet by some warrior tribe."

"Intense," Eloise said. "How did you escape, pray tell?"

"Apparently, I was at school off world."

"Oh, of course. And you were the only person, or alien, or whatever, who was studying off world?"

"Yeah, the Plot Bunnies attacked the author before they were fully grown, I think."

"Well, there hasn't actually been an original plot in a couple hundred years, you know. If you distill everything down into The Seven Basic Plots—"

"Yeah, I remember your, whatever, presentation thing on that."

"Really? Because you slept through half of it." Eloise hit the monitor again as the screen flickered with red and green stripes.

"So, what's up with your life?"

"Same old, same old." Eloise let Columbine change the topic, bending to reach the connector cables. "Trying to get my computer to cooperate. And the Principal is getting me ready to spend the rest of my life unloved and alone."

"Stop being a drama queen. You know you're going to get your letter."

"The School obviously doesn't think so."

"What do they know?" Columbine brushed it off. "They think everyone's doomed to be at the School, like, forever because they are. Do you think we could get dinner? I'm moving out tonight, and then I'm going to be God knows where in space, so I doubt I'm going to get cell reception. We need to have a goodbye dinner."

"That was quick." Eloise froze, fingers half into a mess of cords.

"Yeah, the author isn't much for planning, apparently. What's it called? Pantsing, or something?" She didn't give Eloise a chance to respond. "Food?"

Eloise pulled her hand back, words barely wanting to come. "Yeah, of course."

"Great. See you at the dorm."

Eloise nodded as Columbine hung up without a goodbye. She glanced at the paper still sitting where she had set it. An invitation out of the School. With at least a little time to plan. Not like this. So last minute. Eloise cut the power to the malfunctioning computer altogether, snatching the paper like it would bite if she didn't catch it unaware. Columbine would be moving on with her life—living whatever life her Pantser author gave her. Perhaps it was time for Eloise to move on with hers.

Chapter Three

ELOISE SWALLOWED, LOOKING AT THE LARGE OFFICE building. After the years she had spent among the white, gray bricks that monopolized the School, the mirrored windows of the tall building were nothing short of intimidating. The morning sun glinted off the windows, turning them silver and making Eloise squint.

Did she really want to go in? The butterflies were starting deep in her stomach. She hadn't felt them in years, but there they were, like they had all hatched after sleeping for a decade.

She straightened her skirt and took a step toward the building. The doors slid open at her approach. Hesitating for a split second at the unexpected movement, she recovered, taking a deep breath as she moved into the large, airy lobby.

The receptionist looked up from her modern desk, the top seeming to be freshly polished stainless steel from the way it glinted. "Welcome to the Recording Office Pavilion. How may I help you today?"

Eloise moved toward the desk, her borrowed heels clicking noisily on the marble floor. "Hello, I have an appointment with Mr. Marley."

"Name?" The receptionist picked up an equally shiny clipboard.

"Eloise."

"Eloise . . ." she prompted, running her finger over the board.

Her cheek twitched slightly. "Just Eloise."

"Oh." The receptionist looked Eloise over. "Right. You're *that* Eloise."

Eloise nodded with a tight smile. "That's me."

"Here's your pass." The receptionist slid the laminated card across the desk. "Mr. Marley's office is on the top floor. Elevators are straight back. Don't stare."

Eloise frowned. "Stare at what?"

"Mr. Marley is . . ." the receptionist started, her words trailing off. "Well, you'll see."

Eloise nodded shortly, fighting off the nervous urge to pump the woman for information. "Thank you."

She walked by the desk and pressed the button to call the elevator. The gold doors opened to reveal a glass carriage, letting her watch as it sped her toward the seventieth floor. Playing with the hem of the blazer the School had given her, Eloise watched as the ground got further and further away. She released a shaky breath. Columbine had to be terrified on a spaceship, if this was how Eloise felt after just fifty-some stories. The elevator slowed to a halt and chimed, the doors sliding open.

Suddenly, the receptionist's warning made sense. The name Marley clicked in Eloise's head. She had never really considered what happened to people who became ghosts in their stories. But if Mr. Marley were any sort of barometer, they were gray and see-through for the rest of their lives. Dread hit her stomach; maybe she would be picked up, but as a ghost of some girl in a haunted house. Her name had peaked, when? 1920 in the author-world? Plenty of time to say she had been a ghost. Eloise swallowed nervously.

"You must be Eloise." Mr. Marley cut into her thoughts. Standing from behind his large desk, he offered his hand.

She glanced down at the gray fingers, doing her best not to show her hesitation in touching them. At least the man wasn't wrapped in the chains Eloise recalled from *A Christmas Carol*. The tailored charcoal suit offered some sense of normalcy. She forced herself to offer her hand in return. Though not quite hitting something solid, her palm didn't pass straight through. She still didn't quite trust a full grip, though, shaking his hand once before dropping it again. "Very nice to meet you, Mr. Marley."

"Please, have a seat." He motioned to the square leather chair on the door-side of his desk, his words sounding particularly proper in his British accent.

Eloise did as she was told, alternating between watching him and looking at her hands, trying to tread the careful line between attentive yet not staring.

Mr. Marley picked up what looked like Eloise's school file. "I trust you've been told a little about what we do here?"

Like anyone at the School didn't know what happened at the Recording Office. "You keep copies of all the manuscripts being written."

"And more and more every year, it seems." Mr. Marley sighed, flipping a few pages in the file. "Your grades are very impressive, I must say."

"Thank you . . . sir." Eloise bit her tongue, the honorific feeling awkward in the modern office.

It didn't seem to register with Mr. Marley one way or the other. He kept his eyes on the file, silence stretching on as he read. Finally, he set it down and stood once more. "We've recently had an influx of new projects we need recorders to watch, you see. Perhaps you've seen an uptick in Assignments at the School?"

Eloise forced something like a smile as her hands clenched in her lap. "I haven't been keeping track."

He motioned for her to follow him, his gray form seeming to float even though his feet connected with the wood floors. "Anyway, it is our job to keep an accurate account of what is happening to those in-story. If we don't have recorders overseeing the manuscripts being produced, we would have no way to know if someone needs to be marked as having died in the line of duty, or if they've just dyed their hair, you understand?"

Eloise nodded, stepping back onto the elevator as Mr. Marley pressed the button for a floor a good few dozen down.

"It is a relatively simple job," he continued, moving into a long hallway. "Each office is equipped with both a television monitor and a computer, which are connected to in-story feeds. You will be able to hear what is happening; it is your job to ensure the computer is recording the words correctly. Do you believe you can do that?"

"Of course." Eloise did her best not to sound affronted.

He nodded, stopping in front of an open door. Motioning for her to enter, he remained in the hallway. "We have a desk set up for you there. If you have any questions, you can ask Kaitlyn down the hall. Welcome to the Recording Office."

Eloise gave another tight smile, watching him go before she looked back at the room. With no large windows like in Mr. Marley's office, the space was as dull gray as the ghost himself had been under the halogen lights. No glass or stainless steel here. Still, her stomach flipped as she moved toward the desk, seeing a much more modern computer than anything she had ever used at the center of it. She leaned to look under the desk, not finding a tower at all. The way the wires ran from the flat screen to the wall, she could only imagine that was the entire computer. And it still took up less than half the space her malfunctioning monitor in the dorms did. The television sat on a stand by the desk—that, at least, was a little more familiar with its protruding back—her name along the bottom. She ran her fingers over the engraved letters before looking at the matching gold plaque at the top. *Working Title: Life in New York.* She took the words in before stepping back to look at the relatively large screen. Pressing a couple buttons along the bottom, she waited to see what would happen. The screen stayed blank. She frowned, trying a couple more.

"Hey there."

Eloise spun at the voice, almost knocking into the stand. She glanced back, ready to steady the TV if it threatened to tip, before looking at the tall, dark-haired man standing in the doorway. She opened her mouth, took a second to recover, and hopefully managed it before she looked like a complete idiot. "Hi. Sorry. I was just—"

"Rumor had it we were getting a new recorder." He smiled, his straight white teeth coming into view. "Thought I'd drop by and introduce myself. I'm Barnaby."

Her eyebrows creased before she could stop it. "Barnaby?"

"Yeah, yeah." He sighed, leaning against the door-frame. "Historical Fiction. Stupid name. You are?"

"Oh." She hesitated briefly before holding out her hand. "Eloise."

He moved forward to take her hand, and she realized how tall he really was. Standing directly in front of him, she was forced to tilt her head uncomfortably far back to see his face.

"We haven't seen many Eloises around here," Barnaby said, then paused. "Well, except for 'at the Plaza.' You aren't—"

"No," she cut him off. "No, I'm not."

"Thought I'd ask." He shrugged. "Maybe someone did a sequel and aged you up. So, they've stuck you on the New York project now."

Eloise blinked at the change of topic, then looked back at the monitor when it clicked. "Oh. Yeah. I'm not really sure . . . Mr. Marley didn't really go into detail about how to . . . start."

"Yeah, well, he's been a little . . ." Barnaby waved his hand away from his head in an out-of-it sort of gesture, "since he finally found someone who could get rid of all the chains and stuff. Dela thinks he still has to focus a little too hard on not having his jaw drop open all the time without the bandage. But it's really not hard. You don't even have to press anything anymore. They put a new program in so the TVs turn on automatically when someone starts writing, so you don't have to worry about it. And if your author's anything like mine, you're going to have a lot of downtime."

"What?" She glanced from the monitor back to him.

"My author's had writer's block the last few months, so I've been spending most of my days bothering everyone else who's actually trying to work." The bright smile returned.

Eloise opened her mouth and tried to think of something to say. "Sounds like a nice gig?"

He shrugged. "I got bored sitting around home all day, so I got a job. Now, I'm bored sitting around work all day."

"More people around here to bother, I'm sure?"

"True," he said. "Very true."

The monitor blinked to life, the computer following suit, loading a document without being directed. It started typing:

New York par tees have not changed much cents the time when the English kicked the Dutch out of the city. There a time to see and be seen, a time to scope out the newly single . . .

Eloise stared at it, moving closer to watch the words seemingly type themselves. She sat on the black swivel chair, eyes never leaving the screen. "That's . . . really cool."

"Personally, I prefer dialogue." Barnaby moved behind her. "I never got used to some disembodied voice describing everything I did. Still sort of creeps me out."

Eloise tried to think of an answer that didn't make her sound entirely clueless.

He continued before she could. "But you get what you're supposed to do, yeah? You used to have to type everything, back in the dark ages, before they put in voice recognition. Saves a ton of time this way, but it obviously still has some bugs. So you just highlight anything wrong." He reached over her and selected *par tees*.

"And replace it."

Parties appeared in the typo's place, Barnaby typing quickly, even one handed, from his odd angle behind her.

"Seems simple enough." Eloise waited for him to pull back before she began to type herself, correcting the text easily. The television continued to speak, detailing the party taking place in a stunning New York apartment. Eloise glanced over, but instantly regretted it as she saw the equally stunning characters milling around in evening gowns and tuxes. Maybe she hadn't completely thought this through. Now, she wasn't teaching people who were going to go off and have lives. She was watching people who already had lives in progress.

She caught another typo nearly before the program had finished typing it. Yeah, she was definitely moving up in the world.

"You're quick."

Eloise jumped, nearly forgetting that she wasn't alone with her thoughts. She glanced at the man still standing in the same place behind her, watching over her shoulder. Releasing a breath, she tried to ignore the awareness of having him there. She pushed a piece of hair behind her ear and stared at the screen. "It isn't that hard. I was actually the best in my class in editing."

"I take it that was pre-story?"

Eloise froze, glad she wasn't looking at him as she recovered. She pressed her lips together, fixing a wrong *there* before answering. "Yeah. Pre-story."

Thankfully, he didn't ask any follow-ups. "We're all getting some drinks after work tonight. Office thing. Care to join us?"

"Oh." She finally turned away from the computer to look at him. "Well, I wouldn't know anyone—"

"You'd know me." He laughed. "And it would be a good time to meet everyone else. They are your coworkers."

"I don't really drink much."

"So nurse a beer or something." He shrugged with a smile. "We're not going to force you to do shots, if you don't want to."

She still hesitated, instinct saying it was a bad idea to spend more time around the actually post-storied than necessary. Especially potentially drunk time.

"Come on," he urged. "It's not often we get new blood around here. We could use it. Believe me."

She shifted, the combination of his dark eyes and easy charm suddenly seeming much more persuasive than she might have liked. She nodded, scratching her neck to cover the flush she felt rising there. "All right. What time?"

His smile widened. "We all meet down in the lobby at five. Just head down when you're done for the day."

Chapter Four

Eloise stumbled back into her room much later than she had intended. Apparently, it would be easier than she had previously thought to avoid talking about her . . . situation, even when a little buzzed. Okay, a little drunk. She giggled to herself, doing her best to recall the night. She hadn't had so much fun since back when they'd had enough people to have parties at the School.

It was nice to be out with people again. Even if those people all assumed she was like them. Post-storied and bored.

Eloise sat with a loud thud in her desk chair and looked at the old computer sitting there. Of course now, it had decided to turn on. Not like she had been trying to get it to work for a week. She went to kill the power, but then paused.

An email sat open, waiting for her. She frowned, looking around the room. The door had been locked. No one should have been able to get in. And why someone would want to break in just to read her emails was beyond Eloise. She hardly controlled state secrets. She shook her head, her slightly intoxicated brain too clouded to bother trying to figure it all out. She blinked, trying to bring the words into focus.

Hey Ellie!

I found a way to connect to the gen. network when the author isn't writing—apparently I have computer skills now. Yay author?—so I thought I'd check if I could get an email through. Hopefully this doesn't tear a hole in the universe or something, but I think that's a slim enough chance that I'm going to try. If we all die, well, my bad.

It's weird *hearing the author's voice talking about what you're doing. "Columbine looked over the glowing panel and pressed a series of buttons, sending them into hyperspace." No wonder MCs in Epics come back looking like* their minds have turned into mush. Living with narrative for nine hundred pages would be enough to make anyone insane. I'm surprised more people aren't in the Hospital.

In other news, I thought it would amuse you to know that the author is apparently making me a virgin. And made a point to say it. I know, right? Well, I suppose what everyone says is true—what happens pre-story, stays pre-story. Though, I still think the authors are pervs. They're always so hung up on our sex lives. And that one manuscript Scott was in? I hope to God, if I do become a romantic interest, the author can write a sex scene better than that half medical analysis/half bad porn dialogue. I suppose we'll see.

But you don't want to listen to me spout on about sex forever—as far as I know, at least. Have you gotten your letter yet? If you have, you have to let me know ASAP. Seriously, I need to know where you're ending up. I bet it won't be space, but still. If you haven't, I'm sure it will be there soon. Don't get all depressed on me, since I know that's where you're going if you haven't. You're not allowed to do that when I'm not there to cheer you up.

Ugh, the ship is powering up, so I guess we're going to start going again soon, but I'll be back later. The author never writes for more than an hour at a time, so there's plenty of downtime. I hope this gets to you fine and doesn't, you know, end the world as we know it.

Love you, hon. Hope this gets to you, and that I hear from you soon!

Columbine

Eloise yawned. Her head slumped against her hand. It was too late to respond. And who knew if her computer would get it back to wherever Columbine was. Better to wait until she was back at work anyway. She rested her forehead on her arm, closing her eyes. She'd move to the bed in a moment. The desk was just too comfy.

Chapter Five

ELOISE TOOK A SIP OF THE DARK, STRONG COFFEE, eyes locked on the document on her desk. Someone walked past the office door. Eloise started, pretending to stare at her blank monitor. Whoever it was didn't stop. Releasing a breath, she set the mug down, hesitating for just a second before she flipped another page over. Should she be reading it? Perhaps not. But even with the lingering guilt, she couldn't stop herself.

Catherine blushed as his body came out of the water, the droplets sliding down his muscular chest to his tapered waist, but she couldn't take her eyes off him. She had never seen a man in the nude before, and he was something to behold—tanned and muscular, with a line of hair . . .

"Hey there."

The voice made Eloise jump and flip the manuscript over to hide it. "Barnaby!"

The man in the doorway smiled. "Didn't mean to scare you. What were you reading?"

"Oh, nothing." She shook her head, trying to fight off the heat rising in her cheeks. "I was just . . . passing the time. My author's MIA again."

"Right." He smirked. "That's why your face is on fire?"

"It's just warm in here." She attempted to shuffle the papers away.

"Right," he repeated, snatching the manuscript from her. "*The Duke's . . .*" He paused, stared at the typeface on the page, and then looked back up at her.

"I looked you up." She blushed to a point she didn't know was possible, feeling it reach her ears. She drew her shoulders up, trying to disappear into her torso. "I didn't know you were in one of *those* books. You just said historical fiction."

He nodded. "How far along are you?"

"Far enough to have had a very thorough, um . . ." She bit her lip, glancing down before she caught herself and forced her eyes back to his face. "Far enough?"

He continued to nod, leaning back against her desk.

"It's actually not bad writing," Eloise continued to babble. "Especially for erotica."

"Erotic Romance, technically." He glanced at the manuscript, expression more amused than upset as he looked back at her. "You know, you could have just asked."

Eloise swallowed and tried to force her shoulders back down to something normal. "I'm sorry. I'm a chronic researcher. You can ask anyone at . . . anyone I went to school with. I'm definitely better at that than with people skills. Obviously."

He sat in the chair at the empty desk behind her, flipping through the pages.

Eloise scanned his face. "You're not upset?"

He shrugged. "My life is public record. Same with all of us."

She tried not to think on it. "You're a duke?"

"From the nineteenth century." He motioned with the pages.

"You look good for your age."

He laughed. "Thank you."

Pressing her lips together, Eloise looked back at her computer screen. Everything was still sitting unhelpfully dark. Nothing to save her.

"You have another question?"

She looked back at him, eyebrows raised.

"You look like you want to ask something else."

Eloise hesitated, then shook her head.

He smiled. "What is it?"

Eloise prayed for a last minute reprieve from the monitor, and finally released a breath when nothing magically clicked on. She motioned to the manuscript. "*The Duke's Bride*. Are you married?"

Barnaby made a face, something between annoyed and laughing. "Catherine and I didn't last long post-story."

"Oh." Eloise swallowed, feeling the heat starting to rise back up her neck. "I'm sorry. I shouldn't have—"

"Don't be." Barnaby sat forward, smile back in place. "The author wrote us to be much more sexually compatible than romantically, it turns out."

"Well, that's halfway there I suppose." Eloise smiled uncomfortably.

He just laughed.

Eloise cleared her throat, scratching at the side of her neck. "I take it you don't hold stock in the theory that only an author can set you up with your true love then?"

"I'm pretty sure the whole One True Love thing is a trope someone came up with that just caught on. I'm not sure it exists outside books."

Eloise just nodded, looking away again.

"I take it you weren't a romantic lead."

She froze for less than a second, then shook her head.

"Well, you're not missing much there."

"No?" She looked back up, meeting his dark eyes. Situated in his uncomfortably handsome face, they were not doing anything to help her barely contained blush.

"Here, I can reenact the entire experience." He stood, taking her hands to pull her to her feet. "Basically, the narrative starts: *She walked into the room, and he lifted his head, spotting her across the ballroom in . . .* well, it doesn't really matter, it's always some frilly, overly romanticized thing. Use your imagination. *He stepped close to her, taking her hands in his and brought his lips down to hers.*" Barnaby tilted her chin to face him and pressed her lips to his gently. "And then there is always some overdramatic narrative about worlds colliding and stars exploding and . . . that's all there is to it, really."

She blinked, trying to recover, entirely certain she was once again as red as when he'd walked in. Perhaps it would be wise to stay away from Romantic Leads in the future. Or at least until she completely found her footing away from the School. She swallowed. "I, well, I can't say I've ever had a kiss that made planets collide."

"That's because planet-colliding kisses *certainly* only happen in novels." He smiled, stepping back to lean against her desk again. "It would be very dangerous for all parties involved if that was what happened every time people did. We'd have to have a national ban on kissing to protect the common good."

The laugh escaped before Eloise could register it. She placed her hand to her mouth as she recovered, dropping it to her side again self-consciously. "True. But figuratively even, most of my exes, pre-story of course, were all pretty crap kissers."

"None of them were written to be good." He shrugged easily. "I was."

She opened her mouth. The monitor flickered on behind them before she could get a response out. Of course, now that she didn't need it.

"Well, looks like you have work to do." He moved toward the door.

"You're just leaving?" She looked back at him.

"You know how it goes. Places to go, people to bother." He turned back to face her. "How about we get dinner after work? We can keep talking then."

She blinked, somehow keeping her mouth from dropping open like an idiot.

"If you're interested," he finished.

The words came out before she could properly think about them. "Are you asking me out?"

The corners of his eyes crinkled with amusement. "Five-thirty, in the lobby?"

"That's not an answer to my question." She frowned.

"Six better? Need some time to pretty up or something?"

Eloise raised an eyebrow and gestured to her plain, business casual blouse and skirt. "You don't think I'm pretty now?"

"True, you are." He smiled. "Some time to do whatever women do to get dressed up then."

She wasn't going to make it back to the School and office in half an hour. Not that it mattered. She didn't have anything to wear that was better than her work clothes anyway. She caught up to her thoughts. She was actually considering going.

Bad idea, Eloise.

Opening her mouth to say "no," she looked back up at him. Met those eyes again. Her lips moved before she could stop them. "Five-thirty's fine."

"Great. I'll see you then." He flashed a final smile and left the small room.

Eloise watched him go, breath caught in her chest. What the hell had she just done? Sharp beeping cut into her thoughts, the computer screen flashing unhappily at her neglect. Taking a seat, she shifted the mouse to clear the alert and ran her eyes over what had already appeared before glancing at the television. Turning the volume up slightly, she settled in to watch the action.

Life in New York wasn't especially original or well-written, at least in Eloise's opinion, but it was cute. And after tamping down at least a little of her jealousy, it had been nice to see a little of New York. Well, at least the author's take on New York. Whether the author had ever been to New York, or seen more than a vague picture of New York once in their lives, was anybody's guess.

Another five minutes, and the narrative suddenly stopped mid-sentence. The characters on screen froze. Eloise's eyebrows knitted as she looked between the computer and the television. Just as she started to stand, the last few sentences on the computer highlighted and disappeared. She blinked, frowning as the people on the screen jumped back to where they'd been a paragraph ago. The computer cursor blinked for a couple seconds, and then the people on the screen started up again, this time with a new dialogue.

That had to be the most disconcerting thing in the world, having everything pause and rewind like that. It was awkward to even just watch. The people paused again, and then the monitor turned off altogether.

Eloise rolled her eyes. That was a whole lot of nothing. Glancing at what was left on the page, she rewrote a word, and then diminished the program. She sighed, looked at the TV, and then manually rebooted the computer screen to get to her emails. Before the program could even fully load, Columbine's message popped open. The screen flickered to blue a couple times, finally settling with an angry tone. Whatever Columbine had done to break through, the computer didn't seem to like it.

Eloise rested her chin on her palm, steeling herself to read.

Hi Ellie,

Apparently my author, after getting six chapters out, has gotten a case of writer's block. Believe me, it is the most infuriating thing in the world. At the moment, we're floating in the same goddamn place in space in a ship where half the doors don't actually work because the author hasn't created the rooms behind them yet. We're lucky he mentioned the bathroom in the captain's quarters or there would be real problems around here. I'm surprised we haven't started killing each other yet. Though it wouldn't really matter if we did. None of us can die if the author doesn't want us to.

This one girl here, Sandy, lost it the other day—not that she was the most stable person to begin with—and she jumped out the ship's airlock. I wasn't on deck at the time, but Kiplinger (the mechanic who, of course, is only referred to by his last name, originally James, I think?) told me they were trying to fish her out, but the second she stopped moving out in space (apparently your head doesn't actually explode) she reappeared, looking exactly the same and very much alive on deck. There's apparently no escape from the story until the author says you can go. It's scary. I wonder why more people don't warn you about it before you are Chosen.

Other than that, I've just been sitting around, trying to keep my mind off things. Honestly, I think people play up how great being in-story is when they get back from it. Or maybe, there's just a whole collective amnesia when you leave because you're just so happy to have it over and done with. I'll keep you updated if things get better, or if we ever get going again.

Much Love,
Columbine

Eloise stared at the screen for another moment, then hit the power with a jerk. The screen went black, the computer whirring softly as it shut down. She glanced at the manuscript still sitting on the other desk. It made her stomach twist. Standing sharply, she grabbed it, shoving the stack of papers into an empty drawer. She would have to return it to the records room sooner or later. For now, she would pretend it didn't exist. And if she could make it through dinner without discussing any more lives in-story, she would possibly survive the night, sanity intact.

Her mind flashed back to Barnaby standing in the doorway, the flush threatening to return.

Possibly.

Chapter Six

Barnaby took a sip from the wine glass in front of him and studied the woman sitting across the table. Though not as flustered as she had seemed this morning, she still hadn't said much since they'd made it to the restaurant. Even now, Eloise's face remained half hidden by the large red menu the waiter had handed her. Still, there was something fascinating about her. She was beautiful, of course—one of those typical beauties authors seemed to love writing. That had been obvious even under the harsh halogen lights in the office, and perhaps was more so in the low candlelight of the restaurant. But there was something more. Something he almost felt like he was missing as he watched her.

Her blue eyes slid up and met his over the menu. "What?"

Barnaby came out of his thoughts, leaning back slightly in his chair. "Just looking at you."

The menu lowered slightly. "Any reason?"

He tried to think of the answer, but only ended up shrugging. "You look beautiful. Do I need another reason?"

The menu lifted again as her eyes dropped, though the crinkle at the corners belied a hidden smile. "Are you this suave on all your dates?"

"Can't say I've been on a lot of dates."

She glanced up. "No?"

"We had a pretty messy divorce, Catherine and I." He swirled the wine in his glass. "It seemed wise not to jump right back into the dating scene."

She nodded, wetting her lips briefly as she finally set the menu down. "Why did you break it off? If you don't mind my asking."

He considered his answer. "You know how it is. Romance is much easier to keep alive when you have an author writing your relationship for you. Same with any in-story relationship, really. I doubt you've kept up with everyone you were friends with in yours?"

Her eyes widened slightly, the same troubled look he had noticed before flicking over her features for just a second before she managed to hide it. She gave a shrugged nod.

Barnaby paused, trying to understand whatever it was he'd missed. "Is something the matter?"

Eloise shook her head, opening the menu in front of her again.

He just watched, smiling as the silence began to stretch on. "You seem very interested in our dinner choices tonight."

"Oh." Her eyes moved up to his, the dim light almost hiding her blush. Almost. "Sorry. I was just thinking."

"About what?"

She hesitated, that odd, caught look sliding away as her pretty smile came back. "You're going to laugh at me."

"I laugh at a lot of things," he said, continuing when she didn't: "Try me."

She released a breath, then shut the menu with a definitive thump. "You know how we have at least a portion of our life controlled by the authors, yes? While in-story, we're stuck waiting for someone to write. And when they write, our actions are completely dictated."

He nodded.

"Well, when we write things, do you think we control the actions of whomever we've written? Like . . . this menu. I mean, I know it's only food, but do you think there's another step down from us? That the food doesn't actually exist there if they don't have it written down?"

Amusement started to work its way across Barnaby's face. He did his best to keep it down. "I'm not sure it works that way."

She shook her head, seeming to read his expression against his better efforts. "I told you you were going to laugh at me."

"I'm not laughing," he said, covering his mouth for a second before gaining full control over the threatening smile. "It's actually an interesting thought."

She looked at him. "You're humoring me."

"No," he insisted, "it is. I've never thought about it before. Perhaps there's a world populated with those who were written about by those of us who were writers in-story."

"Or writers post-story?"

Barnaby furrowed his eyebrows, running the idea over in his head. "Do you know anyone who's kept writing post-story? I can't think of anyone. At least, not writing fiction."

Eloise frowned, taking a moment. "Do you think there's a reason?"

"Can't say I've ever considered it."

Her eyes dropped as she nodded.

"We could take a field trip and try to find Jo March," Barnaby joked. "See what she has to say."

She gave him a small smile before changing the topic. "It must have been hard, waiting in School with a name like Barnaby. Not exactly popular."

"I guess." He didn't fight the switch. "Though I always sort of figured if someone had thought up a Barnaby at some point, they were going to use it. It's not the sort of name you forget about during outlining."

"But you go by Barnaby still. Not Barney or anything."

"I was never a fan of Barney," he said. "Some of my friends call me Fitz, though."

"Fitz?" Eloise raised an eyebrow.

"My author-given name is Fitzwilliam."

"Barnaby Fitzwilliam?" Eloise finally gave a real smile. "And your middle name has to be Percival or something, yes? All very English."

"We were set in Ireland, actually."

She hesitated. "You don't have an accent."

"Author was from Iowa, I think. Something Midwestern. Never wrote it in."

"Ah." Eloise's gaze flickered to the side, lips slightly parted in a way that seemed more contemplative than perhaps the information warranted.

Barnaby stared at her lower lip until he caught himself. He smiled and continued. "Every once in a while, there would be this really bad faux-Irish accent in the narrative when the author was trying to write phonetically. Luckily, she seemed to give up on that pretty quickly. But, hey, it's easier to be a duke when you come from someplace that actually has landed gentry."

Eloise nodded.

"Well, you know all about me now." He took a drink of wine. "You haven't told me anything about you."

The odd, wide-eyed look came back, just for a second as she took her own sip. She addressed the glass. "Only reason I know that much about you is because I'm a snoop and pulled your manuscript."

He smiled. "So you want me to find your manuscript?"

She laughed derisively, eyes still down. "Good luck with that."

"Obscure novel?"

She tipped her glass back again before answering. "You know, just one of those little high school dramas. Nothing special. And I'm hardly mentioned."

"Supporting Character?"

"Maybe even mSC," she said quickly. "The Recording Office may have bent some rules to let me work for them. I suppose my editing skills tipped the balance in my favor."

"Word is you're brilliant," he agreed.

She paused, eyebrows furrowing.

"Some of the higher ups were talking about you, and since I have nothing to do all day at my desk, I was listening—"

"You were eavesdropping?"

"Apparently, you're not the only snoop." He smiled. "Do you want me to finish?"

"Sorry." She made a motion across her lips like she was zipping them.

"Well, they were talking about you and nearly sounded shocked at how well you're doing."

"Shocked?" She frowned.

"What it sounded like." He shrugged. "Point is you're apparently brilliant."

"Or I'm exceeding low expectations."

"If they bent rules to get you, I'm going to assume they knew you were good."

Eloise just pressed her lips together. Barnaby guessed she was still relatively new to being post-storied; perhaps the fleeting, odd looks were simply her way of dealing with the jolt of coming back out. He could remember that a little too well.

He didn't force a response. "Have you always been smart? Or were you written to be?"

"I've gotten rid of pretty much any author-written traits."

He watched her, treading carefully. "I take it your story was bad for you?"

She kept her eyes on the table, lips pressed tightly together before she finally looked back up. "I suppose I still feel like I'm living on borrowed time."

His eyebrows finally creased. "From a high school story?"

"School can be hell," she said. "And authors can be sadistic."

He watched her, the hardness behind the statement catching him unprepared. "How so?"

"Well." Eloise's eyes flicked away, her hands clasping tightly. "Even just in general. Do you think Dr. Jekyll wanted to develop a dual personality? Do you think Mr. Marley wanted to spend the rest of his life gray and see-through? We are all tools authors use to perfect their art. They make us wait around for months, years, picking us up, killing us off, all for the purpose of getting *their* story told. And we have to put up with it because our entire existence is based on them giving us a story. We have no free will. Either you give yourself over and let those people do whatever the hell they want to do to you, or you're stuck in that damn School and left to fade away. If they want to break us, bash our heads in, slowly flay us alive, we just have to take it. It's like . . . I don't know. Mind rape. *Life* rape."

Barnaby took a moment, letting the words settle. "I didn't take you for one of the Disenchanted."

She blinked. "What?"

"You don't have the same look they do."

"What look is that?" Eloise shook her head.

"I've known some people who come back from their stories dead inside. You can just tell. All the hope is gone from their eyes."

She shifted uncomfortably. "And I don't look like that?"

"Not at all."

Eloise's jaw locked. She took a large drink from her glass. "You study eyes?"

Barnaby paused, not sure he was entirely willing to be drawn off topic this time. "You can tell a lot about a person from their eyes."

"Subscribe to the whole 'windows to the soul' cliché, then?" The bite in her voice slipped away as she seemed to push whatever was bothering her deeper. Whatever had happened, she'd at least been post-story long enough to develop that defense mechanism.

"I suppose," Barnaby answered, trying to think of a way to break back through. But he had to let it pass. Perhaps he'd been out of the dating scene for years, but deep soul-searching on the first date couldn't have come into fashion. He cleared his throat, trying to lighten the serious cloud that had moved over them. "You know, between the mouth and eyes, you can tell a lot about what a person is thinking."

"Have you studied deception techniques?"

"A little," he said, trying not to look surprised she would know. Perhaps brilliant really was likely. "I have to keep myself busy doing something all day."

She nodded, nearly looking distracted. "Expressions are interesting."

"And it tells you a lot." He smiled, unable to keep his own good humor from returning. "Like when I kissed you?"

Her eyes came back to his cautiously. "What about then?"

"Your nostrils flared just a little bit when I pulled away."

"My nostrils?"

"Just slightly." He nodded. "Which suggests you very much liked it."

She looked at him and let out a laugh. "You are a very strange man."

"I feel like I should point out that you're the one who agreed to go out with me."

She shook her head, smile fully back in place. "How long has your author had writer's block?"

Barnaby leaned back in his chair, not minding this change as much with her smiling again. "Three or four months now. He keeps writing a paragraph, then deleting it, and then writing a new one, then deleting it . . ."

"His characters must *love* him." Eloise tilted her nearly empty glass toward her as she glanced at it absent-mindedly. "My friend, Columbine, is in-story right now, and her writer's stalled for the past week or so. Apparently, that week got to one of the girls up there so much she, well, tried to . . ." Eloise looked up again, drawing a finger across her neck.

Barnaby grimaced. "She should have known she can't do that."

"According to Columbine, she wasn't the most stable girl to begin with, and the author hasn't made her any better." Eloise finished off the rest of her drink.

He nodded slowly, then froze. "Wait, I don't think I've ever heard of someone being able to contact people while in-story before."

Eloise paused, empty glass at her lips for a second too long before she lowered it. "Columbine found a way to connect to the gen. net. when the author's not writing—like how our computers connect to the stories at the RO, maybe—so she can send emails. Author apparently made her some tech genius."

"So did Sven's author, but he didn't figure out how to connect from in-story."

Eloise's brow furrowed.

"Sven from the office?" Barnaby tried. "He works with IT."

She shook her head. "I don't think I've met him."

Barnaby let it go. "It's impressive, your friend managing it. I take it you know each other from School?"

Eloise nodded. "I was the brainy one, she was the tough one. Actually led a walkout in kindergarten because she didn't like the Teacher once."

"Is her author keeping her tough?"

Eloise opened her mouth, but then shut it again as she shook her head. "I wouldn't know. She hasn't talked about that."

"Yours obviously didn't have a problem with keeping you smart. Unless that's one of the things you regained."

"Not much was written about me, really, so I guess I kept my default settings. We aren't exactly *tabula rasa* when the authors get us. "

Barnaby smiled. "You're starting to sound like the Philosopher Kings."

Eloise hesitated. "You mean from *The Republic?* Are they still around?"

"Of course," Barnaby said. "You haven't been over to the Ancient Greek Quarters? It's a serious party over there."

Eloise shook her head. "Can't say I have."

"It's insane. A friend and I went to a party we heard about out there one night . . . I ended up leaving after the second couch got set on fire by two drunk 'gods.' My friend—Ian actually, he works a floor down from us— stayed. He showed up three days later, still half drunk, with no idea where his pants went. Turns out someone over there took a liking to him and threatened to turn him into a pig if he didn't go home with her."

Eloise blinked. "That is . . . definitely something."

Barnaby nodded. "Enthusiastic consent is really more of a suggestion over there than a rule."

"Then I think I'm more than happy staying over here with you." Eloise released an incredulous breath.

He smiled, looking at her across the table. "You know, I am too."

Chapter Seven

ELOISE YAWNED, BRINGING HER HAND TO HER stomach as the large breath made the muscles low in her abdomen twinge. Her eyes blinked open slowly, taking in the unfamiliar room. She tensed for a second before sighing when she figured out where she was.

She didn't get up, simply looked the room over carefully, finding just the bed and a couple pieces of furniture. With no knick-knacks and nothing on the walls, it gave the distinct impression that the owner had just moved in. She half expected to see cardboard boxes lying around filled with the things that were too sentimental to leave behind, but not functional enough to bother unpacking.

"Good morning." Barnaby walked into the room with that bright white smile of his.

She sat up and tried to return the expression. It ended up too tight to be natural. Wrapping the blanket around her, she took everything in. She knew better than to make decisions after a full bottle of wine, she really did . . .

"I made breakfast downstairs, if you're interested." He motioned out the door.

She paused, the idea catching her off guard. "You cook?"

"Marginally well." He shrugged easily.

She nodded, looking at the floor and then back to him. "I really don't do this often."

"Do what?" He bent to grab her shirt from where it had been dropped in the doorway and tossed it to her.

"Go home with a guy after the first date." She pulled the shirt over her head. "I generally expect a couple more dinners . . . or at least hard alcohol."

He laughed. "Believe me. I have nothing negative to say, first date or not. Last night was great."

Eloise let out a less than comfortable laugh. "So, I take it you don't believe office romances only end badly."

"Wouldn't know." He shrugged, glancing back at the doorway. "Never had one."

"Never?" She managed to grab her skirt without fully leaving the bed.

"Never."

She accepted it with a nod, finally standing now that she was somewhat put together. She crossed her arms tight across her stomach as the silence began to stretch on. "So . . . ?"

He lifted his eyebrows questioningly.

"Should I . . . go?"

"You don't want breakfast?"

Eloise shifted her weight between her feet. "Just don't want to overstay my welcome, if you'd like me out of your hair." *Your damningly attractive hair.* She frowned as the thought registered, doing her best not to let it distract her. *What the hell is wrong with you, Eloise?*

"I'd like for us to have breakfast more." He smiled. "Maybe take a walk, unless you're in a rush to get home."

She swallowed, the little voice that told her to get out before she made a complete mess of things once again fighting a losing battle as she looked at him. "A walk?"

"We're right by the Border. One of the sets right on the edge, Paris, I think, is in a Christmas cycle. I've been meaning to drop by. Unless you're ready to get rid of *me?*"

Eloise opened her mouth, tried to force something out. The Border. The Wall. Where their world ended and the stories started. A place where they certainly wouldn't want the likes of pre-storied her. But then again, she was working a job. Had spent the night . . . here, in what she had to assume was MC housing. She wasn't locked away in the School any longer. And looking at the man across the room from her, there had certainly been a reason she'd ended up back here in the first place, wine or not.

She smiled, clenching her fists quickly before she forced her arms to her side. "Sounds great."

Just beyond the last line of the MC neighborhoods, the short stone wall stretched out as far as Eloise could see in either direction. Other than the scope of it, however, it looked entirely benign—a patchwork of earth-toned field-stones barely reaching Eloise's waist. Even as short as she was, she could have easily jumped it. That was, if she ever became bold or stupid enough to brave no-man's-land in pursuit of a story. She swallowed the lump in her throat, trying not to show her discomfort. Things would have to be desperate for her to ever consider it. They all knew the tales. A few had tried and never been heard from again, swallowed up before they made it halfway across the odd black ground, so dark it was almost difficult to believe anything was there.

And that was why they had stopped allowing pre-storied anywhere near it.

Barnaby rested his hands along the top, seeming blissfully unaware of Eloise's unease. "Oh, definitely Christmas."

Eloise started from her thoughts. "What?"

"See the Paris set?" He pointed.

Taking her eyes off the black, Eloise followed his finger. Lazy snowflakes floated past the tight-packed skyline, catching the colorful lights strung along the streets. Her mouth formed a perfect "O." If she didn't stop gawking soon, she'd start getting questions she wouldn't be able to answer. She recovered, eyes still searching the set. "It's lovely."

He looked at her. "Yes, it is."

She looked at him, and couldn't help but laugh. "Can you say cliché?"

He snorted. "I was going for romantic."

"Well, you ooze romance just by being yourself. You were the *romantic* lead of a *romance* novel, after all. You don't have to use clichés. After editing class, I have a sincere dislike of those."

He smiled, looking back out at the sets. "Which one's your favorite?"

"Favorite cliché?"

"No." He laughed, glancing at her. "Favorite set."

She blinked. That made even less sense than asking about clichés. Once assigned, everyone was transported directly into their sets by the OAT. Same on the way back out, at least as far as Eloise had been told. There didn't seem to be much time for sightseeing in all of that. She spoke carefully, in case she had missed something. "I haven't exactly been over to compare?"

He laughed. "No, to watch."

She turned back to the sets, scanning one after the other, stretching out to what had to be well past the horizon. She shook her head, not seeing a way to easily lie. "I can't say I've been here enough to pick one."

"Why not?"

She shrugged and chose her words carefully. "I suppose I've always found it depressing. I mean, everyone being so focused on the sets. It can't be healthy. If we spent half as much energy on our world as we do on theirs, ours could be more beautiful than anything they could create."

He glanced at her. "Not to be argumentative, but I doubt it."

She looked away from the sets, raising an eyebrow to prompt more.

"Our world is a mirror of theirs," he continued. "We take what we can from the stories. Whatever trickles down. Our clothing, our buildings, transportation, even our furniture is made to look like what they have shown us. Why do you think the Greeks have all their columns and most of the Dickens-era characters look ready to meet Queen Victoria?"

"You don't look Victorian." She glanced at his jeans.

"Neither was my author."

"And Mr. Marley?"

"You didn't see him before the chains came off."

She looked back out at the sets, far across the no-man's-land, pressing her lips together tightly before she spoke again. "Well, either way, that doesn't mean we don't have the mental capacity to be creative. We could create our own world, that wasn't a facsimile of theirs, if we put a little more effort into it."

"The authors give us our mental capacities."

"No, they *change* our mental capacities," Eloise corrected, trying to keep her tone level. "We manage to get through School without their help."

"But that doesn't really count."

"And why not?" she snapped.

He looked at her for a long moment, brow furrowed, before he answered. "Because . . . it's School?"

Eloise clenched her jaw, releasing a slow breath through her nose before turning away from Paris and the unsettling black. "I should get home. Thank you for dinner. And breakfast."

"Hey." He caught her wrist as she moved for the sidewalk. "What's wrong?"

"Nothing." She shook her head. "I just need to go."

Still, he didn't release her as he studied her face. "You're not long out of your story, are you?"

"No." She didn't bother to figure out whether her answer made sense.

He continued to search for something.

She did her best not to give it to him.

"How old are you?" he finally asked.

"Does it matter?"

He turned her to face him straight on, tilting her chin up gently. "You're just . . . younger than I realized?"

"Does age really matter post-story?" she returned.

"How long have you been out of your story, then?"

She shifted, half of her ready to pull away, the other half not willing to. "Not long."

"That's not a real answer."

"What does it matter?"

"Just . . ." He seemed to weigh his words before continuing, tone gentle. "It all becomes less fresh after your first decade out. Maybe I didn't think about you not having gotten there yet?"

Eloise finally stepped back. "I'm not the Wife of Bath, but I'm not a child, Barnaby."

"I never said you were," he said, letting his hand drop. "Just young."

"How old are you, then?" she asked, voice sounding too petulant to her own ears.

"I was mid to late twenties in-story?"

"You know that's not what I meant."

He smiled, once again looking much too attractive. "My book was written in 1986? 1989 maybe? You can do the math."

Much older. She didn't feel the need to get into specifics. She pulled her shoulders back with something like false confidence. "Do you think I'm too young for you?"

"Do you feel too young for me?"

Anyone else, and the return question might have felt passive aggressive, but Barnaby . . . he honestly just seemed to be asking. She released a breath, scratching the back of her neck before she caught herself.

She forced her hand down with a smile. "I think last night should be your answer there."

He smiled back, kissing her lightly before he met her eyes again. "At least let me walk you home?"

She shook her head, perhaps too fervently, but otherwise didn't let the question throw her. "It's a distance. No need for you to go so far out of your way."

"I don't mind."

"Really." She finally took a step back.

He didn't try to stop her this time.

"I'll see you at work?"

He looked at her for another moment, and then finally nodded. "I'll come around to bother you."

Chapter Eight

Dear Columbine,

I haven't heard from you lately, so I hope that means your author has gotten over his writer's block and you're back to shooting aliens, or having space sex, or whatever it is your author is having you do. I've still got to imagine that having sex with some voice narrating you has to be weird. Barnaby insists that you at least start to get used to it after the first couple times, and being from a romance novel I suppose he would know, but still.

Anyway, things back here have been fine. Truthfully, the reason I'm writing is because I think I'm getting in over my head with the Barnaby situation. I think I'm falling for him. And not the, "we had sex and it was really good so I'm sort of enamored" falling for him, but really falling for him. And with him not actually knowing the truth about things . . . I mean, I sort of fell into it because, I don't know, I just can't say no to him half the time in this entirely illogical, not at all me way, and I'm not exactly dancing through the office announcing what I am, so the not-storied thing didn't happen to come up in the midst of my entirely idiotic fumbling. But now, I don't know how much longer I'll be able to keep up the lie. And I have no idea how to tell him.

Honestly, I should probably break it off. It's what I would do if I were thinking logically, just cut my losses. But I don't know if I can do that either.

You know you were always better than me at all this relationship stuff. Hopefully, when you have the time, you'll be able to write back. It's a little different now that you're not just down the hall . . .

Well, I hope you're having a good time off in space. Hopefully all suicidal tendencies amongst the crew have been abated now. I can't wait to hear from you.

Lots of Love,
Eloise

Dear Columbine,

I haven't heard back from you recently, so I hope that means you're busy (in a good way) and not being attacked by Martians or something. Let me know if your author has put in any of those stereotypical little green men with big bald heads. If he has, you have to find a way to get a picture to me.
I'll just keep an eye out in case you get some free time.

-Eloise

Dear Columbine,

Hopefully everything's all right. I haven't heard back from you in a few weeks now. Hopefully your author is just writing up a storm, and you aren't hurt or anything. Send me a line when you have the chance.

-Eloise

Please send me a line to let me know you're all right sometime, if you can.

-Eloise

Ellie,

Things are crazy. I'm fine for now, don't worry. I'll write more when I have time.

-Columbine

Barnaby rested against the doorway, watching Eloise's face. Half-lit by the computer screen, she looked paler than normal, cheek resting dejectedly in her hand. He knocked on the doorframe lightly. "What's wrong?"

Eloise bolted upright, swiveling in her chair to face him.

He smiled. "I swear I never mean to scare you when I do that."

The surprise slid away as she released a breath, giving him a tight smile. "It's okay. Sorry. I really need to turn my desk toward the door. I just keep forgetting to."

He took the chair from the other desk that had still yet to be filled with a new recorder and pulled it up to her. "Are you all right?"

"Oh, I'm fine." She glanced back at the computer screen, alt-tabbing off whatever email she'd had open. "I'm just worried about Columbine."

"Still haven't heard back from her?"

"No, I just got one." Eloise motioned weakly at the computer. "But it's rushed. Doesn't sound like her."

"Maybe the author just changed her personality a little."

Eloise pressed her lips together in a thin line.

Barnaby braced himself. Definitely should have known better than to bring up author changes by now.

"Maybe . . ." she continued, displeasure seeming to be a low simmer for the time being. "Not that that's a great option either."

He touched her arm lightly, trying to move on before that changed. "I know. But I'm sure she's fine, and that she will continue being fine."

Eloise nodded, even though the taut, worried look didn't leave her face.

"How's work going?"

She looked at the blank television sitting further back in the office, letting him change the topic without complaint. "Nothing's happened for a few days now."

"Welcome to the life of the barely employed."

She shook her head, a hint of a smile finally coming back to her mouth. "After half a year, you'd think they would have reassigned you already, with us supposedly being short on recorders and all."

"They can only reassign you if there's been no action on your story for more than three months. Even if my author keeps deleting everything, there's technically been action. Just nothing for me to check at the end of the day."

"Working out better on your end than for the people in there, I imagine." She looked down at her hands, seeming amazingly interested in a chipped nail.

He just nodded, not bothering to start off another debate. "What do you want to do for dinner tonight?"

Her eyes flicked back up. "We have food at home."

He smiled. *We.* He had to suppose that that was about right, as often as she had started staying over—after all, it only made sense with how much closer to work he was than wherever she was out toward the mSCs. But somehow, just a few months in, things had become "*we*." Something told him that wasn't usual. But he couldn't bring himself to be too bothered by it. "We do, but I thought we could go out."

"What's the occasion?"

"I can't just want to take you out?"

She gave him one of her small smiles. "Fair enough."

He let the answer settle and smiled. "Though, I do have a surprise for you."

Eloise tilted her head. "What?"

"It wouldn't be a surprise if I told you."

She shook her head, good humor beginning to return. "You're seriously going to say that, and then make me wait until dinner?"

He shrugged, holding his hands out innocently.

Eloise's eyes narrowed slightly, but the corners of her mouth belied a smile. "Are you going to ask me to move in? Because I'm basically there already. I mean, I've taken over that bottom drawer of your dresser and everything."

"You could have an entire side of the closet if you wanted. I barely use it. But no, that isn't the surprise."

She studied his face. "Am I going to get it if I keep guessing?"

"Depends," he said. "How long do you have?"

She released a long breath, sitting further back in her chair. "You're lucky you're cute."

"I prefer roguish."

"Well, I suppose you're that too."

Catching his foot under her chair, he rolled her forward. "Since neither of us has any work to do, do you think anyone would notice if we took off early?"

"Are you trying to get us fired?" Her own leg went out in an attempt to push back against him, but she couldn't quite manage with him being nearly a foot taller than her.

"Just bored." He tried to dampen the laugh in his throat.

"And so you're acting like a child." Her own giggle started as her struggle got her absolutely nowhere.

Barnaby's friend, Sven, poked his head in the office, glancing between them. "Am I interrupting?" he asked, Norwegian accent still thick even after decades.

"No." Eloise finally pushed herself free, flushing slightly as she pushed a piece of hair behind her ear. "Did you need something?"

"I was looking for Fitz, actually." Sven motioned at Barnaby.

Barnaby straightened, smile still in place. "What's up?"

"Catherine's wandering around looking for you." Sven looked a little too amused. "Thought you'd want to know."

Barnaby's brow furrowed for a second before he recovered. "What's she doing here?"

"Just said she needed to see you, from what I heard. The grapevine is leading her down here." He lifted his hand. "Hi, Eloise."

She waved back, then looked at Barnaby.

Barnaby sighed and pushed himself up. "I'll be right back."

"What?" Eloise's mouth twisted like she was still trying not to laugh. "You aren't going to introduce me?"

Barnaby shook his head. "You don't want to meet Catherine."

"And why is that, Barnaby?" Small, brunette, and looking as young as ever, Catherine appeared in the doorway.

Barnaby forced a smile and turned to face her. "Catherine. Didn't know you were planning on dropping by."

"Did you move offices again?" Catherine asked, glancing at Eloise.

Barnaby shook his head, deflecting. "Did you need something?"

Her large brown eyes flicked back to him. "I need the ice bucket."

He blinked, wondering if that sentence made sense anywhere but Catherine's head. "The what?"

"The ice bucket. I was looking for it last week and didn't find it. You must have taken it."

Eloise stifled a laugh.

Catherine frowned, her gaze once again shifting to Eloise. "Is something funny?"

"I just can't imagine him using an ice bucket." Eloise stood, offering her hand. "Eloise, by the way."

Catherine looked Eloise over quickly. "I take it you're the new girl."

Barnaby sighed. "Eloise, Catherine. Catherine, Eloise."

Catherine shook her head. "What is your propensity for blondes lately?"

"How's Christophe?" Barnaby returned quickly.

They settled into their well-known draw. Catherine crossed her arms. "Anyway, the ice bucket is gone."

"I didn't even know we had an ice bucket, Cat."

"It didn't get up and walk away."

"Don't know what to tell you." Barnaby sighed. "Maybe the cockroaches stole it."

Catherine scoffed. "I don't have cockroaches."

"Obviously. They're living in the ice bucket now. Probably have managed to put together some little cockroach-sized furniture at this point, if it's been gone since I left."

Eloise snorted as she tried bite down another laugh.

Catherine's gaze snapped back to Eloise. "This isn't funny."

"You have to admit it's a little funny." Barnaby smiled.

Catherine kept her eyes on Eloise, who was flipping through some papers, failing to pretend she wasn't listening. "I don't know how you stand him."

The corners of Eloise's lips twitched as she stood, lifting a folder. "I've got to run this down the hall. I'll let you finish up."

Catherine watched as Eloise left the room, then nodded after her. "Robbing the cradle?"

"She's written about your age." Barnaby took a seat again.

"She's short."

He laughed. "And you're a giant?"

"I'm taller than she is."

Both written around what Barnaby would guess was nineteen and neither reaching above his shoulder, Catherine and Eloise likely could have been swapped as romance heroines if only the author had chosen a blonde rather than a brunette. Barnaby sat back, not entirely comfortable with the easy comparison. "Do you still need something, Catherine? Or is this really about you wanting to yell at me over an ice bucket?"

"Christophe said you were dating a sixteen-year-old."

Barnaby shook his head, going to stand again. "Goodbye, Catherine."

"It's a little disturbing that the older you get, the younger your tastes seem to run."

"She's not sixteen." Barnaby shuffled Catherine toward the door. "And if I see an ice bucket, you will be the first to know."

Eloise had only moved a few yards down the hall, the conflict more fascinating than perhaps it should be. For two people literally written for each other, things had obviously become very bitter once the author had stepped out of the picture. Perhaps opposites had been meant to attract in-story. She could always check the pages still in her desk, if she could bring herself to read more of their book. But just seeing the one conversation, she could easily believe they had been shoved into a Belligerent Sexual Tension trope.

A knot formed in the pit of Eloise's stomach. She had to admit, from all the stories she had seen, that this, in itself, was a trope playing out. The divorced couple separated for some poorly explained reason who still fought because they were still in love with each other. Eloise tapped her fingers, frowning. Things had fallen together so easily, she hadn't really had much time to consider her and Barnaby—not outside the lie hanging over her head every time she let herself think about it. But if their relationship was the easy one, with his and Catherine's "they fight because they're in love," had she turned into the False Romantic Lead in her own life?

"Catherine chased you out?" Sven broke Eloise out of her thoughts, coming up behind her with a full water glass.

True, Eloise could have just said she was running to the water cooler, if she had thought of it. "I don't think I was helping, hanging around. Does Catherine come by often?"

"Not really." Sven took a drink. "Mostly just when she's down visiting Christophe in HR."

"Someone she's now dating, I gather?" Eloise turned to fully face him.

Sven nodded. "Has been for a while. I'm pretty sure people were taking bets upstairs as to when she'd find out about whatever's happening with you and Fitz."

Eloise raised her eyebrows.

"You didn't expect people not to notice that he's almost exclusively in your office when he goes wandering these days?"

"I suppose not," Eloise said.

"And that you've been showing up at the same time most mornings."

Eloise raised her eyebrows.

Sven just smiled.

Another thing Eloise hadn't much considered in the whirlwind her life had been the past few months. But office gossip—that was a cliché in itself, if she had suddenly managed to turn her life into a Rom Com.

Sven glanced at the office, then back at Eloise. "Does he know?"

She paused, the question not clicking. "Know what?"

"That you're pre-storied."

Eloise's eyes widened. She did her best to recover, stumbling over her words. "Wh-where did you hear that?"

He shrugged good-naturedly. "Mr. Marley had me help recover some files last week. I happened to notice it while on his computer."

Eloise gaped, but did her best not to look like a fish as she pulled herself back together. "You aren't going to tell—?"

"Not really my business to tell anyone." Sven offered a quick smile. "Just, with whatever's happening between you two, Fitz, at least, might deserve to know."

"I know." She looked back at the office as Catherine nearly fell, walking backward out the door, still talking as Barnaby seemed to shepherd her out. Eloise swallowed. "I'm just . . . figuring it out."

Sven nodded, clapping her shoulder lightly as he moved back to his own office.

ELOISE GLANCED OVER THE MENU, MIND SEEING the words without taking the time to really comprehend them. The afternoon, the last few months, everything she had somehow managed to ignore for the most part turned over in her head. As awful as all the worry over

Chapter Nine

Columbine was, it had at least been an anchor, offering some sense of focus as the rest of the world kept spinning. Becoming whatever it now was.

Coming out of her thoughts long enough to order, Eloise turned her menu over to the waiter and looked at the man seated across from her. "So?"

Barnaby raised an eyebrow. "So?"

"Are you going to make me keep waiting for whatever this surprise is?"

The corners of his eyes crinkled as he smiled. "Need to work on your patience, don't we?"

"Barnaby."

He laughed, going to a bag under the table. "Fine."

She frowned as he placed a small stack of papers between them. She glanced back up. "You realize you can't divorce me without first getting married?"

He shook his head. "They aren't divorce papers."

"What are they then?" She picked them up.

"Just look."

She scanned them quickly before looking up, a knot forming in the pit of her stomach. "Census papers?"

"To pick a last name." His bright smile didn't help. "You didn't have one listed at your desk at work, so I figured you didn't get one in-story. I thought it might help you feel more settled now that you're out."

Eloise's mouth opened. No words came out. Swallowing, she tried not to entirely freeze up. "Barnaby, I don't think I can—"

"All you have to do is pick something you like." He didn't let her finish. "Could look some up when we get home if it helps. I know it's a headache normally, but I have a friend in the Census Office who can get everything filed for you, so no run-around. No lines or interviews or anything."

She nodded slowly, setting the papers down gently, as though they would combust from her holding them too long. Who knew, perhaps they would.

"I admit I was hoping you'd be just a little happier." He studied her face more closely than Eloise cared for in present circumstances. "I know you like the idea of being your own person."

Well, she had been telling herself she would find a way to tell him anyway. Still, the surprise kept her mute. She should have been able to think of a better lead-in than this.

"What's wrong?" he asked.

But to lie here . . . there was no coming back from that. Better for her to tell him than have whatever friend he had in the Census saying just why he wouldn't be able to put the papers through. She pressed her lips together, running her tongue along the inside seam uncomfortably before finally forcing something free. "It's . . . very sweet of you to try to help, Barnaby. You really shouldn't have gone to the trouble."

"No real trouble." He shook his head, eyebrows still slightly creased as he watched her. She could only imagine what he might be seeing.

"It's really very sweet," she repeated. "It's just . . ."

She trailed off as she noticed the waiter standing beside them. Of *course* someone would be there in the middle of her Can't Spit it Out trope. It was her day of tropes, after all.

"Sorry to interrupt." The man glanced between her and Barnaby before looking back at Eloise. "Are you Eloise, by chance?"

Eloise blinked, not even trying to figure out what it could possibly be now. "I am."

"A woman up front asked me to give this to you." The waiter held out an envelope.

Eloise glanced at the paper, then looked back up without taking it. "What woman?"

"She didn't leave her name before she left."

Eloise reached for the small, white envelope tentatively, not sure she could bring herself to open it after everything else.

"Secret admirer?" Barnaby glanced at it before looking up again, a hint of his customary smile back, even in the lingering tension. Hopefully that good humor would hold for the rest of the night.

"Obviously." Eloise slit the envelope open, pulling the sheet of paper out before she could think better of it.

Dear Eloise,

I had an advanced copy of tomorrow's paper sent to me for my class tomorrow, and I thought you might want to know now rather than coming across it at work or something when you aren't expecting to.

I'm not really sure how else to say this, I suppose there's not a good way to, but I found Columbine listed as Fallen in Action. I know you two were close.

I'm not sure if you're going to be back anytime soon, but if you need anything, just let me know.

Sincerely,
S.

"Eloise?"

She heard Barnaby's voice, but couldn't bring herself to look up.

"Eloise?" he asked again, his hand going to the edge of the paper when she still didn't answer.

Eloise didn't bother to stop him, watching the note—not even a proper letter, it was so short—slip from her hands. She stared at the candle in the middle of the table, now in her line of sight without the letter, not bothering to truly watch as Barnaby read for himself.

He looked back up, all hints of the earlier smile gone. "Oh, Eloise."

Her name finally snapped her out of her trance. "I'm sorry. I . . . I need to go."

"Eloise." Barnaby stood.

She didn't wait, digging through her purse as she moved for the front door.

The gust of fresh air caught her as she stepped outside, her feet freezing to the curb as she pushed through the mess in her purse, looking for her wallet.

"Eloise!" Barnaby followed, stuffing his own wallet into his back pocket as he stopped next to her.

"I . . . I can't find my bus pass."

"Eloise." He caught her shoulders, moving off the curb to stand in front of her.

She took a shaky breath, looking up at him for a second, and then the dam broke, tears coming until she was gasping sobs.

"Oh, Eloise." He wrapped his arms around her as she folded into his chest, head resting against his shoulder.

She sniffled, doing her best to force the sobs down. "I . . . I'm sorry. I—"

He hushed her, rubbing her back lightly. "Come on. Let's go home."

It was midnight by the time Eloise managed to cry herself out, but she still couldn't fall asleep. Sweet as he was being, Barnaby tried to stay up with her, but even Eloise had to call enough enough. She closed her eyes, lying still, pretending to sleep until she heard Barnaby drift off beside her.

His breathing quiet and steady, she turned onto her back, staring at the ceiling. Even with her body aching from her tears, she half wished she could go back to crying. It was better than the numbness that had taken over. Unable to take it anymore, she found her shoes in the dark and grabbed a jacket from the closet. She moved downstairs, gaining speed as she reached the front door. Buttoning one of Barnaby's coats, she held it tighter around her, finding it easily long enough to cover her pajamas. She stepped outside, taking a gulp of the cool air before she moved down the steps to the street.

The neighborhood was quiet as she walked past the line of identical townhouses, skirting the patches of orange light under the streetlamps. House after house sat dark, their owners more than likely asleep. Probably for the best. No need for Barnaby to explain the crazy woman stalking the neighborhood at two in the morning. She had to look like an escaped mental patient, eyes puffy, shuffling along in a jacket that was at least five sizes too big.

Eloise finally slowed, the Wall coming into view before she realized where she'd been headed. She paused, looking at the sets stretched out toward the horizon. As dark as it was behind her, the sets seemed to keep their own time, some dark, some bright as noon. People milled around in a few. Snow still fell on Paris, though it didn't seem to grow any deeper once it reached the ground.

Nothing had changed.

Nothing ever changed. Columbine, in all her wonderful, bossy brilliance had become just one more name taken away for whatever god-forsaken reason the author wanted. Someone to mourn for a second, and then be glad it hadn't been you. People would read about it—in the papers in the morning, out in the author's world when, or if, the author ever finished—but life would go on. Just another character sacrificed in the name of the plot. Just another forgotten name.

Eloise kicked the Wall, jumping back as pain shot up her leg. Something metallic pinged as it hit the ground. Frowning, she set her hurt foot down slowly. Nothing by the Wall should have been metallic, let alone rung out like that. She glanced at the pretty two-story houses behind her. Just as dark as the townhouses she'd passed. Pulling the jacket tighter, she sent another look at the sets. Curiosity drove her forward. Moving to the Wall, she pulled herself up, balancing on her hipbones as she looked directly under her.

Something glinted silver-blue on top of the black no-man's-land. She frowned. Things didn't normally sit in no-man's-land, did they? It didn't seem likely, at least.

She hesitated. The numb anger deep in her chest pulled tight.

Well, if there was any good time to test the curse of the no-man's-land, it was now.

Pulling herself the rest of the way up onto the Wall, Eloise straddled it, taking a last deep breath before she dropped to the other side. She paused as her feet hit the ground. Nothing happened. The ground didn't swallow her whole, nor did some cosmic alarm start screaming. She bounced on the balls of her feet. The ground was actually springy, like it was made out of some kind of rubber. She took a couple steps to test it, and then paused again. The black wavered further out, like the rubber sat on liquid, but she still didn't fall through. She looked out at the sets. People still moved around, not looking much larger than dolls at this distance, acting out scenes as if she weren't there.

Eloise clenched her fists. Screw the stories. Screw the authors. She wouldn't go. Even if her letter came, she wouldn't. The author could write his damn story without her. She'd rather fade away. At least she would still be her while doing it.

Turning back to the Wall, Eloise looked at the object still sitting there, shining in the moonlight. Carefully, she picked it up, turning it over in her hand. A smooth, curved disk. She ran her fingers over it, feeling a seam running along the edge. Her fingers hit a latch on the far side, the only protuberance on the otherwise symmetrical shape. She pressed the button.

The case sprang open. A thin needle wavered on a flat face, barely visible in the moonlight before it settled on a direction. She turned the outer casing until the front was in line with the needle. A compass. Pressing her lips together, she looked back at the sets, and then shoved the compass into the pocket of the jacket, climbing back over the Wall.

Barnaby sat up, eyebrows furrowed as she clicked the bedroom door shut. He looked her over. "Where did you go?"

"I just took a walk." She unbuttoned the jacket and tossed it over the dresser. "I couldn't sleep."

"You should have woken me." He yawned.

"No need for us to both be overtired and cranky tomorrow." She moved back to her side of the bed, sitting as she kicked her shoes off.

"Eloise—"

"I just needed to be alone." She turned to look at him, stomach twisting at the concern on his face.

"Eloise," he started again.

"I hate them." The words came out before she could think better of it.

He hesitated, frowning. "Who?"

"The authors," she said. "I hate them."

He opened his mouth, then shut it again. "Do you want me to get you something to help you sleep?"

"You think I should drug myself?"

"You need sleep," he said, face serious. "You're going to be a wreck tomorrow as it is."

Eloise looked down. "What do you think of Ashe?"

"Ash?"

"The last name," she said. "A-S-H-E."

He took a moment. "For you?"

She nodded, staring back off at the wall.

"Eloise Ashe," he tried it out. "I like it."

She nodded again.

"Do you want me to turn in the papers with that?"

She swallowed and shook her head as she lay back down. "Not yet. But . . . thank you."

Barnaby kissed her forehead, pulling her against him as she finally did her best to fall asleep.

Chapter Ten

ELOISE WOKE ALONE IN BED, THE SUN COMING IN the window. She blinked, her head still foggy as she tried to place what felt wrong. Leaning across the mattress, she turned the clock to her. She jumped out of bed as the numbers made sense. Her foot hit one of her shoes, throwing her forward. Catching herself on the dresser, Eloise released a breath. Obviously, today wasn't going to be much better than the last.

The door flew open, Barnaby looking at her with concern. "What happened?"

"I . . . tripped." She straightened. "Why didn't you wake me for work? Why aren't *you* at work?"

"I called us both in." Barnaby ran a hand through his dark hair. "Are you all right?"

The rush of adrenaline passing, she turned, leaning against the wall as she attempted to stop her mind's racing. She finally met Barnaby's eyes. "You didn't have to do that."

"Neither of our stories have been moving much. I figured sleep was more important."

Eloise closed her eyes, sliding down until she was seated with her knees to her chest. "I'm sorry. I didn't mean—"

"You don't have anything to apologize for, El." He moved to sit next to her.

She looked over, shaking her head. "You're too good for me, you know that?"

"That's not true."

She gave him a small smile. It dropped off quickly as she looked at her knees. "There are things you don't know about me, Barnaby."

"Like what?" He pushed a piece of hair behind her ear.

"I . . ." She took a deep breath, then released it heavily. It was as good a time as she was ever likely to get. "I'm pre-storied, Barnaby."

His eyebrows furrowed, hand stilling where it was at the side of her head. "What?"

"I was going to tell you last night . . ." she continued in a rush. "I really was, but . . . well . . . I'm so sorry."

"But . . ." He hesitated. "You're at the RO."

"They made an exception for me."

Barnaby opened his mouth, shut it again, and finally stood.

"Barnaby—"

"It's not fair to spring this on me now, Eloise," he cut her off, turning back to face her. "What am I supposed to say when you're already like this?"

"I can go home if you'd like," she offered weakly, looking down at her hands. He had to need time to think. Perhaps she did as well. Everything was just . . . too much. She did her best to shrink into herself. "If you need to digest, I can go—"

"I'm not going to send you out like this." He motioned at her before his hand went into his hair.

"You'd have every right to." She took a shaky breath, doing her best to remain composed. Easier said than done, with everything. "I wouldn't blame you if you did. Really."

He shook his head, finally dropping his hand as he released a breath. "Come on."

She frowned, glancing up as her eyebrows furrowed.

"Come on," he said again, tone harder. "You need to eat something."

"What?"

"Are you coming or not?" He moved for the door, pausing on the threshold.

With nothing else to do, she stood, following him down to the kitchen.

Silently, Barnaby set food on the table before moving as far away from her as possible without leaving the room.

Tension settled over them. Eloise kept her eyes on the plate in front of her, taking small bites of her eggs. Even that seemed too heavy with her stomach in knots.

He finally moved back to the table, resting his hands on the back of one of the old chairs. "You should have told me before this, Eloise."

She swallowed, staring at her mostly full plate. "I know."

"Why didn't you?"

She released a breath and forced her eyes up to his. "I didn't know how."

"Didn't know how?" he repeated.

She tried to think of something that didn't sound stupid, but ended up only shaking her head.

Jaw clenched, he sat. "You could still get a letter. You can't be twenty-five?"

"I wouldn't go," she murmured.

He paused. "What do you mean you wouldn't go?"

She took another small bite, trying to settle the bile churning in her stomach. Still, as she considered the words, she couldn't bring herself to retract them. Author changes, Columbine, an entire office set up just to watch everyone try to make it through manuscripts with some part of themselves still intact . . . how could she stand going through that? How could *any* of them stand it? She pushed the eggs around her plate as she repeated, "I wouldn't go. I'd rather fade away."

"And I don't get a say in this?"

Eloise froze, meeting his gaze. "What?"

"You're just going to sit here and let yourself die?"

She shifted in her seat, body tense. "You'd rather I get killed in-story?"

"Not everybody dies."

"Enough do."

"And if you don't go, you *will* die," he snapped. "How is that better?"

She swallowed the lump in her throat, too many things coming at her at once. "At least I'd get to die on my own terms."

"Goddammit, Eloise." He stood, the chair scraping across the tile floor.

"I'm sorry." She watched him, half unsure why she was apologizing, half entirely certain she needed to.

"So, I'm just supposed to sit here and watch you fade?"

She closed her eyes, taking a breath before she opened them again. "I really, really like you, Barnaby. More than I think I ever meant to. And . . . that was incredibly selfish of me."

He looked at her, arms crossed.

"I should never have gotten you involved in this." She gave up eating, setting the fork on the table. "It was awful of me. I know."

His jaw worked, clenching and relaxing as he stared at the wall. "We could talk to someone. See if we could put you in a romance. To be romance, the MCs can't die."

She was already half in one, if the tropes stalking her were any indication, right down to her and Barnaby stumbling together without a second thought, even if there should have been many. Would his popping up at her office count as a Meet Cute? Perhaps they didn't have a chance no matter where they were. It would figure, the rest of their lives being so out of their control. She forced the words out. "You can't just choose where you're sent."

"We could try."

"And who knows what they would do to me, even if I lived." She threw her hands up, voice threatening to crack as more and more thoughts began to press down on her, mixing with the anger, frustration, love—more emotions than she thought it possible to feel all at once.

"They'd make you fall in love with someone." He scoffed, running a hand through his hair. "What else?"

"I love *you*." She couldn't stop the words, couldn't bring herself to care at this point.

He finally looked back, held her eyes for a long moment before he finally shook his head. "What did they used to say in School? Nothing pre-story counts?"

"I'm not going in a story." She stood, conviction growing, the only thing feeling at all solid.

He didn't respond, conflicted eyes piercing through her. Somehow, it struck worse than anything she could imagine him saying.

The guilt came rushing back in waves. For letting herself forget what she was. For letting this happen. For being nothing better than a fraud. She crossed her arms tightly across her stomach, fighting off the trembling starting in her hands. "I can leave. Take you out of this entirely. But I'm not going. Whatever happens. I'm not going to go off and let them make me something I'm not. Tell me I'm in love with someone I'm not. Not after this. I can't."

He sat, entire body seeming to deflate as he rested his head in his hands.

She swallowed and tried not to lose her own composure, watching him sit there like that. "Please say you understand?"

He released a breath, addressing the table. "You're asking me to just sit here and watch you die."

"I'm asking you not to hate me."

He looked up, eyes meeting hers without lifting his head.

"I'll go." She glanced at the window, then back at him. "Quit. I'm not supposed to be here anyway. You don't have to be involved. You honestly never should have been. I just . . . don't want you to hate me."

"I don't hate you, Eloise." He closed his eyes, shaking his head slowly. "I very much the opposite of hate you."

The statement settled over them, the silence weighing heavily as neither of them could seem to think of anything left to say.

"Should I go?" Eloise asked softly.

He looked at her, deep conflict playing out over his face. He finally stood, shaking his head. "Let's go upstairs and talk. I think we have a lot to work out."

Chapter Eleven

ELOISE FLINCHED, SOMETHING BRUSHING THE SIDE of her face. So she had managed to sleep at some point. Both apparently too drained from breakfast, her and Barnaby's discussion had dissolved into not much more than a short, "We'll work it out. Somehow." The rest of the day had seemed to be a test of who could avoid saying anything important. For nothing but silence and small talk, it had been exhausting; exhausting in a way that left her too tense to sleep. She forced her eyes open unwillingly and waited for them to focus.

Barnaby gave her a weak smile. "I'm going to head in to work for a couple hours."

Eloise blinked, working to get her hands under her as the words made sense. Her body protested, the numbness seeming to have turned into a deep ache in her bones. "Should I—?"

"Go back to bed." He shook his head. "I just didn't want to disappear while you were still asleep."

She swallowed. "Barnaby—"

"I'll be back soon." He kissed her forehead quickly, not giving her the chance to object as he moved for the door.

Eloise didn't bother arguing. His heavy footsteps moved down to the first floor. The front door opened and closed with a slam. She released a breath, turning to look at the window. Sun shone brightly through the slats. A nice enough day to walk rather than drive to the office. The change in routine still didn't sit well with her.

We'll work it out.

It was the best outcome she really could have hoped for after telling him. She hadn't lost both Columbine and him entirely in under twenty-four hours. Still, she couldn't bring herself to find the thought comforting. As much as they avoided it, they wouldn't be able to ignore what she was forever. Whether he realized that on his walk or three years down the road, they wouldn't be able to make things normal again by pretending nothing had changed.

Perhaps the honorable thing to do would be to go. Let him out of the relationship without making him say he couldn't handle it. The sting now would have to be better than asking him to put his life on hold while she aged and disappeared.

She pulled her legs up to her chest. That would be the most honorable thing. She just didn't know if she could be that selfless.

Dropping her forehead to her knees, she groaned. When had she become such an idiot? Perhaps the goddamn author changes wouldn't have been as noticeable as she thought, if this was her now.

Perhaps Barnaby had brought some romance novel tropes home with him, and they had rubbed off. True, he hadn't technically been Rom Com, but romance was romance at some point.

Releasing a shaky breath, Eloise forced herself out of bed, not bothering to put on more than the tank top and boy shorts she had ended up sleeping in. The bulk of Barnaby's clothes from last night remained where they'd been dropped on the floor, likely a byproduct of hurrying to dress this morning. Shaking her head, she gathered them up, dumping them all into the hamper by the dresser. The jacket she had worn out still lay where she had placed it, apparently forgotten.

She picked it up, at least pretending to be productive. The compass fell from the pocket, bouncing slightly on the carpet as it landed. Eloise stared down. Looking entirely benign where it sat, something about it still made Eloise's chest tighten. Placing the jacket back where it had been, she sank to the floor, sitting cross-legged as she picked the compass up. The metal felt as cool and smooth as it had out by the Wall. Steeling her nerve, she found the seam between the two halves, pressing the little latch.

The little silver needle wavered, finding north from where it floated under a glass dome. She studied the markings around the edges—a flourished zero at the top near the clasp, a ninety, one-eighty, and a two-seventy marking the other sides of the circle. Raised black enamel wrapped the edge in what looked like some mix of Arabic and Tolkien Elvish, not that she could have read either. She ran her fingers over the lettering. Whatever it was, wherever this was from, it was a beautiful piece of craftsmanship.

Snapping it closed, she frowned as the smooth surface on the top of the case seemed to engrave itself out of nowhere. She watched the winding curves form, unable to put it down. Slowly, it warmed, a blue glow starting under the new pattern. She released her hold, squinting against the light, but it didn't drop, sticking to her palm as though seared there. She tilted her hand, tried to shake it off, unable to keep her eyes open as the heat became painful. A final jerk and the compass came free, hitting the ground with a thud.

Dust puffed up. She coughed, trying to bat it away as she babied her hand at the same time, eyes not quite readjusted. Something small and hard dug into her thigh. Eloise froze, the hair rising on the back of her neck. Slowly, she forced her eyes to focus. Trees surrounded her, taller than she had ever seen before. She took a deep breath, debating the likelihood of a complete mental break. Running her hand along the ground, she felt the dirt, hard and gritty. If it was a mental break, her subconscious hadn't gone halfway. It even smelled like outside—all grass and pine and petrichor.

She stood cautiously. "Hello?"

Nothing answered.

Wrapping her arms around her midsection, she took a few steps forward and tried again. "Hello?"

A tall, blond man broke through the trees with a crossbow leveled at her chest.

Eloise's hands went up on instinct as she looked at him, wide-eyed.

He stared at her for a long moment, frowning before lowering the bow. He called back over his shoulder, "Over here. It's just some girl."

Slowly, more faces appeared through the trees. First, a tall woman with long brown hair pulled back into a braid. Then, a shorter black-haired man and two small children with bright red hair.

The woman crossed her arms over her chest, studying Eloise for a moment. "What are you wearing?"

Eloise glanced down at the tank top and boy shorts, shifting uncomfortably. "Well, I didn't know I was going anywhere."

"Maybe we're actually going to start going again," one of the redheads spoke in a surprisingly grown-up voice. "I mean, if he's adding another character . . ."

"Why would he send her like that?" The brown-haired woman motioned to Eloise's clothes.

"Trying to make it up to us?" The dark-haired man smiled, eyes dropping over Eloise quickly. "Well, at least to the guys. Unless you swing that way, Hebe?"

The brown-haired woman, Hebe, glared before pulling a robe, much like the one she was wearing, out of a pack. She tossed it to Eloise. "Here."

Eloise took it without question, sliding it on and tightening the belt around her waist. On Eloise's small frame, the hem draped to the ground, the sleeves covering her hands. She tried to make it fit at least well enough that she wouldn't trip before looking at the group standing around. "Am . . . am I in a story?"

"Where did you think you were?" Hebe shook her head.

"I . . ." Eloise trailed off, mind stalling.

"Don't worry about it." The dark-haired man stepped forward. "The transport can scramble your head sometimes. I'm Savitr."

She took his offered hand, shaking it once. "Eloise."

"Eloise?" Hebe frowned.

Eloise looked at her. "Yes?"

"That's a rather . . . normal name."

"Is it?" Eloise looked at the rest of them.

"The author likes to pretend he's Tolkien," Savitr said, motioning to the redheads. "Hence the hobbits."

"We're not hobbits." The girl of the pair frowned.

"Well, you get mad when I call you midgets." Savitr glanced at her quickly, looking back at Eloise before the girl could sputter some indignation. "The author keeps pulling 'different' sounding names. Savitr." He motioned to himself. "Hebe. Pan and Echo." He pointed to the male and female redheads in turn. "Though, Owen . . . that's pretty normal."

Hebe glanced at the blond man, then looked back. "Owen's still more sword and sorcery than Eloise." She moved forward; she had to be at least six feet tall with the way Eloise had to crane her neck back. "What's your backstory?"

Eloise couldn't find anything to say, just shook her head.

Hebe scoffed, turning back around. "Two-to-one odds we're going to be sent on a 'rescue the damsel' quest next."

"How many fantasy damsels do you know in tank tops?" Owen finally spoke, voice low and melodious.

"I'm sorry," Eloise broke in, holding her hands up. "So this is a high fantasy?"

"You didn't even get *that* briefing?" Hebe looked Eloise over.

"If you paid attention to *Lord of the Rings* in class, you really don't need it," Savitr cut in before Eloise could answer. "Ragtag bunch of fantasy races going to find some MacGuffin to save the world. As I said, we've got hobbits."

"We're Chiumbe," Pan said, "technically."

"And Owen and Hebe are basically elves," Savitr continued over him. "Though, the author apparently either also likes Greek myth or DC Comics, since Hebe's basically our Amazonian Action Girl. She's lucky she hasn't run into any Wonder Woman slash fiction."

Hebe opened her mouth, the entire group disappearing with a pop before she could make a sound.

Eloise's shoulders tensed as she looked around. The entire group had vanished.

On the third night, the troupe came across a woman in the woods.

Eloise started, glancing up at the sky through the canopy before hearing twigs snap in front of her. The group reappeared, moving through the forest as though they were in a trance.

She was a small woman, with soft blonde curls framing her delicate features. She wore a pale blue dress that matched her eyes, looking much too clean to have been out in the woods for long.

Eloise felt a tug and held her hands out as the robe Hebe had given her faded away in favor for a long, pale-blue dress reminiscent of a medieval garment.

"Hello," the woman said.

Eloise frowned, the narrative pausing until she offered up the word tentatively. "Hello?"

"I am . . ."

"I am," she said.

The narrative stopped.

She looked up at the sky and offered, "Eloise."

"Eloise of the Siofe." The narrative took over. "Welcome."

"Elf kind?" Hebe slid off her horse.

Hebe spoke without a pause as her feet hit the ground, like it was a script she had learned while hypnotized.

Eloise's skin crawled.

"They sent me out to find you." Nobody spoke, so Eloise parroted the line.

"Who did?" Owen moved over to her.

"The Siofe." She smiled easily. "We know you've been out here for some time." She moved toward the white horse hitched to a tree behind her.

Eloise's head snapped to the side, looking at the white horse that had suddenly appeared, hitched to a tree like it had been there the entire time. The group in front of her watched expectantly when she didn't move.

"I have no idea how to ride a horse," she tried to explain.

The group remained looking at her, frozen.

She moved toward the white horse . . . the narrative repeated insistently.

Eloise stepped hesitantly forward.

"Follow me." She mounted, and started off through the trees.

Well, this was going to be fun. Bunching up her skirts, Eloise somehow managed to pull herself on top of the horse without falling off the other side, clutching the mare's neck as it took off toward wherever the author was directing it.

Chapter Twelve

BARNABY PLAYED WITH THE SLIGHTLY BENT PAPERCLIP, far too aware of how closely Sven was watching him.

"You all right, Fitz?" Sven finally asked, glancing at his monitor quickly before looking back.

"I suppose." Barnaby twisted the metal a final time before setting it back down on the desk—as useless as it might now be.

"Is Eloise sick?" Sven asked. "She hasn't been around for a couple days."

"Her friend from School was just killed in-story."

"Oh." Sven gave an understanding grimace. "That's hard."

Barnaby nodded. "She's in bad shape over it."

Sven looked at him carefully. "You think she's going to be all right?"

Over Columbine, sure. Who among them hadn't gotten over a friend's death? It was all but expected. With her stubborn insistence on staying pre-storied, however . . . . She certainly wouldn't be all right if he couldn't convince her to go in. If only he had some way to pick out a sappy novella for her, something quick that would see her safe to the other side. Perhaps Columbine's death was just too fresh. Once that wound wasn't so deep, perhaps Eloise would see reason.

"Fitz?" Sven broke into his thoughts.

"I don't know," Barnaby finally said. "She's . . . not doing well."

Sven sat back in his chair, rocking slightly. "I don't think I've seen you this worried over a girl before, Fitz."

Barnaby gave a dry laugh. "You know, I don't even know why I asked her out. Because I was bored and she was cute, I guess."

"I'm sure relationships have started on less."

Barnaby ran a hand through his hair, irritated. "God knows how this all happened. I wasn't looking for anything serious."

Something about the way Sven watched Barnaby across the table said Sven knew something he wasn't saying. The man finally just shrugged. "They say you just know when it's right."

"They also say that only an author can match you with your 'True Love,'" Barnaby returned. "And, I'm sorry, but if I never hear another romance cliché in my life, it will be too soon."

"Clichés are clichés for a reason," Sven said. "They would never have formed if there weren't some truth to them."

"There's a difference between truth and convenience." Barnaby sat back, crossing his arms. "Love at First Sight makes for easier storytelling than showing a real relationship."

"Are you saying you and Eloise were Love at First Sight?" Sven lifted an eyebrow.

Barnaby snorted. "I don't know about that. Though, is there a straight trope for Lesbian U-Haul Syndrome?"

"Fourth Date Marriage?" Sven suggested.

Barnaby shook his head, moving to stand. "I can't say I have a particularly positive view of marriage, at the moment."

"I'm sure we could find that trope, too." Sven leaned across the desk, grabbing one of the reference books off a shelf. "The Commitment-phobic Bachelor, maybe? Or former Uninterested in Love? I'm guessing it's not Armored Closet Gay—"

"Don't try to Bachelor trope me." Barnaby rested his hands on the back of the chair.

Sven found a page and turned it. "Seeing you and Catherine, I don't think you're holding off for a Divorce is Temporary."

"Barnaby." The voice cut Barnaby off before he could respond. Mckayla's head came around the door. "Your author's writing again."

He turned, sharp retort for Sven still hovering at the tip of Barnaby's tongue. He cleared his throat, trying to swallow it. "He's writing, or 'writing'?"

"Been going for about twenty minutes now and hasn't deleted anything, as far as I could see."

Barnaby released a breath before looking back at Sven. "I suppose I have to see this."

Sven just smiled, sticking his book back on the shelf.

Riding the elevator up the two floors to his office, Barnaby took a seat, moving the little-used monitor away from the window to get rid of the glare. He looked at the horses and sighed. Months of waiting, and here was yet another traveling scene.

He glanced at the computer, scanning the lines as they continued to roll down the page.

They arrived at the city of Ljótr. The buildings, for the most part, were built into the trees. Owen looked at the platforms around the beautiful houses. They glowed as if they were built of crystals. He then looked at the girl who slid off her horse gracefully, whispering something into its ear before sending it off. "You live here?"

"Yes." She smiled.

"Where is everybody?"

"They are watching."

So, the man actually was writing. For the characters' sakes, Barnaby could only hope the author would give up his epic aspirations and send the lot of them home sooner rather than later. Barnaby glanced back to the TV monitor. He did a double-take. Despite being dressed in a flowing blue dress, the woman still looked much too familiar.

The words stopped, and everyone but the blonde woman on screen froze.

"Hello?" she said after a pause, looking up. "If anyone can hear me, I really don't like this anymore."

Barnaby took a sharp breath, his chest feeling too tight. The words came up slowly on the computer screen, like the processor didn't know what was happening.

He placed his fingers on the keys, and hesitantly tried typing: Eloise?

His voice echoed on the screen. He pulled back sharply.

Eloise started, looking around, seemingly everywhere but at the screen. "Barnaby?"

He looked at his keyboard, typing slowly. You can hear me?

"Yes!" A relieved smile broke out as she continued to search. "Where are you?"

At work, he typed. What the hell are you doing in there?

"I don't know." She pulled something silver from her pocket, holding it up toward the sky. "I found this at the Wall, and then I was looking at it today, and I ended up here."

What is it? He squinted, glancing between his computer and the TV. The feed's to your right. Not up.

"Oh." She searched in the correct direction at least, holding the thing out in front of her. "It's some sort of compass? I was looking at it, and then suddenly, I was in here."

Barnaby tried to wrap his mind around what he was seeing. You weren't assigned there?

The smile faltered. "I told you—"

Her answer was cut off as the people started moving again.

Hebe slid off her horse, patting its neck as it whinnied. "Watching what?"

"You." Eloise looked up at the platforms.

"I thought they knew we were coming." Hebe fingered her crossbow.

"You aren't going to need that," Eloise admonished. "Our archers will not shoot if you do not."

"I don't see anyone." Savitr looked around.

"Because they do not wish you to see them. I beseech you, leave your mounts at this place. They will be seen to."

The television screen went black.

Barnaby turned back to the computer, trying to keep the file from closing. He barely remembered the old boot-up procedure from before everything had become automated and at least managed to keep the document open, even if the TV remained dark. Cautiously, he tried typing again, the computer beeping angrily as he added to the document. Eloise?

The screen flickered back on like it was struggling, the light dim.

Eloise held her hands to the sides of her head, not quite covering her ears. "Why are you yelling?"

Owen looked up, no longer frozen. "Who the hell is that?"

Eloise brushed Owen off. "Barnaby?"

Sorry, the screen went off. Barnaby typed, releasing a breath. I was trying to override the automatic shutdown.

"But you can still see us?" she asked.

The TV is at least trying to stay on, yes. Now, how did you get in there?

"I really don't know." Eloise shook her head. "Can you get me out?"

How could I do that if I don't know how you got in there in the first place?

"I told you," Eloise said, voice sounding suddenly too young as it wavered. "I found this silver compass thing at the Wall and just stuck it in my pocket. And when I was cleaning today, it dropped out of the jacket. And while I was looking at it . . . well, one minute I was sitting in your room, and the next I was in the middle of this forest."

"Not that any of us are complaining," one of the shadowy shapes said.

Who's that?

"Savitr," Eloise said. "He's been flirting with me."

"He flirts with everyone," Hebe droned.

"And that's Hebe," Eloise explained.

I figured, Barnaby typed. Sounded like her. Eloise didn't seem to answer, so he kept typing. Let's start at the beginning. You got that compass by the Wall?

"Yes," she said, voice beginning to sound garbled. "I just leaned over and grabbed it."

He frowned, trying to put his thoughts together even as the document threatened to close. Leaned over? It was on the other side of the Wall?

"Yes," Eloise said slowly. "But it was just right there. I was barely on the other side."

In what universe did you think reaching over the Wall and taking something was a good idea?

"I wasn't thinking." She sat with a thump. "I was upset."

Barnaby closed his eyes, then hit the side of the monitor as the document flickered. It came back up, but just barely. You didn't get any letter?

"No," Eloise said. "Never talked to anyone at the OAT. I don't think I'm supposed to be here at all. I've been acting along, but it doesn't seem like I actually have to do what he types. That isn't normal, is it?"

"We have to," Owen volunteered.

I could try to call someone at the OAT.

"You don't think they'd try to keep me in here if you do?" Eloise frowned.

Do you think you'll get out at all if I don't? He could hear his irritation echoing back from the TV.

She didn't respond.

Barnaby released a breath. Fighting with her now wouldn't help any more than it would have the day before. I'm going to find a way to get you out of there, Eloise. I promise.

"She's storied now," Hebe's garbled voice answered. "What are you going to do about it?"

Barnaby hesitated. I don't know yet.

"We're stuck in here," Pan finally spoke. "Why should she get special treatment?"

You can't force her to be there if she isn't supposed to be.

Hebe scoffed. "If her being here gets this damn story done any sooner, you better believe I can, and will."

Barnaby tried to type, but the cursor froze, flickering in quick succession and then going down entirely.

"Goddamn . . ." Barnaby hit the side of the screen. The TV went black. "Goddammit!" He pushed back, running a hand through his hair sharply.

Meghan from the office next door poked her head in. "You all right?"

Barnaby nodded, gathering his things. "Yes. Sorry. I just have to head home. Minor emergency."

"Is everything okay?" She frowned, pushing a piece of deep red hair out of her face.

"Yeah." He picked up his keys off his desk. "You'll let people know I had to go?"

She nodded, watching him move past.

Barnaby headed for the garage, cursing in his head. He'd walked. Of course he had. It had made sense at the time.

Now, he had to figure out what the hell he was going to do.

"Barnaby?" Eloise called, the world gone still once more. "Barnaby?"

"Think we might have lost your boyfriend." Hebe shook her head, moving to hitch her horse.

"He'll be able to see us once the author starts writing again." Eloise stood, trying to affect something like confidence in her voice.

"And he still won't be able to do anything," Hebe said. "You're written in now. Welcome to hell."

"It's not that bad," Echo said, her small body dwarfed against the thick tree trunks.

"What do you call sitting around the damn forest for half a year waiting for something to happen?" Hebe narrowed her eyes, then motioned widely. "And now, we're in another damn forest."

"There are houses." Eloise looked up at the glowing homes above their heads.

"We won't be able to go in." Owen frowned, jaw locked. "He hasn't written anything but the façade."

"He has to write that there are insides to his houses?" Eloise's eyebrows furrowed, the idea somehow horrifying.

"It's his world," Echo said. "He has to write everything."

Eloise shook her head, doing her best to remain calm as she moved back and forth. "I can't be here."

"Sorry to tell you, but you are." Hebe went through her pack. "Might as well settle in."

Eloise looked around at the rest of the group, clenching her fists for a moment before she forced herself to relax. "What are we looking for?"

"What?" Owen frowned.

"You said you were after a MacGuffin," Eloise continued. "So, it's some sort of Holy Grail search. What are we looking for?"

The others didn't speak.

Echo finally looked up. "It's called the Asfera."

Eloise nodded. "And what does it do?"

The others looked between them, eyes settling on Owen one by one.

"We don't know," Savitr supplied when Owen just shrugged.

Eloise raised her eyebrows. "You don't know?"

"There used to be a wizard traveling with us," Owen took over. "He supposedly knew, but never told us. Just, it's supposedly important to the fate of the world, and everyone's after it."

"A true MacGuffin then." Eloise looked down, not bothering to ask what had happened to the wizard—dead, lost, or resurrected, she didn't really want to know. "Do we know where it is?"

"Off across the mountains." Owen motioned vaguely.

Eloise looked, not able to see more than twenty feet past the trees. Still, the thought hit. Perhaps it was their way out. "Do you think we could go after it?"

Hebe frowned. "Go after it?"

"If you know it's across the mountains, there must *be* mountains already," Eloise continued. "Who says we couldn't go and get it?"

Echo gaped, looking at the others. "Can we do that?"

"We'd be shot right back here as soon as the author started typing again," Hebe answered.

"I might not be," Eloise said, doing her best to work out some sort of plan as she spoke. Anything that wouldn't simply be sitting around and acting out whatever this author scripted for her. Or sitting around in this forest waiting for the others to find their MacGuffin. Kind, ethereal woman in the forest . . . the author most likely was planning to High Queen her, especially judging off the Phosphor-Essence the town was giving off. There was no way the author intended to write her in as an MC at the moment. Not for a high fantasy. He'd likely be done with her after she doled out some It May Help You on Your Quest bits of advice. And then where would she be?

"It might be worth a shot." Savitr once again broke the silence.

Hebe narrowed her eyes, clearly less than amused with the man. "I doubt she's going to sleep with you just because you support her crazy ideas."

"It has to be better than sitting around here just waiting," Echo said, shrugging apologetically when Hebe shifted the dark look to her. "Don't you think?"

"You're insane." Hebe shook her head.

Savitr glanced at Eloise, then back at Hebe. "I say we put it to a vote."

"Since when has this been a democracy?" Hebe returned.

"Based on the author, Owen's in charge." Savitr nodded in Owen's direction. "You want to leave the decision to him?"

"The author isn't here," Owen said, holding his hands up. "If we're already off book, we might as well vote."

"Owen." Hebe placed her hands on her hips.

"It's not really up to me, Be. If that's what everyone wants to do . . ."

Eloise jumped back in before Hebe could respond. "The worst that happens is you walk some more. I imagine that's what the author is having you do now, unless there are Eagles involved?"

Hebe gritted her teeth, but the group remained silent.

"And," Eloise finished, "it would at least be us doing it. Us, because we chose to. Not because we had to."

The looks went back around the group, nerves plain on Pan's face, some hope on Echo's. Savitr continued to nod. Owen and Hebe held each other's eyes.

Hebe huffed, but turned back to her horse. "Don't come crying to me when we all end up right back here."

Eloise did her best to offer the rest of the group a smile as they all ignored Hebe's grumbling, turning the compass in her pocket nervously.

Chapter Thirteen

BARNABY TAPPED HIS FINGERS ON HIS THIGH, THE line moving glacially toward the counter at the far wall. The last time he had been in the gray waiting room, he'd been too nervous to care how slowly they inched forward. Waiting just a little bit longer before hearing what he was in for hadn't seemed like a bad thing when he'd been assigned just before turning twenty.

This time, he was well into debating whether his RO ID would have any weight whatsoever if he pushed his way to the front. He made a turn around the next metal barrier that kept the line somewhat orderly, looking at the workers sitting at their little partitions. He didn't recognize most—likely a gathering of Lawful Neutrals, those written to uphold the law simply because it was the law—so jumping the line would do no good. Barnaby released a breath. He'd just have to hope he'd be lucky and end up with someone who tended toward good rather than obstruction.

Another slow turn, and the front of the line was in sight. "Next."

Barnaby started forward, stopping in front of a man who seemed to be wearing a uniform from the First World War.

"Letter?" The man didn't stop typing long enough to look up.

"I'm actually not—" Barnaby started.

The soldier sighed and finally slid his eyes to Barnaby. "We can't see you if you haven't gotten your letter."

"I've already been assigned, thanks." Barnaby fished his wallet from his pocket, pulling out his ID, whether or not it would actually help. "I'm with the RO. I need to speak to someone about a woman who just appeared in one of my stories."

The soldier's eyebrows lifted, his face suspicious. "Why would the Recording Office need anything from us?"

"Because I don't think she's been properly assigned there." Barnaby pulled his ID back. "Could you at least look her up? See what it says on your end?"

"I don't have the authority to share those records."

"You can't run a search and just see if she came through here?"

"I don't have the authority to share those records," the soldier repeated.

And there it was, the Lawful Neutral. Great. Barnaby saved his breath, knowing better than to argue. "Who does have the authority, then?"

"You will need to fill out a request form and go to the second floor."

Barnaby somehow refrained from sighing. "And where are the request forms?"

"Table by the door." The soldier pointed.

Barnaby turned, looking back across the snaking line. His jaw clenched.

"Next."

The further they walked, the odder the landscape became. The thick trees that had surrounded the façade of the village phased out, turning into little more than sketches—the vague idea of what was meant to fill the space, but nothing *real*.

"We're going off the grid," Pan said to no one in particular.

Eloise had to agree, the thought adding to the knot in her stomach.

"Keep this up, and we're going to end up wandering around in a big white box of nothing," Hebe mumbled.

Eloise kept her eyes forward. With an epic of this sort, something meant to be like *Lord of the Rings*, she could only hope the author at least had an outline he was following. It didn't seem like the kind of thing that would be easy to make up as he went along. Even if the group around her didn't know much about the mighty MacGuffin, the author certainly had to. It had to exist somewhere already. Didn't it?

She released a breath. Hopefully, the author wasn't attempting an epic using the "write until it makes sense" method.

When . . .

The disembodied voice tried to start, but seemed muffled from their spot amongst the sketchy landscape. Eloise tensed, looking at the rest of the group. They looked ill, pale—Pan even doubled over—but no one disappeared, no one froze. Not yet at least.

When they . . . The narrative sputtered, mumbling Eloise couldn't fully understand buzzing over them.

She took her chances. "Hello?"

Everything went silent.

"Hello?" she tried again. "Can you hear me?"

"What are you doing?" Echo looked up, fingers rubbing her temples.

"Well, if Barnaby could hear us . . ." Eloise went back to searching the sky.

All right, real funny, the voice from the narration started again, all loftiness gone. Who is this? Chris?

Eloise paused, then answered, "Who's Chris?"

Great joke. I'm restarting my computer.

"Wait, wait." Eloise held up her hands, though she had no idea whether or not an author would be able to see her without a screen. "Please. I'm not sure what will happen to everyone if you close your story."

A long pause. What?

"You see . . ." She tried to think of something to say that didn't sound entirely mental, and couldn't come up with much. "Well, I'm Eloise, and I don't really think I'm supposed to be here, so it's doing something odd. Everyone else—Owen, and Hebe, and all them—might jump back to where you left them, but I really have no idea what might happen to me now that you've started trying to write me into the story."

You expect me to believe I'm typing to a character I just made up?

"But, that's the thing. You didn't make me up," Eloise continued. "I mean, do you really think 'Eloise' fits well with whatever Galadriel-esque character you were writing? I just got sucked in here somehow."

No answer.

"What's happening on your end?" Eloise asked. "You can't actually see us, I take it?"

See us?

"We have a feed to see into stories where I'm from. I'm guessing you don't? I would wave if it'd help."

Everything went quiet again.

"Really." Eloise closed her eyes. "I don't know what you're seeing right now, but really, I'm not someone playing a prank. I . . . well, I don't know what I could do to prove it, but we're currently at the edge of whatever forest you had us in. It's not really described yet, so I don't have too much to go off, but it looks like rocky plains? Rohan-ish, perhaps? And you have a really well-formed mountain off in the distance. I'm guessing that's where the Af . . . Afsi . . ."

"Asfera," Savitr supplied.

"Where the Asfera is?" Eloise completed.

The mumbling came back.

Eloise tilted her head, trying to listen. "I can't really hear what you're saying?"

It disappeared.

Echo looked around, the rest of the group deathly silent. "Do you think he's gone?"

Eloise released a breath, then tried to inhale, as futile as it might be. "If you're still there, would you mind writing us somewhere a little more comfortable? Everyone's been stuck camping, waiting for you to write the past few months. If you could write us a nice hotel or something, that would be great."

The voice returned. Write you a hotel?

"You control the set." Eloise crossed her arms tightly over her stomach. "It's why things are a little patchy here where you haven't fully described it. If you could just write something like: 'Suddenly, they were all teleported to the Four Seasons,' we could at least be inside while we sort things out."

If this is Chris, I'm going to-

"It's not," Eloise cut the author off. "But if I knew Chris, I would let him know."

A final long pause, and the narrative picked up. Suddenly, the band arrived at a hotel. They walked into a well-furnished room and took seats around a long table in the center.

The small hotel, which couldn't have housed more than a few rooms, landed in front of them with a thud. Eloise smiled, the expression sliding away as she watched the group around her finally lose their battle against the narrative. One by one, they marched forward, going to take their seats in the room the author had given them.

Eloise followed a step behind, taking one of the empty chairs toward the door. Even as sparse as the space was— little described, entirely generic—it was better than standing out in the odd, half-completed field. "Thank you."

Now, the voice started, still seeming to hover above her even inside the building. If this isn't a joke, and I'm not saying it isn't, how are you talking to me?

Eloise looked at the others, all frozen in place, and shook her head. "I suppose it's because I wasn't supposed to be here? You see, most people get assigned to stories. There's this whole long, really bureaucratic process that I won't go into, but I wasn't assigned, I just showed up."

Showed up how?

Eloise took the compass out, turning it over in her palm. "Magic? Plot Device? I really don't know how to explain it. Then again, I don't know how people normally get sucked into these things either. I've never been in a story before."

Is everyone else in there supposedly like you, too?

Eloise looked up. "Like me?"

The author didn't type for a long moment. Real?

"Oh, yes." Eloise nodded, glancing back at the compass before she returned it to her pocket. "We're all real. Just . . . it seems like you freeze if you're meant to be in the story when the author's typing. I guess ending up here like I did didn't kill my 'free will' switch or something."

So . . . I'm controlling real people. Supposedly.

"All of you are," Eloise agreed. "Do you have a name for me to call you?"

A name?

"Well, you know I'm Eloise. But you're currently just a disembodied voice."

I'm Dan.

"Good to meet you, Dan." Eloise sat back in the chair, looking around the table. She did her best to ignore the blank stares of her companions. "I'm sorry for interrupting your story."

It's all right. I've had writer's block for a while anyway.

"So everyone was saying."

Was everyone in there just supposedly waiting around for me?

"More or less." Eloise stared at her hands, trying to keep her tone neutral, just in case anything was tagged on the author's side. She wouldn't make friends sounding as bitter as she felt. "It's your world, we're all just living in it."

Should I kill you off, or something? Get you out of there.

"Oh God no." Eloise's eyes widened, fingers gripping the arms of the chair. "Don't do that. You kill us, and we're truly dead."

You wouldn't just . . . wake up or something?

"It's not like we're dreaming. We don't wake up right before we hit the ground." Eloise released a tense breath, doing her best to ignore the spark of adrenaline.

How do I get you out of there, then? Just write you out?

"I don't know." Eloise shook her head. "My . . . boy-friend, I guess, is working on that from his end. But I don't even know how I got in here in the first place."

What happens to people in old stories? Does everyone just end up sitting around?

"If the author doesn't finish," Eloise agreed. "Once stories end, though, people are normally sent home. The ones who *weren't* killed off, at least."

So, what should I do?

Eloise pressed her lips into a thin line. Nothing seemed like a particularly good option for the time being. She sighed. "I guess you should try to finish the story?"

Chapter Fourteen

BARNABY DID HIS BEST NOT TO RUB HIS TEMPLES, sitting in yet another small gray room as the woman across from him slowly looked through the stack of papers he had completed.

"Do you have her succession number?" The woman glanced up.

"What?" Barnaby shook his head, the entire afternoon starting to feel like an exercise in futility.

The woman—Mrs. Finch, from the placard on her desk—adjusted her glasses and turned the paper back to face him. "You've only written a first name. We need a succession number to look this girl up."

"I don't know her succession number," Barnaby said, his words tense.

"Do you have a way of getting it?"

The RO or the School would have to have it. How he'd convince anyone to let him see those files without letting everyone know what was happening, however, he had no idea. And hell if he would deal with those lines downstairs again. "Can't you just look up if there were any Eloises transported this morning? It would have happened today."

"I'm afraid there's nothing I can do without a completed form, Mr. Fitzwilliam." Mrs. Finch slid the papers back to him, offering a smile. "Please feel free to return once you have all the necessary information."

"Really." Barnaby didn't move. "I think this woman was placed in this story by mistake. If—"

"The Office of Assignment and Transport does not make mistakes, Mr. Fitzwilliam." Any kindness slid off her face. "We pride ourselves on the utmost competence."

"I didn't say it was incompetence," Barnaby backtracked. "I'm just trying to figure out—"

"Once you have the proper forms, I will be happy to help see what files the Office has on this girl. Until then, I'm afraid my hands are—"

"Mrs. Finch?" The woman at the desk across the room looked over. "Mr. Pontmercy is paging you."

Mrs. Finch paused, looking flustered as she turned to her computer. "I don't show anything."

The other woman twisted her monitor, pointing to some alert. "Sounds like it's important."

Mrs. Finch froze, tensing before she stood, hands pressing out the wrinkles in her forties-era dress. "If you will excuse me, Mr. Fitzwilliam. We look forward to your return when you have the proper forms."

Barnaby opened his mouth, but couldn't think of anything else to say as Mrs. Finch moved out the door with quick, short strides. Barnaby pinched his nose, releasing a breath before he began to gather the papers Mrs. Finch had rejected.

"Sorry about her." The woman across the room stood, moving toward Barnaby. "This is what happens when you take everyone written to be stereotypical bureaucrats and stick them in a building together. I think they all end up here because everyone knows the transportees will be too nervous to complain."

Barnaby looked up with a frown. "I'm sorry?"

"Alice Wembley." The woman held her hand out with a smile. "Anti-bureaucratic bastion in the storm."

The frown didn't move, but Barnaby took her hand. "Barnaby Fitzwilliam."

"Good to meet you, Barney." Alice took Mrs. Finch's seat. "Mind if I call you 'Barney'?"

"Actually—"

"So, what's happening?" She didn't let him finish, already pulling the papers back.

Barnaby hesitated.

Alice glanced up and smiled. "Sorry, my mind works really quickly. You'll catch up. You're looking for an Eloise?"

Barnaby went with it, going for his ID again. "I work at the RO, as a recorder. Today this woman, Eloise, appeared out of nowhere and, well, it doesn't seem like she's supposed to be there. The screen kept on after the author stopped talking. I could communicate with her. I've worked in the RO for at least a decade, and I've never seen anything like it."

"Sounds exciting." Alice turned to the computer, typing quickly.

"I don't know about that." Barnaby watched the side of her face. Blonde hair cut short into a wavy bob, she looked like a dame out of a gangster novel. Her clothing, however, said she'd had a modern author. He shifted back in his chair. "I'm sorry, but you don't seem like the type of person who generally works here."

"You mean I'm not stodgy and boring?" Alice tossed him another smile before going back to typing.

"Something like that."

"I bore easily." Alice shrugged. "It's really more fun than it should be, causing trouble around here."

Barnaby nodded.

"Now, that's interesting." Alice leaned closer to the screen.

Barnaby rocked forward to see. "What is?"

"There's no 'Eloise' marked for assignment, and no transports set today . . . but there was a spike in activity earlier this morning. Like someone—or something, for that matter—transported . . ." —she scrolled through a long spreadsheet with charts— "in a residential neighborhood."

Barnaby tensed. "That could be her."

Alice read a little more, pressing her fist to her mouth before she glanced at the door. She clicked the mouse, copying the file to an email. "I'll send this to myself and look more into it. Mrs. Finch will probably figure out she wasn't actually paged sooner rather than later. Do you want to leave your contact info? I can let you know what I find out."

"Uh, yeah." Barnaby fumbled for a piece of paper, not willing to question the first good luck he'd had all day. "Thank you."

"No problem." Alice took the paper Barnaby offered her. "It's been a really boring week so far. I could use some excitement."

Barnaby nodded.

"You might want to head out before Mrs. Finch comes back and catches you hanging around." Alice smiled, motioning to the door with her chin. "I'll be in touch."

"Thank you," Barnaby repeated, gathering his things. Now he just had to figure out how get back in contact with Eloise.

Eloise looked at the food that had been written onto the table. She couldn't help but feel it was fake, something she shouldn't truly touch. But the chair under her, the roof over her head, those had both been created the same way, and they certainly felt real enough. In-story, the author was god. God could certainly create as he needed. Maybe, then, it was just fear of Food Chains. Too many times reading Persephone and the Pomegranate playing out, perhaps.

The words echoed in her head, a story read long ago. *Bite no bit, and drink no drop . . . while in Elfland you be.*

With Dan gone, the others around the table finally started to stir, their dazed, empty looks returning to normal as they came around.

Hebe looked at the space and spoke first. "Where the hell are we?"

"Same place we were." Eloise picked up an apple experimentally, only to set it back down. Far too symbolic. "Once the author caught up to us over here, it seems you slipped back into the narrative, but he at least gave us a place to stay while he outlined some."

"Outlined?" Hebe frowned.

"Unless Barnaby figures out another way to get us out of here, it seems like our best hope is to actually get this story finished." Eloise shifted, finally taking her eyes off the food. "I was helping him outline."

"So *you're* writing the story now."

"Obviously not." Eloise glanced away from Hebe as Pan and Echo finally snapped to. "I've just read enough to be able to walk him through finishing a standard high fantasy. A little harder than normal, since he doesn't especially want to kill any of us off anymore, even the Red Shirts he was planning. Good for us, but means the epic battle is off the table."

"He can't just write 'The End'?" Pan asked.

"Well, a cliffhanger doesn't help us any." Eloise stood. "The story might start waiting for a sequel. Fantasies are known for their series."

"They walked outside, tripped over the MacGuffin, and all went home." Hebe stood with her. "How about you pitch that with your next little author chat?"

Eloise met the taller woman's eyes, doing her best to seem in charge even with the height difference. "I'll see what I can do."

"Can we eat this?" Savitr broke in, pointing to the food spread across the table.

Eloise nodded. "There are some real beds as well, if anyone wants to try to sleep. Dan seemed very contrite over leaving you all sitting in the woods for months."

"Dan." Hebe crossed her arms. "So, you're on a first name basis now?"

"Leave her alone, Be." Owen shook his head. "Are you really going to argue against her getting us out of here?"

Hebe's nostrils flared, but she sat again, ripping a stem of grapes from the bigger bunch.

Echo finally looked up, offering a small smile. "Thank you, Eloise. I hope you get out of here soon."

"Let's hope we all do." Owen sighed, digging into the food himself.

Barnaby stared at the computer screen, the little wheel spinning the same way it had been for the past hour, absolutely nothing loading. He groaned, rubbing his eyes. Even the little clock on the screen had frozen. That, or time was now passing so slowly he couldn't tell the difference from one minute to the next.

Footsteps moved down the hall, Sven stopping in the doorway with a yawn. "Now that I'm here, will you tell me what the hell is going on?"

"You made it." Barnaby stood. So at least time *was* actually passing. "My computer's stalled. Can you fix it?"

Sven looked at him for a long moment, eyebrows furrowed. "It's five in the morning. What are you even doing here?"

"It's a long story." Barnaby shook his head, motioning back to the screen. "I was trying to get a document to open, and now the screen's frozen."

Sven's expression didn't change, but he moved to look. "You're trying to open the connection to the feed?"

"I guess." Barnaby ran a hand through his hair.

"It's automatic." Sven looked back at him. "You'd have to override the entire system to get in." He paused. "Have you slept at all?"

"I've been working."

"You were gone for a day and a half. How far behind can you possibly be?"

Barnaby pressed his lips together, then released a long breath through his nose. "This needs to stay between us."

"All right . . ."

"Somehow, Eloise got sucked into my story."

Sven blinked, but didn't seem to comprehend Barnaby's words. "What?"

"I left her at home this morning. No, yesterday morning," Barnaby corrected, "and then came in here to find her in my story. She got sucked in somehow."

Sven opened his mouth, then closed it again as he cleared his throat. "Did she ever tell you . . . what she was?"

Barnaby met Sven's eyes and read it all over the man's face. "She told you?"

"Told me . . . what?" Sven returned.

Barnaby locked his jaw. He didn't have time to deal with annoyance at the moment. "That she was pre-storied?"

The slight grimace on Sven's face slid away, relief showing through. "Since she was, maybe she was just assigned?"

"I was down at the OAT all afternoon." Barnaby shook his head. "They didn't have any record of either assigning her or transporting someone today." He groaned. "I mean yesterday."

Sven's brow furrowed, but he nodded.

Barnaby had to ask it. "Why did she tell you?"

"She didn't," Sven said.

"Then how—?"

"You're not the only one who bugs me for IT help. I see a lot of confidential files." Sven looked at the computer. "So, what's happening exactly?"

Barnaby released a heavy breath, and then gave Sven the full run-down in as few words as possible. "And so I'm back here, trying to get in touch with her."

"You've been here all night?"

Barnaby opened his mouth, hating to admit it. "More or less."

Sven studied Barnaby, something unreadable passing over his face before he sat at the desk. "Let's see what's happening."

"Do you think you can override it?" Barnaby moved behind him.

"Given enough time, I'm sure I could."

"What's enough time?"

"We'll see." Sven bent, twisting to get to the wires running to the wall.

Barnaby leaned back on the desk, rubbing a hand over his face.

"You should try to get some sleep, Fitz." Sven glanced up. "We could do this in the morning."

"It is morning."

"You know what I mean." He went back to his wires.

"Just . . . how could this happen?" Barnaby asked himself, Sven, perhaps no one in particular.

"I've never heard of anything like it before." From under the desk, Sven answered all the same. "What did the OAT say about it?"

"I didn't have the right form in triplicate. They wouldn't tell me much."

Sven reappeared topside. "You're really going all out for this girl."

"You expect me to just leave her in there?" Barnaby tried to stifle a yawn, but didn't quite succeed.

"There's a difference between trying to help and staying up all night trying to rescue her."

"So, you're saying I'm an idiot?"

"I'm saying you might still be more of a romantic than you give yourself credit for." He started typing.

Barnaby didn't answer, listening to the computer beep and whirl, seemingly struggling against whatever Sven was doing to it. "Any luck?"

"I've got the computer working again after whatever you did to it." Sven continued typing. "Now, I'm trying to rewrite part of the network program."

Barnaby nodded, eyes nearly losing focus as exhaustion began to set in. He motioned to the door. "I suppose I'll go make us coffee, if we're going to be at this a while."

Sven just hummed, not looking away from his work.

Chapter Fifteen

ELOISE LOOKED AROUND THE PARK. THE TREES STOOD still in the bright day. A water feature sat silently. No ripples, no waves. The ducks that floated off on the far end of the pond didn't move, didn't quack, didn't even breathe. Eloise touched a flower, smelled it. There was a general floral scent, muted, indistinct, whatever had been included with the general thought of a flower rather than a distinct scent the author had written in. Sighing, she looked down the packed dirt path. A single wooden bench sat a little ways off. She moved over to it, tucked one leg under her, and took a seat.

What do you think?

She stretched out, resting her arms along the back of the bench, looking up at the generic blue sky in the general direction of the voice. "It's nice."

Only nice?

"Very nice," she amended. "It just takes a little getting used to."

What do you mean?

"It's a lovely space." She tried to think of a way to describe it. "It just doesn't feel *real*, if that makes sense."

Anything I can do?

She shook her head, staring back across the park to where it tapered off into the sketchy plains and little hotel. He could do anything. Put them on a tropical island or in a beautiful palace. But as much as he typed, as much world-building as he offered to write in, it would still never be real. Perhaps that was what had brought Columbine's storymate to attempt suicide. Not just the waiting, but the artificialness of it all. Life spinning out of your control while living in a diorama. Eloise could easily see it taking a decade to get past the strain of it all on the other side. She crossed her arms, cold even in the pleasantly warm air. "How's the outline coming?"

Dan took the change in topic without comment. I'm doing my best to come up with something that isn't too hard on you all, but I originally went into this planning an epic . . .

Eloise nodded, waiting.

Does it have to be a real ending for this to work? he finally asked. I could just come up with something and ... The End.

"That's what Hebe was suggesting." Eloise pressed her lips together, looking at the bath-toy ducks.

Should I, then?

Eloise tapped her fingers on her upper arm, considering it. "Perhaps. I think part of me is waiting to see what the people in my world say—assuming they'll be able to get through. Last thing we need is for the entire story to implode on us or something."

Makes sense.

She didn't speak.

What would happen if it did?

"Did implode?" Eloise frowned.

I mean, there must be something outside my map, yeah? Or are you just floating out there?

Eloise took her time as she thought. "The sets are all next to each other. At the edge of yours, I'm guessing there's another one."

Would I destroy both, then?

"I have no idea."

If I didn't keep writing at all, would you be able to walk home? Back through the sets, I mean.

Eloise's chest tightened, the idea so foreign it didn't seem to sit entirely right in the corner of her mind.

Eloise?

"I really don't know," she said. "I don't think any-one's ever tried."

Another option there, maybe.

"Maybe," she agreed, shifting uncomfortably. "Though I have no idea which way I'd even go. I could be thousands of miles into the sets, as far as I know. Trying to get sent back is likely the easier option."

I'll keep planning, then. See if we can get you all closer to the end tomorrow.

With the world currently set to turn to twilight any-time Dan left, Eloise wouldn't have known "tomorrow" from anything else, but movement had to be a positive thing. "Let me know if you need any plotting help."

If Dan answered, he didn't type it. And so Eloise just sat, watching the not-real world around her.

"I've got something." Sven barely glanced up as Barnaby returned, this time standing behind the TV.

"What is it?" Barnaby set the mugs on his desk hap-hazardly, lucky they didn't decide to spill as he moved forward.

"Take a look at that." Sven motioned to the computer before leaning over to study the TV screen. "Everything the author was typing was popping up, but so was anything Eloise said. I've never seen anything like it. I'm trying to keep the feed up."

Barnaby sat at the computer, typing quickly. Eloise?

The display sputtered, but a word popped back up. Barnaby?

The television sparked, Sven pulling back sharply before he fixed another two connections. "Got it!"

The set flickered back to life, Eloise searching the sky from what seemed like a park bench.

Barnaby frowned, mumbling under his breath as he typed. Where are you?

"A park." Eloise's voice came over the TV. Sven turned up the volume as she continued, "I don't think it has a name. Dan asked where I'd like to wait while he worked things out."

You call the author "Dan" now?

"It is his name."

"This is amazing." Sven looked between the monitor and the computer, catching Barnaby's eyes. "Other than Eloise being stuck in there, I mean."

"Did you go to the OAT?" Eloise asked over the end of Sven's sentence, seemingly oblivious to Sven speaking.

Of course. She couldn't hear him. Barnaby turned back to typing, his own words coming over the television once again. I'm waiting to see if I hear any more, but they didn't send you in there.

Eloise pressed her lips together, concern pulling her face taut. "Do we think that's a good or a bad thing?"

Barnaby paused, releasing a breath. I'm not sure. It's just a "thing" right now.

Eloise nodded, focusing on her lap. "They won't know how to get me out of here, then, I take it?"

We're working on that, Barnaby assured her, feeling Sven standing over his shoulder.

"The author's going to try to end the story," Eloise said. "I told him that would generally send us all home. I've just been waiting to hear from you."

End the story how?

"Hebe's pushing for: 'And then they tripped over what they needed, went home, and lived happily ever after.'"

"Hebe's another character?" Sven glanced between the two screens, finally picking up one of the mugs.

Barnaby nodded, not bothering to answer otherwise. That would be the quickest way.

"But do you think it would work?" Eloise looked up, once again nowhere near the feed.

You think it wouldn't?

"It just . . . doesn't feel right." She crossed her arms. "Like it's not a real ending."

If the author's willing to do that, I think an ending's an ending.

Eloise pursed her lips. "Then it's just whether or not I'd be sucked out with everyone else."

You should be, if the set shuts down. Barnaby turned to Sven. "You didn't have the OAT involved when you came back out, did you?"

"Not as far as I know."

Sven agrees.

"I do?" Sven asked.

Eloise's eyebrows pulled together, a little difficult to see as the screen grew darker. "Sven's there?"

He's helping with the computer. Barnaby glanced behind him, motioning Sven back into action with the television.

Eloise just nodded, keeping any comment she might have to herself. "So, you think I should tell Dan to just wrap up?"

Barnaby's fingers remained on the keyboard. He couldn't quite bring himself to pass a verdict when he wasn't any more certain than she was.

"His other suggestion was trying to walk back," Eloise continued when Barnaby didn't answer.

The sentence didn't fully make sense. Walk back?

"All the sets are next to each other," Eloise said, voice even less sure than before, making the words nearly sound like a question. "We'd have to reach the end of this set eventually, if we kept walking."

And you'd hit no-man's-land, Barnaby typed before he could think it.

"We could walk that, too." Eloise said. "It looked a little wobbly, but it was more rubbery than anything else when I stood on it by the Wall."

What the hell were you doing on no-man's-land?

"Don't yell at me." She frowned, the screen threatening to go out, even with Sven still working on it.

I'm typing, I can't yell. He shook his head and forced himself to type more slowly. You won't be able to walk it. You'd be swallowed up.

"I'll ask him to try to end the story then, next time he's here." Eloise sighed, standing even as the screen flashed black, then came on weakly. "I can't just sit here and hope."

The document joined the TV, flickering unhappily, cursor freezing. Barnaby fought to keep it typing. I'm starting to lose you again.

"Author's been gone too long." Sven shook his head, looking over the wires. "I'm doing my best."

"I'll check on the others." Eloise started to move, her voice sounding like it was coming through water. "When Dan comes back, you should come back too?"

Hopefu-

The document froze, the computer giving a long, angry beep before it shut down altogether.

"Damn machine." Barnaby ran a hand through his hair, leaning back in his chair as his teeth clenched.

Sven fiddled with a few more connections, then finally moved back in front of the monitor. "I can keep messing with it, but it might be out of my pay grade, getting it on when the author's not there."

Barnaby nodded, checking the time. "Whatever you can do."

Sven looked at the monitor, mouth pulled to the side before he looked back at Barnaby. "I do think you owe me at least a bagel, though."

Barnaby laughed, the sound dying off quickly as he glanced at the dead screen. He stood, clapping Sven's shoulder. "I think that can be arranged."

Chapter Sixteen

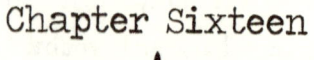

BARNABY STOOD OUTSIDE THE STILL-CLOSED COFFEE shop, leaning back against a wall. A deep headache threatened at the base of his skull. Perhaps he actually should have had some of the work coffee he'd made before heading out for breakfast. He'd never been a morning person as it was, barring a short, author-imposed stint in-story. And he was obviously getting much too old for all-nighters—permanently frozen in his twenties or no.

He glanced at the shop. Still no lights save the one in the back. Obviously, Sven was a better friend than

Barnaby had given him credit for, willing to come help out before even the coffee shop had the decency to be open. Barnaby dropped his head back on the wall, closing his eyes. Hopefully Eloise's author friend would be back soon, and Barnaby could put the past twenty-four hours behind him.

He could switch to wondering what the hell Eloise had been thinking—wandering off in the middle of the night to mess around on no-man's-land. Deciding she would ignore being assigned, as if that were a possibility. Even the death of a friend wasn't an excuse for that.

Even being as young as she was. She'd never even been assigned.

He opened his eyes. He preferred not to focus on that.

The sun poked through the buildings across from him, more and more light slowly sliding over the mess of shops and office buildings. He released a long breath. So, it was officially morning. The shop would have to open soon. Hopefully.

Barnaby's phone buzzed in his pocket, making him straighten. Fishing it out, he checked the unfamiliar number on the screen. He hesitated. On a normal day, he'd send it to voicemail. This morning, he swiped it open.

"Hello?"

"Hi, Barney?" The woman's voice came over the line. "It's Alice, from the OAT?"

"Oh," Barnaby said, his brain feeling too sluggish to take in the surprise. "Hi. How are you?"

"Hope I'm not waking you," she continued, sounding just as chipper as the day before. "I came in a little early to poke around while the nine-to-fivers were still out."

"No, I'm up." He glanced behind him as the shop lights came on, taking a few steps away, as if he needed to protect the phone call. "Did you find something?"

"Oh, definitely something." Alice laughed. "I'm not entirely sure what, but I thought you'd be interested."

Barnaby waited for her to continue, prompting her when she didn't. "Okay?"

"That odd spike with the girl you were looking into? Looking back at the transport records, this isn't the first time there's been something like that. The last one was years and years ago, but it's the same random spike, and they've all generally been in residential areas. There've been at least three others, the first seeming to happen around the 1920's."

Barnaby furrowed his eyebrows, mind turning the information over. "What does that mean?"

"As far as I can tell, it means that, in the last century, there have been at least four things—human or other-wise—transferred into stories without OAT involvement."

"How is that even possible?"

"That, I don't know, Barney." Her smile came through the phone. "But I thought you'd be really interested in this next part."

The knot that formed in his stomach said he didn't actually want to know. "Yeah?"

"Yeah. After two of the three spikes, we show the affected stories ended, but had no transports *back*."

Barnaby's body tensed. "What?"

"Crazy, right?" she continued. "I show the story end markers here, but I can't find any spikes saying anyone was transferred out of them. Like they were stories without characters or something. Some of the files here are corrupted, but both happened within a couple days of those odd spikes. I'm trying to find out more, but I might have to wait until Mrs. Finch signs in with her password for the rest of this stuff."

"Thanks." Barnaby tried to swallow the lump in his throat. "You'll let me know if you find anything else?"

"Can do, Barney."

He said goodbye and disconnected the call, glancing back at the coffee shop. His feet took him back toward the RO. Sven would hopefully understand that breakfast needed to wait.

Hebe paced back and forth along the line of beds, not seeming to be in any better a mood than when she and Eloise had met. "When did the author say he was coming back?"

"All he said was 'tomorrow.'" Eloise shook her head, sitting against one of the worn oak headboards, Echo on the mattress beside her. "But what does that really tell us? There's no way of telling time in here."

"We've been here for months, Hebe." Savitr looked up from his spot on the window seat. "I don't think another couple of hours will kill us."

"You never know," Hebe mumbled, continuing to wear a hole in the carpet.

"He knows we're waiting." Eloise followed Hebe with her eyes. "He'll be back eventually."

"Sorry if you find my questions intrusive," Hebe said sarcastically, glaring at Eloise. "Not all of us have a direct line to our lord and creator."

Eloise just shook her head, placing a hand on her stomach as it continued to churn unhappily.

"Are you all right?" Echo asked.

"Just nerves, I think." Eloise offered a weak smile. "None of this has really agreed with me."

"Try being here for months on end," Hebe grumbled.

Echo rolled her eyes, giving Eloise an apologetic look.

"Do we have any more food?" Savitr stood.

"Just what's left from breakfast." Pan motioned.

Savitr started for the door. "Anyone want anything?"

Eloise shook her head, looking down. From the silence, no one else had much of an appetite either.

Swallowing, Eloise opened her mouth, pausing as she slid her eyes back up. Halfway into a step, Hebe had frozen. Savitr was the same, nearly out of the room. Eloise's mouth snapped shut, the unpleasant churning turning into full nausea. "Hello?"

No one answered. A low, mechanical buzz made the walls vibrate.

"Dan?" She stood slowly. "Barnaby?"

The room shook, an angry clicking going straight to Eloise's bones before things stilled again.

Eloise?

The familiar voice let her release a breath. "Dan?"

Sorry, my computer was doing something odd. Are you all ready to go?

"I actually got through to my people." Eloise crossed her arms at the sudden, unexplained chill. "They said you can use Hebe's idea. You know, if you'd like."

Just ending everything?

Eloise nodded, then realized he couldn't see her. "Yes."

Does it matter how?

Eloise released a breath. His guess was likely as good as hers. "Did you have a final line you wanted to use?"

Nothing concrete. I just sort of knew I wanted everyone to go home.

"All right." Eloise looked at the people frozen around her. "Why don't you write a few paragraphs of Deus Ex Machina to say everything's fine? So there's at least some closure?"

What about you?

"I'll act along," she said. "Just tell me what to do."

Barnaby watched the numbers on the elevator click by, not waiting for the doors to fully open before he hurried down the hall.

Sven looked over from the desk, glancing down at Barnaby's hands. "No breakfast?"

Barnaby motioned him away, moving forward. "Have you got the computer working?"

"I tried, but the program wouldn't let me through. I'm lucky the processor didn't break, with some of the noises it was making."

Barnaby looked at the TV screen, his chest tightening at the silent action playing out. "Then, what's happening?"

"Author came back." Sven motioned. "The sound cut out, but Eloise told him to send them home, so everything should be fine in—"

"No, no, no, no." Barnaby moved to the keyboard, leaning over Sven to reach it. The computer beeped as he struck a key, but wouldn't react.

"It locked up when the author started typing." Sven caught Barnaby's forearm, pushing him back. "What's wrong?"

"She can't have him end it." Barnaby's eyes went back to the screen. "My contact at the OAT called. Apparently, this has happened before."

"Someone being sucked in?"

Barnaby nodded as he tried clicking somewhere else. The screen just beeped at him again.

"What happens if they end it?"

"I don't know." Barnaby looked back at the television. "I'd just really rather we find out before they end it and no one comes back."

Nudging Barnaby out of the way, Sven tried some combination of keys. He only got a series of angry beeps as well. He moved under the desk, voice muffled. "Keep an eye on the screen. Tell me what it's doing."

"All right." Barnaby watched the frozen page, then looked at the television as it started to flicker. "The TV's trying to go out."

Sven's head popped back out. "I'm not doing anything to the TV."

Barnaby's jaw went hard, adrenaline pumping. He clenched his fists and did his best to keep his voice calm. "Better see what you can do quickly, then."

Something beeped, loudly, drowning out Dan's narrative in spurts.

Eloise? He came back.

"Yeah?" She released a shaky breath.

Anything else you need before I do the last line?

She tried to force herself to smile, glad no one was there to see it. "I think we're fine. Thanks."

All right, then. It's been a pleasure.

"Truly," she agreed, eyes watching the others around her in their ending tableau.

And, once again-

Another sharp beep.

-all was well.

The world trembled, the others slowly starting to move. A wind picked up, pushing Eloise's skirt between her legs. It roared. More angry beeps flew through the air.

"What's happening?" Echo yelled.

"I don't know," Eloise called back, another jerk nearly sending her off balance. The world blurred, morphed, came back. She had to close her eyes, the wind making them sting, the waves causing a splitting pain to travel up the back of her head.

Eloise . . .

Her ears tried to pick up the familiar voice, but couldn't quite manage as she crumpled, body curled in to protect herself from the tempest around her. Slowly, the wind died back down, the shaking turning to a gentle lull before finally stopping.

Eloise? Barnaby's quiet voice filtered through the ringing in Eloise's ears. Are you there?

Eloise lifted her head slowly, eyebrows rising at the black and white landscape around her.

Eloise. Can you hear me?

"Yes." Her voice cracked, so she tried again. "Yes, I'm here."

A sense of relief flooded through his words. Are you all right?

Her eyes drifted to the others. Likewise strewn across the ground, they remained the only color against the gray-tone world surrounding them. Eloise blinked, Pan and Echo's red hair shocking against their now gray clothes, their now gray world.

Eloise?

"I'm fine." She tried to get her mind to work once again. "I think. The set's gone . . . gray."

It's closed, Barnaby continued, his voice seeming far off. Are you alone?

"No." She looked at the rest of the group watching her. "The others are still . . . maybe we just haven't transported yet . . . ?"

If you haven't yet, you aren't likely to.

Eloise did her best to swallow the lump in her throat.

Eloise. The voice came more urgently now. The feed's shutting down. Once it goes, I don't think I'm going to be able to get it back.

"Barnaby—"

You're going to have to walk. If you can get into another active set, hopefully I can find you over here. The Wall runs north-south, which you probably already knew, but try to head toward that, if you can. If your compass works.

Owen stood, helping Hebe up before going to check on the others.

I'm going to do everything I can from here, but if you can't get out of that set ... I don't know .... The words started to fade.

"Barnaby?" She stood, nearly tripping over her gray dress.

I'm sorry. I'm so ...

And then it was silent.

"Barnaby?" she tried again.

Nothing. No Barnaby. No story noise. Nothing even from the others standing a little ways off.

She just stood there, letting everything—the landscape, the silence, their choices—soak in.

"What happened?" Pan finally spoke, voice small.

"Having the author end the story backfired, obviously," Hebe snapped, bending to check her gray pack, her body looking nearly tense enough to break.

Silence again.

"So, what do we do now?" Echo asked, the words sitting heavily in the air.

Eloise took a breath, trying to fight off the shakiness in her own voice. Alone, perhaps, she could have stopped, could have thought about how hopeless everything had just become. If she dissolved now, though, with the rest of the group watching her, expecting her to somehow know what to do . . . . She forced a humorless smile, fishing for the compass in her pocket. "I guess we walk."

No one, not even Hebe, seemed to have a comment.

Pulling the metal disk free from her pocket, Eloise flipped it open. The silver and black lettering fit in with the grayscale, but it somehow looked too bright, still itself against the dull world. Eloise hesitated for just a moment, the needle trembling slightly as her hand shook. She finally chanced to turn it. The needle pointed the same direction, no matter how the case spun. She released a breath. If nothing else, it was still a compass. She just had to pray it pointed true north.

The needle once again pointed to zero, and she looked off to what she hoped was west.

"Is that really going to help?" Hebe finally spoke when Eloise didn't, her voice hard. "We have no idea where we are."

Eloise clicked the compass shut, tucking it back in her pocket. "Like Barnaby said, the Wall runs north-south. And, though I can't ask now, if Dan was originally basing this set on Middle Earth, we're likely to run out of map more quickly going west—likely southwest—than east."

Hebe scoffed. "You have the map of Middle Earth memorized?"

"I have all sorts of random things memorized." Eloise closed her eyes to picture it, the focus helping to press her panic down to somewhere she could ignore it. Holding her hands out, she worked it through. "Rohan's in the center . . . center south, I think, before you get to the extended map, with the closest coast west or southwest." She looked at the group once again. "It's not much more than a prayer that Dan was using that map for inspiration, but, do any of you have a better idea?"

Savitr stepped forward first. "Not when it's pray or sit around here forever."

Echo looked at the rest of them, then finally moved next to Savitr with a shrug.

Eloise looked at Owen while he stared at his feet, then to Hebe with her crossed arms and pinched face. "Do we need to take a vote?"

Hebe heaved a sigh, motioning to the set. "Well, it isn't much of a choice now, is it?"

Eloise nodded, rubbing her thumb along the compass in her pocket. It really was up to them now. She only wished she had any clue what she was doing.

Chapter Seventeen

BARNABY RESTED HIS HEAD IN HIS HANDS, ELBOWS on either side of the keyboard. Adrenaline gone, he only felt tired. No, more than that. Exhaustion dug deep into him. And there was still so much to do.

After another moment, Sven reached out, laying a hand on Barnaby's shoulder. "She's a smart girl, Fitz. She'll be okay."

Barnaby still couldn't bring himself to lift his head. "She could be thousands of miles from the Wall. Hundreds of thousands. Who knows how many sets are out there?"

"You—"

"And if something happens in a dead set?" Barnaby continued, finally bringing himself to turn. "Do you really expect her to make it back here? She could die, and I'd never know. She likely will, if you want to start doing the math."

Sven just looked at him, face somber. "You should go home and get some sleep, Fitz. There's nothing you can do here. I'll keep an ear out, see if she ends up in someone else's story."

Barnaby released a long breath and forced himself to stand. "I'm going back to the OAT."

"You need to sleep first," Sven argued.

"Have you applied to be my mother now?" Barnaby gathered his things.

"Do you really think you'll stay awake standing in those lines?"

Barnaby supposed he couldn't argue that. He rested against the desk, the idea of sleeping right there a little more tempting than it should be. He looked back at Sven. "I'm keeping my phone on. Call me if anything happens."

Sven nodded.

Moving to the door, Barnaby stepped into the hall just as the automatic lights flipped on for the day. He continued forward. An hour or two's rest, and then he could get back to trying to figure out what the hell he could do now.

Eloise grimaced, sliding off the back of the beautiful white horse they had somehow recovered. The horse blew, tossing its head back and forth. Eloise patted its neck, bouncing slightly in shallow squats, trying to stretch her sore muscles. "I know. Believe me."

Savitr slid off his black horse with more grace than Eloise had managed. "Are you all right?"

She nodded, glancing behind her before tying her horse's reins to a low branch nearby. "Horseback riding just doesn't seem to agree with me. I'm going to end up bow-legged at this rate."

Owen rode back from where he had been scouting ahead of the group, cantering easily before pulling to stop in front of them. "Try resting on the balls of your feet more."

"Easy for you to say." She sent him a look. "Not all of us are horse-riding prodigies."

"Don't blame me." He offered a smile. "I was written that way."

"What's up ahead?" Hebe asked, her own black mare urging Echo and Pan's ponies forward.

Owen turned his attention to her. "We're coming out of the forest. There's a river or something out a little ways from us, and then . . . well, I don't know what you'd call it."

Eloise paused. "You don't know, like it's some weird landscape, or you don't know, like there's another set out there?"

Owen opened his mouth, but shut it again before he actually spoke. "I truly have no idea."

"Does it look like the no-man's-land at the Wall?" Eloise pressed.

"How would we have ever been to the Wall?" Hebe spoke before Owen could. "We were all pre-storied, and then here."

Eloise pressed her lips together, nodding before she looked back at Owen. "Show me?" She moved to her horse.

It snorted at her approach, stepping back.

Owen glanced at the balking white mare and motioned her over. "Ride with me. It'll be faster."

Eloise sent a final look at her now grazing horse before moving next to him. A slight bend, and he had her under the arms, pulling her over the saddle in front of him.

"Ow." Eloise frowned, rubbing her shoulders. "Manhandle me, why don't you?"

"Sorry. I've seen you try to get on a horse." Owen addressed her even as he looked at the rest of the group. "We'll be right back."

The horse spurred forward. Eloise did her best to grip the edge of the saddle for balance, as he moved much more quickly than she would ever have been able to manage.

Owen galloped up a hill, reining in to a trot when they got close to the top. The trees were more scattered out in front of them, large swaths of gray grass covering the low hills.

He pointed off, beyond a lazy river, at a hazy patch of black near the horizon. "There. Do you see?"

Eloise straightened, flexing her fingers once she released the saddle, letting blood return to her white knuckles. She squinted, her vision blurring for a second. She squeezed her eyes together tightly, trying to fight off the odd sense of vertigo before looking back at the horizon. "Can we get closer?"

"We won't be able to see any better if we start into the hills." Owen shook his head. "That's west?"

She pulled the silver compass out, consulting the little metal needle in it. "That is."

"Do you think that's the end of our set?"

Eloise pressed her lips together, scrunching up her nose as she tried to determine what she wanted to say. She sighed. "I don't know what else it would be. We can hope, at least."

He nodded slowly. "Should we tell the others?"

"Do you think we should get their hopes up?" She twisted to look at him.

He lifted a surprised eyebrow. "Why are you asking me?"

"You were written to be the leader of the group, weren't you?"

"You seem to know better than I do."

Eloise gave a humorless laugh, looking back at the dizzying line on the horizon. "I must be good at faking it, then."

"Sometimes, that's all you really need." He pulled the reins, his horse turning as though it were a part of him. "You're all right if I gallop again?"

She swallowed. "Why wouldn't I be?"

"The saddle still has nail marks in it." He offered a small smile.

She flushed, turning back to face the front. "Maybe just a little more slowly."

Owen spurred off, Eloise squeezing her eyes shut as they headed back the way they had come. When they finally slowed, it was too late to stop every muscle in Eloise's back from tensing. Still, she forced her eyes open once more, looking down the little hill to where the rest of the group had stopped.

"What is it?" Hebe called up to them.

"I think you'll all just need to see this," Owen answered, helping Eloise down to return to her own horse.

Eloise exhaled, trying to get her chest to relax as she returned to the saddle. Just a little bit longer, and perhaps there'd at least be some change to the gray monotony.

A few more ups and downs—certainly more than Eloise would have liked—and the hills they had been traversing all day cut off abruptly, the gray grass fading into black along the edges. The same deep, nearly invisible black chasm as what Eloise had seen by the Wall stretched out at least two-hundred yards before it reached the land across from them—entirely populated with skyscrapers.

The sheer dissimilarity seemed to strike them all silent.

Pan spoke first. "Are we going there?"

Owen's eyes searched the darkness. "If we can figure out a way across."

"What is it?" Echo murmured.

"No-man's-land," Eloise answered, whether or not Echo had been asking her.

Echo shook her head, eyes forward. "It barely looks like anything's there."

"If it's like what I was on before, it's sort of rubbery. Wavy." Eloise did her best to sound confident.

"And if it isn't?" Hebe glanced at Eloise for barely a second before looking back at the open space.

"Then we'll have to figure out a way to make a bridge, I suppose." Eloise tried not to let her exasperation leech into her voice. "I don't know. We might as well see at this point, though."

"That's uplifting," Hebe mumbled.

"I wasn't aware it was my job to play the company morale police," Eloise snapped. "I'm not a goddamn rally girl."

"Should I scout ahead?" Owen cut off Hebe's reply.

Eloise just nodded, trusting that more than her voice at the moment.

Owen spurred off toward the border.

Eloise watched him, finally looking at the rest of the group when she had some control over her irritation. "Well, I suppose it won't do us any good to stand here."

Savitr offered a smile, motioning forward. "Off we go."

For as far off as the black expanse seemed, they somehow reached the border before they realized, the ground opening up all at once. The horses began to pull, doing their best to stay away from the black ground. Owen tried to move forward, but even his well-trained mount refused to follow his urging.

"Do you think they're stuck to this set?" Echo asked.

Owen frowned, looking back at the rest of them. "Looks like we're going to have to leave them."

Silently, they dismounted, redistributing their packs before turning. Standing at the edge of the set, they stared out at the emptiness. Eloise looked down the line and saw the row of unsure faces. She sighed, facing forward. "Fine, I'll go first."

Five pairs of eyes turned to her, waiting with the same expression.

Swallowing, Eloise forced herself to take a decisive step forward. The expanse held, her feet gripping the familiar, rubbery surface for a second before she stepped further out. The white mare whinnied unhappily, taking a decisive step backward. Owen shook his head, releasing his horse's reins slowly, and stepped onto the blackness, bouncing experimentally on the balls of his feet. He looked back at the others still on the edge. "Seems safe enough."

Eloise gave Owen an appreciative smile.

One by one, the others followed, each trying to get used to the strange surface in their own way—Savitr bouncing like he was on a trampoline, Pan and Echo shifting their weight, and Hebe just finding her center of gravity and standing straight. Free of their hold, the horses stomped fretfully, a few already turning back for the gray hills.

"We better move." Owen frowned, surveying the animals. "I can't imagine much good will come from staying out here."

Eloise nodded, moving forward, careful to step lightly on the porous surface.

"What city do you think that is?" Echo moved beside her.

Eloise shook her head. "I don't recognize it from this angle."

"New York?" Savitr suggested.

Hebe snorted. "We can't be *that* close to the Wall."

"No, look." He pointed. "Isn't that Bellevue?"

"What?" Hebe looked at him skeptically.

"Bellevue Medical Center." Savitr motioned again. "Oldest public medical center in the United States. New York."

"I didn't take you for an architecture buff." Eloise glanced at him.

"I was, back in school." He nodded, a slightly pained look passing over his face—nearly shocking compared to his normally teasing demeanor.

"The buildings are tall enough to be New York," Echo agreed.

Eloise lifted her hand to help cut the glare, squinting up at the buildings. A silver tower glinted in the bright sunlight. The next set definitely wasn't in twilight. "Is that the Chrysler Building?"

"So it *is* New York!" Savitr smiled.

Eloise searched the rest of skyline. "But it's the tallest building."

"It is?" Savitr's smile dropped off as he scanned the structures himself.

Echo looked at them. "What does that mean?"

"It means Empire State hasn't been built yet." Savitr barely glanced at the rest of them.

"So, it's a New York set," Eloise concluded. "But a New York from the past."

"1930," Savitr said, "if the Chrysler is completed but not the Empire State."

"1930 exactly?" Eloise asked.

Savitr nodded. "Chrysler was completed May 1930, Empire State May 1931."

"Good to know." Eloise didn't question his apparent encyclopedic knowledge. Not when he never seemed to question hers. "So we're going to Depression Era New York."

"Is that near Modern Day New York?" Echo asked.

Eloise didn't have an answer, and so she fell as silent as the rest of the group, putting one foot in front of the other.

The ground seemed to waver. Slowing, Eloise stared into the blackness, half wondering if she'd started seeing things.

"What the . . . ?" Hebe began to sink where she had stopped a little ways forward. She pulled a foot up, the ground releasing her with a loud pop. The dent from that foot regained shape, as her other one started to sink deeper.

Eloise looked down, the wavering continuing beneath her, like the black substance would soon turn to water. She glanced up and saw Hebe making her way forward, each step seeming to teasingly hit something solid before it began sinking again.

"Run!" Owen's voice sounded somewhere behind the rising panic in Eloise's ears.

No one debated. Feet pounded the black surface as it wavered, solid only for a second before it began to sink. Pulling her skirt up, Eloise pumped her legs as fast as they would go, her lungs burning as the next set began to loom overhead.

After what felt like hours, the odd, rubbery feeling returned under her feet. Another few steps, and Eloise finally allowed herself to slow, feeling the ground hold her weight. She doubled over, her forearms resting on her thighs as she panted. "God . . . I hate running."

Hebe glanced at her, then looked back where they had come—Dan's set still gray and empty across from them. "What the hell was that?"

Eloise looked herself, suddenly realizing that all eyes were on her. She suppressed a grimace. "Really?"

"You're the one who's been on it before," Pan said softly.

Releasing a breath, Eloise opened her pack, rummaging a bit before she found a dull tin cup.

"You can't wait for a drink until we're off this stuff?" Hebe frowned.

Eloise did her best to ignore Hebe's snark, facing the center of the no-man's-land. Gently, she lobbed the cup, the metal arcing before it hit the surface closer to the center. It sat in place for a moment, and then slowly started to sink. An odd glug, and it disappeared below the surface, the black closing around it.

Pan watched it, then looked back at Eloise. "Why did you do that?"

"There's some sort of skin along the top, through the middle there." Eloise motioned toward it with her chin. "Like cornstarch in water. Very, very, scarily dark cornstarch in water."

"Cornstarch?" Hebe lifted an eyebrow.

"It forms a . . ." Eloise waved her hand, trying to think of the term. "A non-Newtonian fluid. Something not quite liquid, but not quite solid either. If you mix cornstarch and water, it's fluid, you can sink into it, but under any sudden impacts, it's solid."

"So, your scientific test was to throw a cup at it?" Hebe said.

"Would you have preferred to go back out there?" Eloise sent her a look. "It makes sense, with those old stories we'd hear in school—the people who were sucked under in no-man's-land? It's land out there, but land you could drown in."

Owen shook his head, heading for the proper edge to the city. "Let's get to actual land before this starts to open up."

Eloise nodded, watching the spot further out—once again perfectly flat—for just another moment before she followed the rest.

Chapter Eighteen

BARNABY LOOKED WARILY AT THE OAT LINE THROUGH the glass door, not quite able to force himself back inside. As perfectly bureaucratic as the workers inside seemed, it wasn't likely he'd find someone who would let him jump the line and just go upstairs. Nor was he likely to find a way upstairs without making it through that line.

He pulled his phone out of his pocket, flicking through his recent calls. Finding the correct timestamp, he moved off to the side, watching the front doors from the street corner as the phone rang.

"Alice Wembley."

"Alice," he said, pausing for just a second to wonder if he should call her that. He brushed it off. "It's Barnaby Fitzwilliam?"

"Oh, hey, Barney. Mind holding just a sec?"

"Sure." He nodded, running a hand through his hair. It was already past noon; he had fallen asleep longer than he intended. Still, he wasn't sure he looked much better for it. Compared to everyone else going about their work days in the stretch of uniform office buildings, he likely looked drunk—or at least strung out. Next time he made it home, he should at least change out of the same, wrinkled shirt he'd been wearing the day before.

"Barney?"

"Yeah?" He straightened, letting his other hand drop back to his side.

"Sorry about that. Mrs. Finch was side-eyeing me for talking on my cell," Alice continued brightly. "What's up?"

"I came by the OAT." He glanced at the doors again. "But with the lines, I thought it might be quicker to just call you."

"Oh, just come around back. I'll let you in the staff door."

Barnaby hesitated. "You won't get in trouble for that?"

"Eh. Worst they can do is fire me." The prospect didn't seem to worry her in the slightest. "Meet me back there in five."

Barnaby frowned but didn't bother to argue, slipping his phone away as he moved to circle the square building.

The employees at the OAT didn't seem to have it any better than their visitors, their dark little door as gray and dreary as the front. Barnaby followed Alice into the dim hallways, each looking the same, as she weaved her way . . . somewhere.

Turning into another stairwell, he watched her back. "I didn't mean to interrupt if you were busy."

She waved her hand. "It's amazing how little work I actually have to do around here. I'll probably hop somewhere else soon enough anyway."

"You're quitting?" he asked.

"At some point." She shrugged, coming to what seemed to be another back door. "I'm just pretty sure my husband would kill me if I was stirring up trouble at home all day. I hop around wherever I feel like it."

Barnaby nodded, squinting as the light hit him, too bright after the gray hall.

"Sorry. Should have warned you." She motioned to a lawn chair. "Please."

Barnaby frowned, looking at the mesh chair before staking a seat. "I take it the OAT didn't set this up?"

"Oh, I think I'd die if I had to sit in that room with Mrs. Finch every hour of every day." Alice took the other chair, pulling a laptop out of her bag. She flipped it open. "I can still get on the network from up here, so if anything major happens, I can sneak back downstairs."

Barnaby studied her for a long moment, then finally had to say it: "You *really* don't seem like you should be working here."

"But aren't you glad I do?" She flashed him a smile before looking back at her computer. "I take it you're here about your story shutting down this morning?"

Barnaby frowned, shifting on the uncomfortable chair. "Was the OAT involved in that?"

"Nope." She tilted the screen for him to look at. "It came up as an error report. That's what got my attention."

He scanned the error code and the short message with it. "What does that mean?"

She shrugged, turning the screen back to her. "Not one they teach us. That's actually just a screenshot from earlier. The entire file went on lockdown when people started poking at it. IT's trying to get in now, I think, but it seems like it's corrupted. Just like the other ones I found."

"What happens when a file's corrupted?"

"I couldn't tell you." She typed something and scooted over to share her screen. "You see these charts?"

Barnaby looked down at the scrolling lines—one red, one blue, one green—moving up and down seemingly at random.

"Everything at the OAT is automated. It's why you

can staff it with people who only really care about forms. You get a form, send the person to the right room, and the machines pop out where they're going. No one decides who. No one decides where. A name comes out, a letter goes off, and then we stick that person in another machine and off they go."

"Are you saying it's a glitch then?" He looked back at her face.

"Couldn't say." She kept her eyes on the line. "I've looked into the machines some, since it's not every day an actual mystery comes walking in the door, but even the guys in IT . . . no one seems to know how they work. They've always been there and always done the exact same thing."

"Always?"

"At least as long as anyone can remember."

Barnaby took the words in, trying to piece the information together in a way that would make sense. "But then, who made them?"

"Can't say I know." Alice leaned back in her chair with a smile. "All very intriguing though, don't you think?"

Barnaby tented his fingers, pressing them to his lips for a moment before speaking again. "Could I be honest, for a second?"

"You haven't been so far?" Alice lifted an eyebrow, face still as good natured as ever.

"Not entirely, I suppose." He forced his hands to drop. "The woman who ended up in that story I was here about yesterday—"

"She's your girlfriend?" Alice finished, then laughed at the surprised look on his face. "Come on now, Barney. She was obviously either your sister, best friend, or girlfriend. You didn't seem to be *enjoying* wading through all those forms they were shoving at you."

"Work could have sent me," he argued.

"And sent you again today to follow up? In yesterday's clothes?"

He released a breath, rubbing at one temple. There seemed little point in arguing if he had been about to admit it anyway. "We've been dating for a few months. And she was at my house when she was transported."

"Into a story you were monitoring?" If she had any other opinion on the relationship, Alice didn't show it in the slightest.

He hesitated. "Do you think I had something to do with it?"

"I can't say I'd know, Barney." She shrugged easily. "It just seems like a pretty big coincidence to me."

"And 'There Are No Coincidences'?"

She laughed. "Depends on whether you think we're in a story or real life."

Barnaby released a long breath. "You know, I'm really not sure at this point."

Alice just continued to smile. "Either way, I would look into it. Seems a little too coincidental, even for real life."

Barnaby nodded, not quite able to share Alice's good humor. "Is there anything you could give me on the other incidents you found like this?"

"There's not much to go on." Alice turned back to the screen, clicking something. "I could print off the charts, but I doubt you'd get much from them if you haven't been trained to use them at all."

"You said the spikes tended to happen in residential areas?"

"True." Alice seemed to guess his meaning. "I could print out the map. And the names of the stories that ended, if you like, though with the files corrupted, there's not too much over here. You could see what the RO has, though."

Of course. Somehow, in everything else, Barnaby had missed the obvious. He could still get into the records at work, even if he couldn't necessarily talk to Eloise. He forced something like a smile. "That would be great. Thank you."

Eloise stepped onto the paved street, craning her neck up to look at the buildings. Though they weren't quite as tall, or as close-packed as she had seen in pictures, the difference between this and Dan's set was jarring.

Savitr walked up to one of the Model As sitting along the street, letting out a low whistle. "I was put in the wrong story."

"I don't think 'Savitr' is a very Great Depression-sounding name." Eloise offered him a small smile as he turned back to the rest of them.

"At least we're back in color." Hebe turned to one of the shop fronts.

Eloise nodded, her long gray dress seeming entirely out of place in the bright, non-fantastical world. She wrapped her arms around her middle, a thought registering somewhere in the back of her mind. It was cold. Even with the bright, clear blue sky over them, the air bit.

"If it's in color, then that means it's an active set?" Pan asked.

Eloise released a breath through her nose at the silence, bristling at the sinking feeling that they were all waiting for her answer. She glanced at the short man. "From what we've seen, hopefully, yes."

They continued forward, Owen and Hebe moving farther ahead to study the empty shops as the rest of them followed on the equally empty sidewalks.

Eloise frowned as a thought hit. "Though . . ."

Eyes turned back to her.

"Where is everyone, then?" Eloise scanned the street. Midday, based on the sun, and yet there didn't seem to be a soul for blocks. The few abandoned cars scattered about were the only break in the concrete and asphalt. "It's New York City. Even in the thirties, it wasn't a ghost town."

"Post-apocalyptic?" Savitr suggested.

"Don't generally have post-apocalyptic historical fiction." Eloise shook her head. "And you'd think the cars wouldn't be so brand new and shiny if that were the case."

Owen returned to the rest of the group. "It isn't really New York, is it? It's someone's representation. Probably based on old photos or something. Maybe they just didn't write in any background characters."

Eloise couldn't bring herself to argue, pressing her arms more tightly against her. "Why is it so cold?"

"Food!" Echo pointed, cutting off any reply as she rushed forward.

Eloise took the distraction, following. A bakery filled the bottom floor of the building on the corner, bread in the window with signs shouting five cents. Pan tried the door, and a bell tinkled gently as he easily pushed it open. The smell of baking bread floated through the cold air.

"Well, whether or not this set's being used—" Owen moved behind the wooden counter, gently squeezing the bread sitting in a glass case, "—the bread's fresh."

"Now we just need to find a deli or something and get some meat." Hebe stepped next to him, tearing off a chunk and taking a bite of plain bread all the same.

Eloise still couldn't bring herself to put any of it in her mouth.

"We should load up on supplies before we go." Savitr raided a pastry case.

"And see if anyone else is here." Eloise turned back to the window.

"I think supplies are more important." Hebe spoke through a full mouth.

"Yes, but if there is someone here, perhaps they could help."

"Unless an author has them busy," Hebe said.

"True." Eloise frowned, looking at the street for a final moment before she turned back to the shop. She tilted her head up to look at the ceiling. "Hello? Is anyone there?"

Silence responded

Hebe glanced up, taking another bite as she looked at Eloise. "Was that supposed to work?"

"It did, more or less, with Dan." Eloise met Hebe's eyes, just for a second. "I don't know how it works here, yet."

Savitr gathered up a loaf, sticking it in his pack. "While we figure it out, let's find that deli. I could really use a pastrami on rye after all our elf food."

Owen nodded, grabbing a couple loaves out of the window. The empty spaces refilled with what had been taken. Owen froze, looking at the loaves in his hands before looking back at the window. "So it's definitely an active set."

"Yours never did that." Eloise pressed her lips together, forcing her eyes up to Owen.

"Before you showed up, it did." Hebe moved back from around the counter. "We only ever had the same three things to eat, but everything always went back to the way the author left it."

"All right, then," Eloise said. "Whose story do we think it is?"

"How could we possibly know?" Hebe shook her head.

"Has to be historical fiction?" Echo said. "Like you said?"

"True, but if it's a gangster story, we should probably start looking for others in different places than if it's about a ruined socialite, I would think?" Eloise tore her eyes away from the self-multiplying bread.

"We could always go to the Chrysler Building," Echo said.

Hebe snorted. "I don't think this is really the time to go sightseeing."

"No." Echo frowned. "If it's the tallest building and we wanted someone to see a signal . . ."

Eloise nodded, slowly catching the idea. "We could find a flag. Or a mirror even, something to get people's attention . . ."

Hebe pursed her lips. "That's actually a good idea."

"You don't have to sound so surprised." Echo huffed.

"So . . ." Pan started. "Where are we going to find a flag?"

Eloise looked around, then motioned outside. "We're in New York. There has to be some kind of flag somewhere."

"Sounds like a plan to me." Owen strapped his bag over his back. "Let's get moving."

Shrugging off his wrinkled shirt, Barnaby glanced at his phone on the dresser as it rang. He tugged an arm free and accepted the call, managing to put it on speaker before extricating his other arm.

"Hey, Fitz." Sven's voice came over the phone.

"Anything happening there?" Barnaby didn't waste time, pulling a new shirt from his drawer.

"Not that I've seen," Sven said. "Did you get some sleep?"

"A few hours." The new shirt went on. "I just left my contact at the OAT. Woman's crazy, I'm pretty sure, but she gave me some good information."

"Okay?"

"I need to get into some of the RO records," Barnaby continued. "Do you think I could now? Or should I wait until people start going home?"

"Do you need electronic records? Or do you need to get into the actual records room?"

Barnaby paused, not actually having considered it. "I'm not sure. They'd be old, I suppose."

"Why don't you come in around closing, then? I'll help you go through them."

Barnaby paused before buttoning his cuffs. "You don't have to do that. You already gave up your morning—"

"Fitz, this is more interesting than anything I had planned tonight by far."

Barnaby looked at the papers Alice had given him and couldn't deny that he could use the help. "I'll see you later, then. And I promise, this time, I'll actually bring food."

Sven agreed with a laugh, the line once again going dead.

Releasing a breath, Barnaby forced himself to turn back to his room, truly looking around for the first time since Eloise had disappeared. Her things were still where they belonged, dresses hanging in the closet, the glass of water he'd left for her untouched on the nightstand. He didn't remember much of his own transport—done the proper way at the OAT—but whatever had taken her hadn't left a mark behind. If she hadn't ended up in his story, he'd have never known what happened to her. She would have simply disappeared. The thought made his stomach twist.

Had anyone known what happened to the other three people who'd been unwillingly transported? Had anyone ever tried to look? Every answer only seemed to raise more questions. And who knew if he'd ever figure them out.

But, leaving his home to enter his story . . . Barnaby had to agree the coincidence seemed too strong to be meaningless.

Glancing at the lone, wrinkled shirt on the carpet, he sighed. Since she was dealing with who knew what, he supposed the least he could do for Eloise would be keeping his clothes off the floor like she'd been trying to. He bent, pausing as he spotted a black residue near his shirt. Crouching, he studied it, eventually reaching out to touch. It stuck to his fingers, oddly gummy.

It began to glow, a bright blue light that nearly burned his eyes. And then it was gone. Barnaby frowned, turning his hand one way, then the other. But beyond the dull ache from the light, it was as if the residue had never existed.

Chest a little too tight, Barnaby gathered his things, hurrying back out to his car. Any other day, he'd convince himself the lack of sleep had played with his mind. Today, he might look for somewhere else to stay until he had more answers.

As the group headed north toward Midtown, the eerie quiet of the city only seemed to grow. Eloise watched block after block pass with the same standard storefronts and empty skyscrapers.

They crossed another wide street before Owen finally slowed. "Does anyone else get the feeling we're being watched?"

The group paused, looking around.

"I don't see anyone." Echo shook her head.

"There are three-thousand windows looking onto the street." Hebe turned slowly. "If someone's up there, they're going to see us before we see them."

"There." Pan pointed.

Everyone turned, scanning the building across the street.

"Where?" Savitr asked.

"That building's different," Pan said, looking between each of them. "It has curtains."

Eloise took in the dash of red in one of the windows in Pan's building, then looked at the rest. Everything else was identically generic; those curtains had no doubt been author-described. She looked back at the group, asking no one in particular, "Should we go up?"

"Why haven't they come down?" Hebe's hand went to the gray dagger at her hip.

"They're likely trying to figure out what the hell we're doing here." Savitr moved into the street. "Let's go introduce ourselves."

The building's interior seemed smaller than it did from outside. A line of interior doors stood claustrophobically close on either side as the six of them made their way inside. Eloise frowned, trying not to get jostled too much as they adjusted to the space—the hall between the two lines of doors not more than three or four feet wide.

Moving single file, they reached a tiny foyer. An old, less-than-safe looking staircase greeted them, winding up in the tight space with short flights and narrow landings.

Hebe looked around, body held tense. "This is . . . quite the place."

"We might have come out ahead sitting in the forest." Savitr pushed a door open, but didn't seem to find anything interesting.

Eloise stepped to the side, glancing up the stairwell.

A little girl peeked over the banister, her bobbed hair hanging around her face, keeping her features too dark to make out. "Hello?"

The others went silent, moving to look themselves.

"Hi," Eloise responded, holding her hand up in a weak wave. "Do you live here?"

The girl nodded, seeming to point further down the hall.

"Are your parents here?" Owen asked, stopping behind Eloise to see over her shoulder.

"They went to get food," the girl said. "Who are you?"

"We're just . . ." Owen faltered, looked at the rest of them. "Passing through."

"You don't look like you're supposed to be here," the girl continued.

Eloise glanced at the rest of the group, their grayscale fantasy attire definitely not suiting for a New York tenement. She forced a smile. "We're not, I suppose. I'm Eloise."

The little girl looked at them for another moment, then finally lifted her hand. "I'm Annie."

"Good to meet you, Annie," Eloise said, trying to see farther down the hall on Annie's level. With the wrapping staircase filling as much of the tight space as it was, however, it seemed impossible without some sort of magic sight. Instead, she just asked, "Is there anyone else here, if your parents are gone?"

"My sisters." Annie looked over her shoulder. "But they're asleep."

Eloise nodded, trying to ignore all the eyes once again watching her. If only she had some sort of manual to study before making any more decisions . . . studying was something she could do well. "Would you mind if we came upstairs?"

"Go ahead." Annie disappeared behind the landing.

"I don't like it in here at all, for the record," Hebe murmured.

"I just hope we don't go through the steps, to be honest," Eloise returned, studying what looked suspiciously like termite damage.

"If the story is active, it can't collapse, at least without the author." Savitr moved over to the rest of them.

Eloise lifted an eyebrow. "Does that mean you're volunteering to go first?"

He hesitated, studying the stairs himself, then motioned gallantly. "Ladies first, of course."

Eloise snorted, looking back at the stairs.

"For God's sake . . ." Hebe moved forward. "I'll do it."

Even with her bravado, Hebe moved slowly, the first step creaking unhappily as she shifted her weight onto it. Still, she didn't break through, didn't lose the railing. Hopefully Savitr was right, and they'd make it the rest of the way up.

Reaching an equally cramped landing on the third floor, Eloise managed to slip by Hebe, looking at the little girl standing in the doorway of what Eloise had to guess was an apartment. Stepping forward, Eloise studied the loose floral-print dress, the Peter Pan collar gapping around the girl's thin neck. For only a year into the Depression, Annie looked like someone out of the Dust Bowl.

Eloise dropped into a squat to be on the little girl's level. "So, your name is Annie?"

The girl nodded, watching Eloise with her big hazel eyes.

"How old are you, Annie?" Eloise asked.

She held up her hand to show five fingers.

"That's a good age." Eloise smiled, taking the information in and filing it away. As well described as the decrepit apartment building was, the girl was no doubt important to the story, but so young, she was unlikely to be the MC of a historical fiction. Unless the author had only ever written a prologue. "Do you have a last name?"

"Schmitt," Annie answered, apparently too young to know she should be proud of that fact.

"Annie, who are you . . . ?" The door wrenched open, a blonde girl—perhaps about thirteen—trailing off when she saw the group. "Who are you?"

"You must be one of Annie's sisters?" Eloise stood again.

"Mary," the girl said, scanning them suspiciously. "And again, who the hell are you?"

"You're not supposed to say that word." Annie looked up.

Mary just pushed her sister back into the apartment by the head, her eyes never leaving the rest of them.

"I'm Eloise, and this is Owen, Hebe, Savitr, Pan, and Echo," Eloise introduced them all in one go. "We were just passing through."

"Passing through," Mary repeated.

"We were stuck in the next set over." She pointed back the way they had come. "Whose story is this?"

"No one's now." Mary frowned, her face turning dark. "We've been living here for at least a decade."

Eloise blinked, the odd, slightly unsettling feel of the set suddenly making more sense. "You're Lost?"

"Yeah." Mary crossed her arms tightly. "Where exactly are you from again?"

"The next set over," Eloise repeated.

The girl's eyebrows pulled together, her gaze finally dropping over Eloise's decidedly non-thirties attire. "How'd you get here?"

"Walked." Eloise didn't know what else she could really say.

Mary's mouth opened, then closed as her face reacted. "You crossed the no-man's-land?"

"We did."

Mary continued to gape, eyes flicking over each of them before she pulled the door open. "Come on in."

The room inside was as small and run-down as the rest of the building. A couch sat in the center of the room by a suitably large radio, while a part toward the back was curtained off as most likely a bedroom. A kitchenette sat to the left next to a door. Overall, not a big space for at least three sisters and probably two parents.

"How long did you say you've been here?" Eloise looked back at Mary.

Mary shrugged. "We don't exactly have days here. You stop trying to count hours after a couple years."

Savitr looked around, shaking his head. "What are you doing still living here then? There must be nicer places you could go if your author isn't writing. You aren't that far from the Upper East Side."

"Author never wrote the Upper East Side." Mary crossed her arms, face hard. "We've only got Fifty-Seventh to Houston Street. And most of that is just the façade. Nothing's written inside." She looked across the room. "Annie, go get Helen across the hall."

"She and Robert are probably kissing again." Annie's nose wrinkled.

"Just get her." Mary rolled her eyes, flopping to sit on the couch.

The five-year-old frowned, but moved for the door again.

Hebe rubbed the handle of her dagger as though she expected some sort of sneak attack. Pan shifted awkwardly. Mary just sat looking at them.

Eloise pressed her lips together, attempting to think of a way to ease the tension. "So, what was your story about before it stopped?"

Mary huffed, looking off at the peeling wallpaper. "I wasn't used all that much. Helen was the MC, off working at a factory or something. I think the author mixed up 1930 with 1830 in half her research. Or perhaps she didn't do any real research at all. Maybe that's why she gave up on us."

A girl with light-brown hair, likely about sixteen, appeared in the doorway with a blond boy, her eyes darting between all of them before settling on Mary. "Who are they?"

"Eloise, Owen, Hebe, Savitr, Pan, and Echo," Eloise repeated quickly, pointing to them each in turn. "You must be Helen and . . . Robert?"

The boy nodded.

"Where the hell did you come from?" Helen asked before he could speak.

"Next set over," Savitr supplied this time. "And we got here by going over the no-man's-land. Do we have that covered?"

Robert raised his eyebrows. "You crossed the no-man's-land?"

Eloise nodded. "You've just got to run across the middle. We're trying to make our way home."

Helen looked at them for a long moment, mouth partially open, before she spoke. "You're trying to walk home?"

"More or less," Eloise agreed.

Helen's expression didn't change. "Do you even know which way to go?"

"We have a compass," Owen said. "And we're heading in the general direction of the Wall."

"General direction of the Wall," Helen repeated. Apparently, everyone in the apartment was very good at that. Eloise had to wonder if it was some sort of story hangover. She shifted, trying to ignore that thought.

"We'll hit it eventually, we figure. You're welcome to come with us, if you're interested," Eloise said, glancing at the apartment as well as she could while still being polite. Every single thing in it seemed to have the same run-down patina covering it. The author had certainly not gone for subtlety regarding this family's lodgings.

"Isn't that dangerous?" Mary asked, finally sitting forward in her seat.

"Probably." Owen nodded. "But we decided we'd rather try than sit on a dead set for the rest of our lives."

"What's going on?" A young, brown-haired girl came out of the room, followed by an even younger blonde one. Apparently, there were sisters everywhere, packed in more tightly than they were in the dorms.

"Annie, will you keep an eye out for Mom and Dad?" Helen looked at the five-year-old.

Annie stamped her foot. "Why do I have to do everything?"

"Because you're the youngest." Helen pushed Annie toward the door. "Wait for Mom and Dad, and get them to hurry up here."

Annie pouted, but let herself be pushed outside once more, the door swinging shut behind her with a loud click.

"Rob, won't you go get your parents and the Bollen-bachers?" Helen turned to the boy beside her. "We need to have a meeting."

He gave her a half salute and slipped out.

"How many of you are there in this story?" Eloise watched him leave.

"I don't know." Helen shook her head. "Fifteen, maybe twenty of us overall."

"We'll have to get more packs if they choose to come with us," Owen murmured, sizing the girls up.

"We haven't agreed to go anywhere." Helen narrowed her eyes.

"If it gets us out of here, I'm game to try it." Mary looked at her sister. "If you and Robert want to stay here, be my guest."

"You don't even know if they can get us out of here, Mary." Helen continued to look forward, stony faced. "Hold your horses."

"We've figured out how to pass the no-man's-land," Eloise said. "We can at least get between sets. I know people in the RO. If we can reach either the Wall or an active set, we have a chance at getting out."

Helen glanced at her sisters, then took a seat next to Mary. "I guess we'll see what everyone has to say."

Chapter Nineteen

Small as the apartment had seemed before, it felt full to bursting with two dozen people piled inside. Eloise fought the urge to hang close to the door. Claustrophobia had never really been a problem for her, but apparently even she had her limits.

Mr. Schmitt sat forward, interlacing his fingers as his forearms rested on his knees. "So, you've made it one set over. Now you think can make it all the way to the Wall?"

Owen answered for them. "The biggest challenge is getting over the no-man's-land, and yes, it could be dangerous, but once you know how to do it, there's no reason we wouldn't be able to again and again."

"This . . . compass." One of the neighbors from downstairs, Mrs. Bollenbacher, looked at Eloise. "How do you even know it works?"

Eloise cleared her throat and forced herself to straighten a little, as it seemed they wouldn't allow her to relinquish explanation-duty entirely to Owen. "The needle keeps pointing the same way, no matter where we've been so far. And traveling west on our set led us to the Lower East Side on yours. They seem to all be lined up."

"But you don't know that," Mr. Schmitt cut in.

Eloise had to admit it. "No, we don't."

"So we could end up walking in circles, if we did go with you."

"We could." Eloise dropped her eyes.

"Still seems like a better solution, to me, than sitting around an empty set from now until the end of time," Savitr interjected.

Eloise offered him a small smile of thanks.

"At least we have food here." Mrs. Bollenbacher crossed her arms across her broad chest, gesturing at Eloise with her chin. "Who knows what we'll find if we start trying to wander sets? It's unheard of."

"Maybe because no one's ever tried," Owen said.

"Or because no one's ever lived through trying it," Helen mumbled from her spot near the window.

Eloise kept her eyes on the scuffed floorboards, tapping her finger irritably on her thigh as she tried to think through the low grumbling amongst the others packed in the room. Her other hand slipped into the pocket of the red coat she had been given—more suited to the weather than her fantasy dress—rubbing the compass case with her thumb. Where she had found it, the fact that it *was* a compass . . . it all had to mean something, didn't it? People didn't just randomly find things like that. Things they'd no doubt need later. At least not . . .

"Not in stories," Eloise said under her breath, eyes coming up when she realized she had spoken out loud. Only Owen and Hebe seemed to have heard, though, and were both looking at her questioningly.

She swallowed, glancing at the others all speaking amongst themselves. "Whether or not we're going the right way, there must be some order to the sets."

Eyes turned back to her, faces confused.

"Why would there be?" Helen asked.

"Just think about it," Eloise continued, still working out her thoughts even as she spoke. "You know there's that saying, 'Truth is stranger than fiction, but it is because fiction is obliged to stick to possibilities; truth isn't.'"

Helen cocked an eyebrow, speaking over the others' silence. "And?"

"Well, we *live* in fiction." Eloise motioned to the apartment around them. "The author's fiction. Everything has to build on something before it and work itself out in a few hundred pages. There's *always* a Eureka Moment. Who knows, maybe this is mine. Authors outline all the answers in the back of the book. Anything that doesn't make sense leading up to that is supposed to be a clue to how everything ties up at the end of each little two-hundred-page package. Sure, sometimes there are just plot holes, but overall, everything has some kind of order to it. Why wouldn't these sets?"

"We aren't in a story." Helen's frown deepened, something hard forming behind her expression. "Our story stopped years ago."

"This one, maybe," Eloise agreed. "But something pulled me in here, and it wasn't a normal transport. And now, being in this set, you have to admit there's a forward trajectory. It's a story, author-driven or not."

"But that would make it real life, wouldn't it?" Echo piped up from her spot on the floor. "If there's no author?"

Eloise did her best not to send Echo a dark look, focusing instead on coming up with her own answer. She finally shook her head. "Not on this side of the Wall. Everything's been too . . . planned."

"Planned by whom?" Helen asked, her skepticism even seeming to outdo Hebe's.

Eloise sighed, looking at the others—most of whom appeared confused, skeptical, even worried—but there was no apparent hostility. Eloise shrugged. "Apparently, we're not far enough in to have figured that out yet."

The words settled, everyone taking them in in their own way before Helen spoke again. "That doesn't really help us much, then, does it?"

"It means we should keep walking, though?" Echo spoke before Eloise could, looking around as the room looked at her. "If this is some kind of story, we're only going to figure everything out right before the end, right? And that's likely to be us getting home."

Helen shook her head. "That's idiotic."

"Or brilliant." Eloise smiled.

"I get that a lot." Echo shrugged good-naturedly, leaning back on her hands.

Eloise looked at Owen and pulled her hand back out of her pocket. "All the more reason to keep moving."

Owen nodded.

"You're *all* idiotic." Helen glanced between them.

"Helen." Mrs. Schmitt finally spoke, sending her story-daughter a chastising look.

"I'd generally be one to agree," Hebe cut in, looking at Helen before she turned to Eloise and Owen. "But there's really no point in sitting and waiting here. At least for us lot."

Mr. Schmitt nodded, slowly standing. "Well, you are all welcome to find a room to rest where you can, if you like. We won't run out of food here. The rest of us are going to need to have a talk."

"Of course," Owen agreed before any of the rest of them could speak. Eloise turned toward the door without another word, her mind still racing.

Barnaby closed his eyes tightly, trying to get them to focus again as he moved into the next stack of boxes. "Weren't they going to digitize all of these?"

"Slow going, I guess." Sven thumbed through a manuscript printed on what seemed to be dot-matrix paper. Still too late for what they needed.

"How is anyone supposed to find anything?" Barnaby glanced at the rows of brown cardboard, none of the boxes seemingly marked, each stacked several deep. If Barnaby hadn't known better, he'd have thought the RO had changed offices at some point, and no one had ever bothered to unpack.

"Most of this seems like stuff no one would really be looking for." Sven motioned with the manuscript in his hand. "Bad first novels, poorly written erotica . . . I think I passed a stack of Yaoi Fan Fiction a couple boxes back."

Barnaby sighed. "Still think this is more interesting than whatever else you had planned tonight?"

"Definitely interesting to see what some people get in their heads to write." Sven moved to the next manuscript. "One of the really great things about Basille—spelled with an extra 'le' for some reason?—was that she could really care less about how she looked ever. Most of the time, Basille threw on the first clean thing she came across and went on her way; but with that, the stacks of Vogue and Cosmo that her roommates had might as well had been graduate level calculus to her..."

Barnaby snorted, rearranging another stack as he tried to check some of the boxes along the bottom. "Issues aside, not the worst I've seen."

"Still, it goes on like that for" —he flicked to the end before tossing it aside— "eight-hundred more pages."

"At least the author finished, I suppose."

The door to the storage room creaked open. Barnaby looked up to see Christophe's familiar tan face. Tensing, Barnaby hoped Catherine wasn't around as well. Despite the fact that he and Christophe both worked at the RO—and Catherine did not—Barnaby had to admit he didn't see Christophe often without his "better half."

Christophe froze in the doorway, dark eyes a little too wide as he recovered. "Sorry, I heard voices."

Barnaby and Sven just nodded.

Christophe flicked his eyes between them before finally settling on Barnaby. "I heard you were sick?"

"Don't have time to be sick." Barnaby got the bottom box free, sliding it in front of him. "What are you doing here?"

"Was just picking up some work before I went and met . . ." His voice trailed off awkwardly.

"Catherine?" Barnaby suggested, lifting his eyes back to the man in the doorway.

Christophe just shrugged.

So at least they wouldn't have Catherine pressing for answers for the moment. Thank God for the small things.

"I have no problem with you two dating." Barnaby pulled the flaps of the box open. Typewritten, that had to be closer. "No need for embarrassment on my account."

"I just know you two still have some . . . issues."

"And they're not really about the people we're dating." Barnaby picked up a manuscript, paging through it.

Christophe nodded slowly, his eyes moving between Sven and Barnaby. "Can I ask what you're doing?"

"Looking for some old manuscripts," Barnaby answered before Sven could.

There was another pause before Christophe asked, "Any particular reason?"

Sven looked up, catching Barnaby's eyes as Barnaby picked up the next manuscript from the box.

"Private, for the moment." Barnaby scanned the title. Still nothing he needed.

Christophe crossed his arms and seemed to debate speaking again before he opened his mouth. "You know the filing system, yeah?"

Barnaby finally paused, looking at Christophe straight on. "Filing system?"

Christophe nodded, looking at the boxes. "Betty, who used to work here, was the one who put them all in here. It's this weird grid thing, but apparently it worked for her."

Barnaby twisted to look at the stacks, then bent to pick up his list from Alice. "Do you think you could help us find a few manuscripts?"

"Are you going to tell me why?" Christophe returned.

Barnaby took a moment, then shrugged. "Eventually."

Christophe actually smiled, moving fully into the room. "Which manuscripts?"

Barnaby handed him the paper, watching as the man maneuvered around the boxes Barnaby and Sven had displaced to work his way into the rows. Sven stood, leaving his box open in front of him and glancing at Barnaby before he watched Christophe wandering the room.

Another five minutes, and Christophe had managed to find all of them, holding the stack of manuscripts as he moved back to the other two men. He stopped a few feet from Barnaby. "Should I demand to be told what this is about before I hand them over?"

"Don't you need to go meet Catherine?" Barnaby said.

Christophe just lifted an eyebrow.

Under different circumstances, Barnaby would have nearly been amused; assertive was not a word he would normally use to describe Christophe Bihonzi. Barnaby glanced at Sven—getting an up-to-you look in response—before he turned to Christophe. "This doesn't leave the room for now, to anyone in the office *or* Catherine."

Christophe's eyebrows furrowed, but he nodded.

"Eloise was transported into a story she doesn't belong in," Barnaby explained quickly. "I talked to someone at the OAT. What they registered happening to her happened to others in these stories. We're trying to figure out how the hell we can get her out of there."

Christophe hesitated, looking at Sven before turning back to Barnaby. "You pulling my leg?"

Barnaby shook his head.

"How . . . is that even possible?" Christophe asked, eyes darting between Sven and Barnaby.

"That's what we're trying to figure out," Sven answered.

"Thanks for finding those." Barnaby nodded to the manuscripts forgotten in Christophe's arms. "May we?"

Christophe glanced down, then handed them over with a jolt. "You think there are people who weren't supposed to be in those stories, too?"

"That's what we're trying to figure out." Barnaby handed one of the manuscripts to Sven before opening one himself.

"Can I look?" Christophe asked.

Barnaby looked back up, raising a questioning eyebrow. "What about your date?"

Christophe pulled out his phone, checking the time. "I'm still running early."

Waiting one final moment, Barnaby handed over the bottom manuscript. "It should be at the end. These all closed soon after the spike that said someone transported improperly."

Christophe and Sven nodded. All three men flipped through the pages as they looked for whatever they could find in them.

Helen's eyes narrowed. Even as the rest of the group remained divided, Eloise could feel those eyes on her. Hebe hadn't been happy with the idea of walking home either. But Helen was something else.

"We've been here for *years*," Mary argued. "Our author could be dead for all we know."

"Or they could come back tomorrow." Helen finally shifted her glare to her sister. "Alexander MacDonald was gone for over a decade with his book."

"You really think you're in the next *No Great Mischief*?" Eloise pulled her coat tighter, holding Helen's gaze this time. "From what I know of that story, the author was actually working those thirteen years. Not leaving everyone sitting around in a, at best, half-completed set."

"What?" Mary continued addressing her story-sister, even as Helen left her eyes on Eloise. "You still think you're going to get to pop home and end up with one of those great MC houses? Is that it?"

Something flickered on Helen's face, but she didn't take her glare off Eloise.

"We're *never* going home," Mary said. "We're never getting out of that little apartment. You're never going to get to brag about that time you were an MC. It's sit here until the earth explodes or walk."

"You don't know that," Helen snapped, rounding on her sister.

"Seems like a pretty safe guess," Mary returned, thirteen-year-old frame puffing up.

"Girls." Mrs. Schmitt finally stepped forward from the little huddle of adults that had formed a few yards down the street. "Shouting won't help."

"You aren't really our mother," Helen mumbled, her narrowed eyes shifting to glare off into the distance.

Mrs. Schmitt crossed her arms. "You apparently need one."

"As fun as all this is—" Hebe dropped back to the street from where she had been scouting on a fire escape "—we need to get moving. So, who's coming?"

"I am." Mary stepped forward without hesitation, moving next to Eloise before she turned to the rest of her storymates.

The others didn't seem quite as enthusiastic. A few of the adults ambled forward. The twenty-something Bollenbacher twins joined with a shrug. Slowly, the group split until a little over half had moved to stand with the fantasy interlopers.

Eloise remained silent, scanning the other half. Her eyes hit the O'Reillys, two mSCs who each had to be over ninety, as wrinkled and bent as the author had seen fit to make them.

Mrs. O'Reilly just shook her head, voice surprisingly strong as she said, "I don't think we're in any shape to go Questing."

"It's not so bad here," another man whose name Eloise couldn't remember added.

Though the glare didn't disappear, the corners of Helen's mouth turned up just enough to look smug.

Robert finally stepped forward, moving next to the Bollenbacher boys.

"Rob!" The slight smirk dropped off as Helen's face reacted.

"It's at least a chance, Helen," he returned.

Looking between the two groups, Annie scampered forward, the other two younger Schmitt sisters following to stand near Mary.

Helen's dark look returned full force as it slid from person to person standing across from her. It finally settled on Robert, something passing between them before she huffed. She stalked forward, speaking through clenched teeth as she looked at Eloise. "If we all die, you know it's your fault."

The words hit deep in Eloise's stomach, the faith she was asking the others to give her pressing down when she wasn't sure she could even really trust herself. Still, she kept her face stoic, hopefully enough so that it could be confused for strength. Taking one last moment to make sure the six who chose to remain weren't going to change their minds, Eloise finally released a breath and looked at Owen. "Looks like we're ready to go."

He gave a weak smile and nodded, the newly enlarged group starting for the edge of the set.

With the west side of the New York set consisting of the Hudson and no apparent bridges, the lot of them went north—trying to find a spot where the streets turned to no-man's-land without requiring a swim. Eloise half wondered if she even remembered how to swim at this point.

They finally reached an edge, though, the wide thoroughfare they'd been following tapering off halfway into the eerie blackness. The group stopped without direction, looking out at it.

"So, which way do we go?" Owen asked, looking down at Eloise.

She gazed across the expanse, seeing a gray castle directly across from them and some sort of field at a diagonal. "That set looks closed." She motioned at the castle. "But we don't know how bad the no-man's-land would get if we tried to cut the corner."

"So we go to the castle first, and then to the field?" Owen came to the same conclusion as Eloise.

She nodded, turning to the rest of the group. The faces looked back at her, a full range of emotions painted across them. She cleared her throat, projecting as well as she could. "It looks worse than it is at the edges. It's just rubbery. In the middle, though, you will start to sink if you don't run. Once you get there, move. Keep going. Don't stop. The ground will become solid on the other side, but you don't want to sink."

The group nodded silently.

"What happens if you sink?" Annie asked.

Eloise looked at the five-year-old, doing her best to tell herself the girl would be at least as old as Eloise outside of story-years, with as long as the family had been living on the set—but couldn't quite manage it with those big hazel eyes looking up at her. She forced a tight smile, deciding to tell the truth. "It isn't likely you'll come back up."

Annie's eyes went wider, but she took the answer, looking out at the castle.

Eloise nodded once and looked at the rest of the group.

"If anyone is going to have second thoughts, now would be the time," Hebe interjected.

Uncertainty hovered over the group like a cloud, but no one retreated.

"All right then." Eloise turned. "We'll see you on the other side."

Chapter Twenty

A CRIME DRAMA, A ROMANCE, AND LITERARY FICTION, the three manuscripts didn't seem to have much in common. Certainly not when Barnaby added the fantasy Eloise had found herself in.

"Do you think there's some connection between the authors?" Sven set his manuscript down.

"Would we actually have any way to check?" Christophe frowned.

"I could try to hack into some files," Sven suggested.

Barnaby shook his head, looking at the three old manuscripts. "What are we missing?"

Christophe's phone rang in his pocket, the man wincing as he stood. Turning his back to the others in the room, he answered, "Hi, honey."

Barnaby snorted, Sven catching his eyes with a knowing smile before they turned back to the manuscripts.

"No, I just got caught up—" Christophe cut off as Catherine's voice—mumbled but obviously upset— came through the line.

Barnaby twisted to pick up the other papers Alice had given him, turning all three manuscripts to face him.

"What's that?" Sven asked, shifting to look.

Christophe paced. "Honey, just calm down . . ."

Barnaby studied the map detailing where the spikes had happened for each story. "Is there a way to find out where each of the recorders of these stories was living at the time?"

"It'd likely be in the General Counsel records," Sven said. "Why?"

"This is where the unplanned transports happened." Barnaby turned the map to Sven. "Eloise transferred from my house into my story. Maybe there's some connection with the recorders, rather than the authors."

Sven nodded slowly. "It would make sense . . ."

"I know," Christophe continued his call. "I know. Just give me twenty minutes, then I'll be there, and we can talk, all right?"

"Can you get into those records?" Barnaby kept his eyes on Sven.

"We're not on the same network." Sven shook his head. "We could go to the General Counsel and try talking to someone there."

"Think I'd get fired doing that tomorrow?" Barnaby began gathering up the manuscripts.

Sven helped him. "You must have vacation time."

"Love you," Christophe said, hanging up before turning back to Barnaby and Sven. "What's happening?"

"We need to get into the General Counsel's records," Sven truncated.

"And it sounds like you need to get going." Barnaby lifted a knowing eyebrow.

Christophe glanced at his phone and grimaced. "We were supposed to go to the symphony tonight. I may have lost track of the time."

"Doesn't sound like you're about to have a fun end to your night." Barnaby took the manuscripts, adding them to his stack of papers. "Sorry for that."

"My fault." Christophe curled his fist, glancing at the door before looking back at Barnaby. "You'll let me know what you find out with all this?"

"Assuming I'm not magically sucked into some other story tonight, sure," Barnaby said, not sure if he meant it as a joke or not.

Christophe made his goodbyes, moving out of the room a little too quickly.

Sven watched, waiting for Christophe's footsteps to disappear down the hall before turning to Barnaby. "Were you trying to get him in trouble with Catherine?"

"Not in the slightest." Barnaby shook his head. "Think I could stay over at your place tonight?"

Sven looked at him for another moment, then nodded. "Sure, man. We can plot our next line of attack."

Eloise panted. The no-man's-land had felt longer this time. Hopefully, that wouldn't be a pattern going forward. She certainly didn't need that kind of Raising the Stakes when there wasn't even a reader looking for cheap tension.

"Everyone made it?" Owen looked over the group, seeming less winded for the run than the rest of them. Whether it was the benefit of being an elf, or simply a former male protagonist with Heroic Build, Eloise didn't know. With Hebe looking only the slightest bit better than the rest of them, it was likely a little of the former and a ton of the latter.

The rest of the group looked around as they took stock of who had made it to the castle set. Eloise forced herself straight to count heads. She opened her mouth to agree.

"I think so," Hebe beat Eloise to it. "Unless the goo got someone and sprang up a clone."

Mary's head snapped up. "Can that happen?"

"No." Eloise shook her head. "At least, not as far as we know."

"Let's lay off the horror tropes." Owen frowned. "Last thing we need is for people to start worrying about Body Snatchers."

"It would really be more of a Replicant Snatcher, if the actual body's destroyed," Eloise said without thinking. "You know, 'You Are Who You Eat.'"

"Thank you, Eloise." Owen shot her a look.

"That does look horror-ish, though, if we're in that kind of story." Echo pointed to the castle on the cliff, a low-hanging fog obscuring much of the landscape in the already grayscale set.

"Should we keep moving, then?" Mr. Schmitt asked, his face still a little too flushed from the last run.

Eloise glanced at the rest of the group. Most had seemed to recover relatively well, though Mrs. Bollenbacher looked like she could do with a rest before they started out over the next stretch of wobbly no-man's-land.

"If everything's gray like this, it means the set's likely closed." Eloise thought out loud, eyes going back to the landscape. The fog certainly left an uneasy feeling in her stomach, but she didn't get the sense that there were any monsters out along the cliffs. In fact, something about the place seemed almost . . . familiar.

"Eloise?" Owen's voice snapped Eloise from her thoughts.

"Sorry." She looked back to the group, entirely sure they had all caught her zoning out. "The set is likely closed, so even if it used to be a horror story, I imagine we'd be safe. At least long enough to let us get our legs back under us."

"And you're sure we won't get eaten by the hound of the Baskervilles or a vampire or something?" Hebe's hand went back to dagger at her side.

"As sure as I've been of anything these past few days." Eloise glanced at Hebe's long fingers curled around the knife hilt. At least her cautions seemed less paranoid here than in the last set.

"That's comforting," Hebe mumbled

"So we might as well rest here for a bit?" Owen asked.

Eloise nodded, letting her eyes drift back to the old castle on the hill. The familiarity still nagged at her. She tried to place what about the set was catching her. She couldn't remember seeing a picture of it anywhere, so it wasn't likely to be Dracula's Castle or anywhere bestseller famous. So it must have been something she'd read. She tried to think of how an author might have described the castle—imposing, looming, intimidating—but without the actual narrative, she still came up lacking.

Owen passed around one of their bottles of water, checking on a few of the more red-faced among them before stopping by Eloise. "Are you sure you're all right?"

"Just . . ." Eloise tried to think of a way to phrase her thoughts. "Does that castle remind you of anything?"

"Other than somewhere Frankenstein's Monster would feel right at home?"

"No, not *Frankenstein*." Eloise shook her head, tapping her fingers on her thigh.

"What?"

"I'm trying to figure out why this set looks familiar." Eloise pursed her lips.

"If it wasn't core curriculum, I probably didn't read it, so you'd probably know better than I would."

Eloise just nodded.

"Should we go check it out?" Owen asked.

Eloise let the idea percolate, her legs urging her to sit for a while with the rest of the exhausted group. But curiosity wouldn't let her ignore the nagging feeling driving her forward. She hesitated all the same. "I think some are still feeling a little seasick from the run."

Owen looked at their mismatched group before squinting into the distance. "We're going to have to go a little farther anyway, if we're going to match up with the next set. It's still hard to make it out from this angle."

Barely able to see the edge of the set herself, Eloise couldn't argue. "We might as well look, then?"

Owen smiled quickly, moving back to round up the troops.

The more they walked, the more Eloise realized just how large the manor was. What she had mistaken for it being close was just it being three times the size she had assumed. She tucked the size away in her mind with the other descriptors she'd begun stockpiling to try to place it. Perhaps if everything weren't so gray, she'd be able to pick out what the author would have focused on for their description. As it was, tightly packed gray fieldstone rose five or six stories, held together with gray mortar, gray window frames punctuating the otherwise sheer stone walls. Eloise marched forward, ignoring the grumbles building behind her the longer they continued the gradual climb up to the manor. Eloise looked right, taking in the cliffs the manor sat a little too close beside. An expanse of water stretched out below it. In-story, it had probably had been a churning ocean. Now, it sat placidly around jagged rocks.

Horror or not, the set was certainly written for drama.

And something hit, the tickle in the back of her mind turning solid. "Not possible," she murmured under her breath as they finally reached the front door.

"What?" Owen looked over.

She turned to the plaque on the wall, peering through the dark, already expecting what she would see there. She read it aloud: "Pentacliff Manor, Leinster County, Ireland."

"This is supposed to be Ireland?" Helen looked around, tone pinched.

"Apparently," Savitr spoke before Eloise could.

"Pentacliff Manor," Eloise repeated.

Owen looked at her. "Do you know it?"

"I think I do." She opened the door and peered inside. Just as quiet and gray as everything else, she barely took the time to motion everyone else forward. "Come on."

Eloise worked quickly, poking her head into every room they passed, looking for confirmation.

The rest of the group followed silently.

"What are you doing?" Savitr finally asked.

"Looking for a Coat of Arms." Eloise continued zigzagging down the hallway, finally coming to a study. Though most of it was in grayscale, the rug and some of the wall-hangings had retained their original deep red color, giving it a strangely artistic, if unsettling, feel. Eloise stepped in, her eyes falling on the crest over the fireplace. A rearing lion sat in two squares, crossed swords in the other diagonal squares. Under it, in a scrolling banner, sat the name.

Fitzwilliam.

Eloise released an incredulous breath.

"What?" Echo asked.

"It's Barnaby's set." Eloise turned, looking around the rest of the room, mind able to pick out the similarities she had read in his manuscript. The thick curtains, the slanted desk . . . . Suddenly, she wished she'd read just a little more. If she could have handled reading him and Catherine, that is.

"Who's Barnaby?" Mary asked.

Hebe sighed, motioning vaguely. "Her boyfriend."

"He was in a historical romance." Eloise touched the desk lightly.

"So, no vampires to worry about," Robert said from his spot beside Helen.

Eloise shook her head, eyes going back down to the red carpet. "But . . ."

"But what?" Hebe glanced over from one of the tall bookshelves.

"If this is his set . . ." Eloise turned to face the rest of the group. "It's been closed for years. Decades, at this point. Why are there still things in color?"

Everyone looked down, those on the offending carpet backing off onto the gray floorboards.

"Maybe that's just how things work in sets that are naturally closed?" Pan suggested. "We haven't actually been to a properly closed one before."

Pressing her lips into a thin line, Eloise nodded again, scanning the rest of the gray walls. "Why don't we rest here? We can keep going once everyone's stretched and had something to eat . . ."

Nobody debated, small groups breaking off as they slowly moved back into the rest of the manor. Eloise watched them maneuver in odd patterns as they avoided stepping on anything colorful.

When it was down to just the original six of them, Eloise frowned at the pairs of eyes watching her. "What?"

"Are you all right?" Echo asked quietly.

"Why wouldn't I be?" Eloise pushed a piece of hair out of her face.

"Obviously, something about all this ties back to your boyfriend." Hebe crossed her arms, but even her normally hard look didn't seem as harsh. "His story. His set . . ."

Eloise nodded. There really was no ignoring the thread beginning to run through their trek. And that wasn't even including having been transported from his house.

"Do you think he was somehow the one that put you in here?" Owen asked.

Eloise's brow furrowed deeply as she looked at him. "What?"

"Just . . . if everything else is connected to him," Owen said carefully. "Could there have been some reason for him to? I don't know how well you know him."

Eloise remained silent for another moment; she couldn't logically count it out in the face of everything else. But if she could believe all of this had been on purpose . . . their meeting, how quickly everything had just seemed to fall into place . . . . She did her best to stamp those thoughts down. Mistrust would get them nowhere as long as they were sitting on a dead set.

Who knew? Perhaps it was just paranoia beginning to set in, with all the talk of Body Snatchers and conspiracy.

Eloise forced a tight smile. "I'm going to have a look around. See what we can find before we keep moving."

The Leinster set seemed caught in perpetual night. Eloise didn't know how long she had been sitting in the bedroom. Bed unmade, gray clothing sitting by the free-standing wardrobe, it seemed Barnaby had still been Barnaby, even caught in-story. But then, she'd only known him a few months in the grand scope of things. Even if she couldn't believe he had somehow manufactured a way to throw her into the sets—not with the way he'd sounded as they lost connection—she couldn't truly expect to know everything about a person in a few months, could she? After the number of times she had rolled her eyes at Columbine's fascination with True Love stories in school, Eloise had to admit that she'd let herself get swept up.

And look where it had gotten her. No wonder she had always hated love tropes.

Eloise paused, groaning. Hating love, just to then have a Heel-Face Turn about it shoved her into *another* love trope.

Obviously, there was no winning.

"Eloise?" someone's voice—Mary, it sounded like—echoed down the stone hallway outside the room. "Eloise?"

Forcing herself off the end of the bed, Eloise moved into the doorway. "Yes?"

Mary started, turning away from looking in another room. She offered a weak smile. "People are looking for you. Seems like we're pretty ready to go?"

Eloise nodded slowly. "Just, give me another second?"

Mary hesitated, but didn't argue. "We're all meeting down in the front hall, when you're ready."

"I'll just be a second," Eloise repeated, watching Mary return the way she had come. Turning back to the bedroom, Eloise moved toward the wardrobe. At least picking up clothes seemed a little normal.

As she draped an old waistcoat over her arm, her gaze caught a trail of black droplets on the wall. She frowned and straightened, following the line up to the frame hanging in the middle of the wall. Barely glancing at the man in the portrait—someone too old to be Barnaby—she looked back at the droplets. Hesitantly, she reached out and touched one. It came away on her skin when she pulled her finger back. The black seemed somehow darker on her still-colored flesh than it had been on the gray wall. She studied it. Gooey, it stuck to the pad of her finger, rolling a bit like rubber cement when she brought her thumb and index together.

She wiped the goo back on the wall, looking up to the frame. It sat oddly somehow, as if something pressed it out slightly on one side.

Of course. Novel. Old manor.

She tugged on the frame, the portrait swinging on its hinges to reveal a wall safe.

"Come on," Eloise murmured, as though the author would hear her some two decades later. "That had to be cliché long before you wrote this."

Pulling on the latch, the safe swung open without protest. The same black goo coated the bottom of it, a stack of papers sticking out in the middle. Glancing back at the door, Eloise picked up what she could of the papers, writing off the pages below the goo as lost.

Tight script marked the old paper, paragraph after paragraph filling the space. Flipping through, Eloise paused at the sight of dialogue. She stared, flipping back to the front. Black and white as anything else in the set, it still didn't seem author-planted. She turned back to the dialogue. Someone had at least started writing a novel in-story. And from the handwriting, it didn't look to be Barnaby.

Sending a final look into the goo, she stuffed the pages into her pack by the bed, strapping it over her shoulder before she moved for the door. One more clue she'd have to add to the puzzle when they stopped again.

Though the lines were not much better than at the OAT, the building the General Counsel occupied was at least better than the gray monotony across town. With its grand arches and white marble, it was supposedly built to emulate the capitol building in some story written ages ago. Despite once again spending a morning inching along toward a desk, Barnaby was glad to have something new to look at.

"Next!" A perky girl, looking not much older than fifteen, motioned Barnaby forward with a smile. She continued before he could fully make it across the space. "Welcome to the General Counsel! How may I assist you today?"

He'd also take peppy over drone, Barnaby supposed. "Hi, I was hoping to get some records."

"Certainly! I'd be happy to help you with that." The girl, Rose, according to the placard at her desk, turned to her computer. "Do you have the name or titles?"

"It would be the public housing records for these addresses." Barnaby slid the first list across the well-polished desk before adding the list of disappearees and recorders connected to the affected stories that Sven had managed to pull up. "And then any documents you might have on these people?"

"I would be happy to look up anything that is public record," Rose continued in the same peppy tone. "Anything else, you will need to get special clearance. Is that all right?"

"Fine," Barnaby said. He'd take peppy over unhelpful, but taking the brightness down a couple of degrees certainly couldn't be that difficult . . .

"Printing out the housing records for you now," Rose narrated, still typing, her bouncy fingers seeming to match her voice. "And looking up the names now."

Barnaby nodded, looking around at the rest of the space as the girl worked. With only the large, round help desk in the rotunda, the space seemed gaping. The ceiling soared above him, exposing the second story, accessible by a grand staircase opposite the door. He could see offices beyond the gilt railing that flanked the staircase and ran down both sides of the balcony. It would be easy to get lost in the midst of all the space and columns.

"Hmm . . ." Rose's bright expression finally started to drop off. "That's odd."

"What is?" Barnaby snapped his attention back to her.

"I have files for the first three people listed here, but the others . . . they have completely empty files."

Barnaby frowned, glancing at his list before looking up again. "What does that mean?"

Rose shook her head. "I've never had something come up like that before. I'll have to have someone look into it. Perhaps the files were corrupted?"

Barnaby nodded, considering her words as he glanced at the list of names. The story files at the OAT and now the personnel files for the people who had ended up in them. Either the spikes had damaged the records across the board . . . or someone had wiped them out.

The smile came back to Rose's face as she looked at him. "Would you like me to print off the first three for you?"

"Yes, thanks," Barnaby said. An obvious thought suddenly hit him. "And could you check one more name for me?"

"Certainly!" She rocked up on the balls of her feet, seeming about two seconds away from literally bouncing.

"Eloise." He ignored her motion as best as he could. "Would likely be the most recent one on file."

Rose typed, the smile faltering once again as she looked. "No . . . it seems there's nothing under that file either." She looked back to Barnaby. "Would you like me to contact you once I've had someone look into it?"

Barnaby gave a tight smile. "I'll just drop by again when I have the time. Thank you for your help."

"You're welcome." Rose frowned at the screen for another moment before she handed him the papers she had printed, smile back in place. "Thank you for coming! Next!"

Chapter Twenty-One

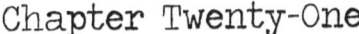

BARNABY STARED AT THE MAP SPREAD OUT OVER HIS table, frowning. His seemed to be the only house that had registered a transport directly on top of it. The one before Eloise's, however, was close enough to that recorder's house to be suspicious.

As for the other two . . . placed properly on the map, there seemed to be no real pattern to those at all—one downtown, and one so near the edge it seemed barely on the paper. He stared at that far point. The other three were at least central, and all four recorders—himself included—were former MCs. It made no sense to find a point so far out it barely qualified as mSC territory.

An idea came to him. Barnaby pulled the map over to bring the part hanging off the table into view. The School. That transport had happened on the road to the School. And the one downtown . . . he double-checked the address, obvious now that he was looking for it. A spot no more than a couple blocks from the RO.

Snatching his phone from the chair next to him, he found Sven's number and dialed.

"What's up?" Sven didn't wait for Barnaby to introduce himself.

Barnaby's mind was already moving too quickly to be thrown. He grabbed his coat off the back of his chair. "I need you to get into some RO files for me, if you can. I'm coming in now."

"What files?" Sven asked.

"I need you to see if the other transports worked there."

Sven didn't respond, silence filling the airspace.

"Hello?" Barnaby picked up his car keys.

"You mean the people who were transported into the stories? If they worked here?" Sven finally asked.

"Yes," Barnaby said. "Like Eloise."

"I'll see what I can do." Sven sighed. "I might have to find a way to get on Mr. Marley's computer, though."

"Do what you can." Barnaby stepped out the door. "I'll see you in a few minutes."

Eloise didn't attempt to keep track of time. Each set was so different, there was no way to tell how many days had passed back home, where day and night followed each other so nicely. Certainly something she'd never thought about taking for granted. Walking when they could, sleeping when they could no longer stand to walk, it could have been a day, a week, or a year, and Eloise wouldn't know the difference.

As time warped, however, so did group morale—moods growing more and more dire. And the longer they went, the less Eloise could be bothered to do anything about that.

Working her way around one of the redwoods in the thick forest, the deep black of the no-man's-land finally came back into view. The group slowed, stopping silently as they looked at the large sand dunes rising out of the next space.

"We're going to be walking forever." Annie broke the silence, sitting with a thump on the gray forest floor.

"If we don't die first," Mrs. Bollenbacher mumbled. One of her sons—Eloise couldn't bring herself to care enough to determine which—shushed her.

Eloise didn't speak, pulling the compass free. It still pointed north, the same as it always did, so they weren't going in circles. They were just seeing how far they'd really transported across the scores of sets.

"At least it looks like it's in color over there," Owen offered, taking up the mantle of group cheerleader. "Maybe it's an active set."

"It's a damn desert," Hebe answered.

"But maybe one of Eloise's friends in the RO might be watching it?" Owen suggested, glancing at Eloise.

She slipped the compass back in her pocket, looking at the dunes. "We might as well see. We can't very well stay here."

People sighed, a few groaned or mumbled, but no one debated the unwelcome truth.

Owen still offered something like a pained smile, looking over the rest of them. "See you on the other side."

No more than a couple-hundred yards into the new set, Eloise stripped to her original tank top and shorts—the heat from the sun beating down in a way she had never experienced. She moved up the next dune, her feet sinking into the soft sand as she tried to move, making her calves burn.

"We're going to have to find camels or something." Hebe panted, stopping at the crest. "We're never going to make it through like this."

Owen scanned the horizon. Eloise hoped he saw more than she did in the never-ending waves of sand.

He shook his head. "There has to be someone here, if it's an open set."

"We have no idea how big of a set it is, though." Hebe frowned, feet sliding as she began to maneuver her way down the next side of the dune.

Wiping the sweat off her forehead with the back of her hand, Eloise started after them. A low mumble stopped her short—something distant, far away.

"Did you hear that?" she asked no one in particular.

"Hear what?" Owen turned to look back up at her.

Slowly, the sky began to darken. The group looked up en masse.

"I think someone's narrating," Eloise said, raising her voice as the wind began to kick up.

"I don't hear anything," Hebe called back.

"It's . . . far away?" More question slipped into Eloise's tone than she cared for.

"Oh . . ." Annie's small voice carried. Eloise turned to look. Her breath caught.

The sand looked red as it kicked up into a cloud. It raced toward them, growing larger and larger as it rolled across the open dunes.

"Everyone down!" someone yelled. Eloise didn't debate it, sliding as best she could down what she could only hope was the protected side of the dune before dropping to the burning sand.

Owen mouthed something at her. Eloise shook her head, unable to make out a single word, the roar of the wind deafening her. The cloud hit, lightning flashing deep inside it as the world turned rusty. Eloise pulled her tank top up, doing her best to cover her mouth as the sand pelted.

The storm seemed to hesitate, sand suspended in midair, and then it rushed forward again. The winds grew stronger, and Eloise felt the sand underneath her begin to slip away. She fought to keep the shirt over her mouth, other hand trying to find something to hold, grabbing nothing but loose sand. It was no use. It all slid away.

And she was left tumbling along the dunes.

Chapter Twenty-Two

"I DON'T THINK I HAVE EVER SPENT SO MUCH TIME in this office off the clock," Sven murmured, hugging the wall.

Barnaby just glanced at him, looking back down the hall to watch Mr. Marley's office. A good twenty minutes after the man normally left, Marley's translucent shape finally slipped away, the elevator chiming a moment later. Still, Sven and Barnaby remained where they were. Barnaby finally looked back, seeing Sven's raised eyebrows.

"If you get me fired, you're the one who's going to be doing all the waiting at the unemployment office for both of us."

"Well, I think I've got line-standing down after this week." Barnaby shook his head, motioning back toward the office at the end of the hall.

Taking a place by the door, Barnaby let Sven pass him, trusting Sven didn't need any help with the computer. Or at least, none of Barnaby's.

"Let me know if you see anyone coming." Sven sat at the desk, pulling the keyboard toward him.

"Can do," Barnaby returned, watching the hall as best he could through the slightly ajar door.

The room went silent, nothing but some typing and clicking filling the space as Sven worked.

The typing slowly died down, Marley's chair squeaking as Sven shifted. "Now that's . . . interesting."

"What is?" Barnaby looked across the office.

"All of the people you wanted to look up?" Sven pulled his hands back as he leaned farther forward. "They all have locked staff files."

"So they did work here?" Barnaby made quick strides across the room, moving to stand behind Sven.

Sven nodded, pointing. "Eloise's is still open. It's how I saw she was pre-storied before. See how it's marked, 'Special Exemption'?"

Barnaby looked at the set of boxes at the top—where his story information would have been—X-ed out in favor of the red stamp. "Is that the same for the others?"

"I've only gotten one unencrypted so far, but . . ." Sven brought up another file, the same marking at the top of that one.

"So they were all pre-storied?" Barnaby straightened, not quite sure how he felt now that his new suspicions had proved correct.

Another file flashed. Sven clicked it open; the third document looked the same as the others. He twisted to look back at Barnaby. "It's certainly seeming that way."

Barnaby frowned, pressing his fist to his mouth as he thought.

An angry beep echoed around the room. The computer flickered.

"Agh." Sven lurched back forward, trying to type again.

"What's happening?" Barnaby watched.

"The program I set running . . . it's like the last file corrupted it."

"What does that mean?"

"I don't know yet." Sven kept his eyes on the screen, typing, then clicking. Each movement just caused another angry beep, the sound finally turning into an infuriated wail.

Barnaby covered his ears, trying to speak over the noise as he glanced at the door. "If anyone's still here, they're headed this way now."

Sven nodded, giving up whatever he was doing as he rolled the chair back. "Time to bail out."

Not bothering with the elevator, Barnaby turned for the stairwell. The wail followed them, then suddenly cut off as they hit the first platform below Mr. Marley's floor.

Barnaby slowed, looked up. "Why'd it stop?"

"Crashed entirely?" Sven kept moving, heading down the next flight of steps. "Whatever it is, we should get out of here."

Barnaby didn't argue, following Sven down a few more floors before they dared to move back into the hallways. Even with the lights off, they moved quickly, the unspoken agreement to put as much space between them and the computer upstairs seeming to drive them forward.

Glancing into one of the offices lining the hall, Barnaby faltered.

"What?" Sven glanced back.

"Look at that." Barnaby took a step toward the door.

"Can it wait until morning?" Sven's eyes flicked to the elevators at the end of the hall, then back to Barnaby.

"Just . . . look." Barnaby stepped toward one of the computer screens, a string of ones and zeros covering the top half. He turned to look at the desk on the other side of the room. The screen there looked exactly the same. "That's binary?"

Sven sent a last glance down the hall, then stepped inside, bending to look at the screen. He pursed his lips and turned to the other screen. "Are they all doing that?"

Barnaby moved to look in the next office, then glanced back at Sven. "They are next door, too."

Sven gritted his teeth, but sat, trying to get the computer to respond.

A few clicks, and the code filled the screen, running for a few moments before the screen went dark again.

A red box lit up, computer by computer. Barnaby took a step forward, looking at the words forming there:

`Confidential Trials. Security Breach.`

`General Counsel Lockdown Protocol.`

Eloise coughed, irritated eyes slowly blinking open. With every inch of her coated in fine sand, her body seemed to crackle as it moved. Still, she pushed herself up, trying to take stock. Her pack was nowhere in sight. She patted herself down quickly, releasing a breath as she found the compass under her hip rather than flung who knew where. Set-up of a crazy convenience trope or not, she'd take it.

Someone groaned nearby, the man nearly unrecognizable in his own layer of sand. Eloise squinted. One of the Bollenbacher twins, perhaps?

She took a stab at it. "Albert?"

The man blinked, dark eyes showing through the crust of sand. He focused on Eloise. "Sorry. Other one."

"Alex," she said.

He nodded, sitting to brush himself off. "Where are we?"

"Still in the desert." Eloise couldn't give much more of an answer than that. They could have blown a few feet or miles, and Eloise wouldn't have known the difference between the sandy hills. At least, with the sun now closer to the horizon, it no longer felt like they were roasting alive. Near twilight had never looked quite so beautiful. She finally opened her mouth, but just ended up coughing again.

"Eloise?" The voice carried over one of the nearby dunes.

She forced herself to stand, as little as her body wanted to. "Owen?"

He appeared at the side of a dune. "Are you all right?"

"Considering." She nodded, spotting Echo beside him. "Are the rest of you over there?"

"Just Echo and me." Owen shook his head. "The others must have gotten separated. Did you lose your pack?"

"Everything but this." Eloise held the compass up, where it sat in the palm of her hand.

Owen pressed his lips together tightly. "I suppose we'll take what we can get."

"We have no food, though?" Alex frowned, beginning to look a little more recognizable as he got the sand out of his dark hair.

"We have Echo's pack." Owen glanced next to him, though Echo had already begun her way up the dune. "It got caught between us in the worst of it. It should hold us at least a few days, if we can't find anyone else right away."

"There's smoke," Echo called down the dunes. "I think there's someone over there."

They looked up, Owen meeting Eloise's gaze questioningly before he hurried to the top.

Eloise couldn't gather the energy to follow. "What do you see?"

"There's some sort of camp," Owen answered. "I can see tents at least."

Eloise blinked, the words taking a moment to sink in. "What?"

"There are people." Owen nodded, as though he understood her shock. "A few dunes over."

Plot-convenient sandstorm. But, Eloise supposed, if it didn't mean starving in the desert, she'd take it. She motioned. "Lead the way."

Barnaby pressed his way through the front door, not speaking until the office locked behind him. "Trials."

Sven looked at him, face a little too pale from all the excitement.

"That means someone is doing this on purpose. *Has been* doing this on purpose," Barnaby said.

Sven nodded slowly, following Barnaby down the sidewalk. "It would seem that way."

"And it seems like I'm going back to the General Counsel again tomorrow." Barnaby didn't pause, barely registering the empty streets around him.

"You think they'll tell you anything?" Sven sped up to stay next to Barnaby's side. "It said 'confidential.'"

"I'll find someone to tell me." Barnaby clenched his fist, then relaxed it. "Somehow."

Sven just returned to nodding, letting the silence of night settle over them.

Barnaby turned the corner and stopped dead. "Shit."

Sven's head snapped to him. "What?"

"I drove." Barnaby looked back the way they had come.

"You'd have to key in to get to the garage . . ." Sven frowned, his hesitation saying he was just as reluctant to get themselves tied more to the building than they already were, considering.

Barnaby sighed, shaking his head. "I'll just have to drop by to pick it up in the morning."

"I'd offer you a ride if I had my car today . . ." Sven stopped a few steps farther down the sidewalk.

"It's fine." Barnaby offered a tense smile. "It's not a bad walk."

Sven checked the time. "You could always stay with me again, if you need. Bus should be here soon."

"I'll be fine." Barnaby lifted a hand in a half-hearted wave, watching Sven look each way at the curb before moving across the street toward the bus stop.

Sven disappeared behind another building. Barnaby sent one last look back toward the RO, and then turned for his neighborhood.

With the last of downtown turning into the bestseller mansions, Barnaby's phone vibrated in his pocket. He fished it out, slowing his pace as he looked at it, frowning when he didn't recognize the number.

He answered all the same. "Hello?"

"Hi, Barney," the familiar voice replied. "It's Alice again. Hope I'm not calling too late?"

"No." Barnaby continued down the street, the houses slowly growing smaller and smaller as he headed for all the *normal* MC homes. "I'm just heading home, actually."

"Good." Alice's bright smile nearly seemed to carry over the line. "I just wanted to let you know that I seem to have finally gotten myself fired."

"I'm sorr—"

"Oh, don't worry about it," she cut him off. "I'm not. I just wanted to let you know what I found before I was shoved out the door."

Mouth still halfway open with an aborted apology, Barnaby waited for her to continue.

"I was trying to track down those odd transports we found, and I found a source."

Barnaby stopped walking entirely, mind trying to take in the words. "A source?"

"Well, as close to a source as I think I was likely to find. The signal came from somewhere over at the General Counsel. If I didn't think the OAT would give me a crap reference, I'd see about getting a job over there next."

Barnaby nodded to himself, supposing he couldn't truly be surprised after everything else that evening.

"You still there?" Alice asked.

"I'm here." Barnaby snapped out of his thoughts.

"I wish I could be more help," Alice continued. "Just like that office to boot me right when things are finally interesting. You'll let me know what you find out, though, yeah?"

"Yeah," Barnaby repeated. "Of course."

"I'll hold you to that," Alice said, voice just as good-natured. "Good luck getting your girl back."

"Yeah. Thanks." Barnaby looked down, releasing a breath as he ran his free hand through his hair. Hanging up, he stared at the phone in his palm.

Perhaps, after all he had learned since this had begun, he'd gotten in over his head.

He supposed there wasn't much he could do about it now.

Chapter Twenty-Three

DOING HIS BEST TO AVOID ANY CURIOUS COWORKERS, Barnaby still couldn't help himself, poking his head upstairs when he returned for his car. Whatever he had expected, a normally functioning office certainly wasn't it. Computers worked ordinarily, and people milled about, getting coffee or slowly working their way to their desks.

If Barnaby hadn't known better, he would have thought he'd imagined last night.

"Barnaby." Christophe appeared behind him, mug in hand. "Didn't expect you in?"

The question under his words hung heavily between them.

"Just dropping by for a second," Barnaby said. "I'm headed over to the General Counsel."

"The General Counsel?" Christophe asked, lifting his mug to his mouth as though it would lessen his apparent interest.

"We might have a lead," Barnaby said. "I'll let you know when I know more."

Christophe just nodded, as though mulling the words over.

Barnaby clapped Christophe's shoulder, moving for the elevator. "We'll talk later."

Tapping his hand irritably on his thigh, Barnaby watched the numbers tick up as the elevator lifted from the ground floor. A last, high-pitched *bing*, and the doors opened. Barnaby took a step forward and nearly ran head-first into the all-too-familiar brunette.

"You're supposed to let people out first, you realize?" Catherine sidestepped with a frown.

"Sorry, didn't know you worked here now." Barnaby didn't bother looking at her as he pressed the button for the garage.

"I was dropping something off for Christophe." She stood in the doorway, holding the elevator in place.

"Great," Barnaby said. "Just saw him down the hall."

Catherine looked at him, glancing at the pressed button. "Where are you going?"

"Nowhere, as long as you keep standing there."

Catherine's frown deepened. "What are you up to?"

"I thought you were here to see Christophe?" Barnaby tried not to let his rapidly mounting impatience show.

The elevator let out a low buzz, unhappy with the door being held so long.

"But I know when you're up to something." Catherine stepped back into the car, the door shutting behind her as the elevator began to move.

"It's nothing that concerns you." Barnaby watched the number tick back down.

"Which is why you've been hanging around Christophe?"

Barnaby hesitated, sliding his eyes back over to Catherine's very angry face. "I what now?"

"You made him late when we had symphony tickets."

Barnaby actually laughed. "Did he tell you that?"

"He said he'd been with you and Sven."

The elevator binged again, this time opening to the parking garage under the building. Barnaby slid past Catherine. "Can't say I had any idea about your plans, Cat. And I can honestly say I have had other things on my mind than trying to figure out ways to get you and your boyfriend to fight."

"So, you just magically decided you wanted to be friends with him?"

"He was helping me with a project." Barnaby clicked the remote on his keys, his car beeping as it unlocked. "No vast conspiracy, I assure you."

"So it's just complete coincidence that he was hanging around with you one night and now is suddenly acting like you?"

Barnaby pulled his car door open, but looked back to where Catherine stood, blocking him from leaving the parking spot even before he could sit. "What do you mean 'acting like me'?"

"Running late? Suddenly keeping things from me?" She crossed her arms.

Barnaby released a heavy breath. "Are you going to stand there all morning?"

"If I have to."

Barnaby checked the time and shook his head. "I didn't know he was running late, for that first part. The second part, he was helping with something involving Eloise that I asked him not to tell you about. No conspiracy greater than that on my part. If there's more he's keeping from you, that's really something you should talk to him—and perhaps a couples' counsellor—about. Not me."

Catherine's brow furrowed. "What about Eloise?"

Barnaby shook his head, sitting. "Go ask Christophe. I've got to go."

"Barnaby," Catherine snapped.

"Really, Cat. Life or death here. Go bother your boyfriend."

"Life or death?" she repeated.

He slammed the door shut. Twisting to look at Catherine out the rear window, he threw the car into gear.

Another frown, but Catherine stepped aside, watching him as he sped out of the parking garage.

Eloise lay awake, staring at the intricately embroidered pillows underneath her in the lingering twilight. The tents had turned out to be a group of mSCs this time, left out in the deserts as nomads. If Eloise never again had to introduce herself and say just what was happening in all its exquisite weirdness, it would really be too soon. Especially if she would have to continue by preaching her way through the desert. The entire exercise seemed just a little too likely to get her crucified for comfort.

And Messianic Archetype really wasn't her cup of tea.

Echo turned over, her small form nearly lost in the sea of rugs and linens across the tent. Eloise had to admit, for finding their lot in life to be mSCs out in the desert, the group had made the most of it. *Arabian Nights* had never been Eloise's particular design aesthetic, but after days—or at least, what she assumed were days—of camping in nothing but gray, gray, and more gray, the lavishly decorated tents on this set seemed to be the height of luxury.

The flap opened. Eloise lifted her head slightly before she pushed herself up onto her elbows. The shapes, a man and a woman, moved toward Eloise's little pallet of pillows. Faces obscured in the shadowy light, they both seemed about Eloise's age, their coloring dark as the rest of the nomads she had spoken to.

"Sorry to wake you." The woman knelt next to Eloise's pallet, sitting back on her heels.

"No problem." Eloise looked between them, doing her best to make out whether these were faces she recognized.

"I'm Sabeen," the woman introduced herself, saving Eloise the trouble of racking her brain for names. "And this is Ali."

"What's going on?" Echo mumbled, turning over once again.

"Sorry," Sabeen repeated, glancing over her shoulder quickly before she looked back at Eloise. "We were just having a meeting, and your friends said you were the one to talk to."

"Talk to about what?" Eloise asked.

"What you're doing," Ali said. "Walking off the sets."

Eloise frowned, checking the flap of the tent to see if anyone else was waiting to hear what she said. She continued cautiously, "From what I gathered, people weren't really comfortable hearing about that stuff here."

"Some aren't, the rest of us, well . . ." Sabeen shared a look with Ali before turning back to Eloise. "Would you come with us?"

Eloise hesitated, but finally nodded, standing slowly. If she suddenly had twelve disciples, however, she was grabbing the first camel out of this set.

Ducking through a flap three tents over, Eloise looked around. With what seemed to be an oil lamp lit in the center, it was possible to properly make out the faces there—Owen the only familiar one in the lot. Eloise counted quickly as Sabeen led her to an open pillow. Seven. Even if she counted Echo and Alex with the group, they were still short of twelve. She supposed she'd take it. Sitting silently on the offered cushion, Eloise looked at the other expectant faces.

"Do you really think we could leave?" one of the men to her right finally asked. Another woman shushed him quickly.

Eloise swallowed, but didn't bother to go back over the specifics. "If you get far enough away from where the author left you, it seems they don't regain full control. It's possible, assuming that happens, you'd be able to leave the set with the rest of us."

Silent faces answered.

"Do you want to leave?" Eloise asked.

"Some won't," Sabeen answered. "But the longer we listen to things . . . we here, at least, are a little worried we're going to end up as Red Shirts if we stick around."

"If we're lucky," another man murmured. "Depending on what those MCs keep doing, we might end up as evil Mooks."

Eloise did her best to force down the lump in her throat at the thought. On a still-active set, this group had the chance of being sent back the natural way, but their deaths would continue to hang over the lot until their author hit The End. And, as mSCs, they were either the safest or the most disposable, depending where they were thrown once the MC showed up. She nodded slowly, looking from face to face. "We still need to find where the rest of our group blew in that sandstorm, but if you'd like to come, you're welcome to join us."

The eyes shifted, just as silent, each member of the story seeming not quite willing to be the first to speak as the question floated between them.

"If they're still active on the set," Owen finally spoke, "it might be best for you to go ahead. Who knows when they'd snap back into the story hanging around here."

Eloise's eyebrows lifted. "Go on without you?"

"Turns out, I'm not bad with the camels." Owen gave a weak smile. "I'm sure if Hebe's gathered up anyone else, she's pushing forward toward the narration. If you head for the edge while I go find her, we can meet where it's safe for this lot."

Author-written or innate, no one could claim Owen wasn't gallant.

"There's no saying how large this set is," Eloise argued. "You could get lost before you reached the edge without the compass. And even if you didn't . . . there's no saying we'd meet up again for certain."

"The rest of us will be okay." The weak smile didn't so much as falter. "Who knows, if we end up in the thick of the narration, maybe we'll be able to talk to the author like you did with Dan."

"You could talk to your author?" Sabeen asked, her dark eyebrows reaching for the headscarf that covered much of her long hair.

Eloise admitted it unwillingly. "Their author, Owen's, since I wasn't meant to be in that set, I think."

The looks of admiration didn't make Eloise feel any better about the messianic connections.

"You go ahead and get anyone who wants to go out of this set," Owen said, voice stronger. "I can take care of finding the rest of our Lost."

As much as getting out of the desert appealed, Eloise couldn't deny the knot forming in her stomach at the thought of leaving him, Echo, and hell, even Hebe.

Ready to bite each others' heads off the past few days or not, they were in this as a team.

"Really," Owen insisted, at her expression. "Who knows, if you take them out of here, maybe the set will start shutting down. I don't think anything bad will come from not having that sun beat down on us, no matter where we go around here."

Eloise bunched the thick fabric over her cushion in her fist, trying to hide her discomfort. "You're sure you'd be okay?"

Owen nodded.

She looked at the rest of the faces. "And all of you want to go? It won't be easy."

"It's better than sitting around here waiting for someone to take our heads off," the man who'd mentioned Mooks mumbled.

Eloise forced herself to swallow, mouth dry in a way she didn't think she could fully blame on the desert air. Still, she nodded. "Ask around camp, then. We'll try to get anyone who wants to go out."

The group of six stood, disappearing under the flap one by one until it was only Eloise and Owen, staring at each other at an angle across the now empty circle.

"Are you sure you know what you're doing?" she asked, face feeling pinched with worry.

"Have any of us known what we were doing since you showed up?" Owen returned.

Eloise had to give him that. She slowly forced her fists to release the fabric. "I'll miss you. All of you."

Owen just smiled as he stood. He stopped in front of her and squeezed her shoulder gently. "We'll look you up, once we all make it home."

Eloise smiled back, watching him duck to clear the flap, heading back outside.

Barnaby sat in the parking lot of the grand General Counsel building, tapping his thumb on the steering wheel. *Confidential trials.* Barnaby had to agree with Sven that it wasn't likely to be something they'd willingly tell him about at the help desk. No, he would have to find a way to see someone important. Someone who would actually know what these "trials" were.

Ideally, the President of the Counsel.

Barnaby released a long breath, trying to work out just what he could do, now that he was outside, sitting in his car like an idiot. If this were a story, he would no doubt have a plan. Possibly some sort of Caper Crew to help with it.

Or he'd just keep floundering like he already was, he supposed. Try to find a side door and press his luck.

He paused, scanning the side of the building. There was, indeed, a side door, under a little overhang toward the back corner. He sighed, wondering whether he was really willing to attempt something that stereotypical.

Well, no reason to fight it now.

Finally leaving the relative safety of the car, Barnaby moved toward the door, doing his best not to look entirely suspicious. He sent a last look back at the parking lot, perhaps failing at "not suspicious" in the process, and then turned the knob.

The door swung open, not locked, not alarmed. Barnaby wasn't quite sure why that didn't make him feel any better.

This early in the day, the people wandering around the General Counsel didn't seem much different than the ones in the RO—heading off to their desks with mugs of coffee, maybe a bagel. And no one seemed to spare Barnaby a second glance, apparently too focused on whatever they were doing to notice him as he did his best to find his way in the winding marble halls. If the entrance with the help desk was impressive, the grandeur only grew throughout the rest of the building, with its high ceilings and dark doors tucked between polished marble columns.

Following a sign for the executive offices, Barnaby came to a wall. Two staircases, one up and one down, framed a walled-off space, like the back end of a room jutting into the hallway. Barnaby frowned at the odd placement of whatever was on the other side of the wall, but there seemed little choice but to maneuver around it at this point. Hearing more footsteps coming from above than from the subfloor below, Barnaby made his choice and descended. Generally oblivious or not, the fewer people around to notice him, the better.

A few cases filled with what looked like bestseller artifacts stretched along the wall to his left, where windows had been on the ground floor. He gave them a cursory glance, but they were dusty, obviously hadn't been touched in at least months, maybe even years. He headed across the long hallway to reach the matching staircase back to the ground floor.

The dark-stained door in the middle of the hall swung open as he passed, the creaking hinges echoing off polished marble. Barnaby turned slowly to look at it. The door slowed under its own momentum, finally stopping. Though it remained open, no one appeared. Rolling his shoulders in an attempt to force out some of his tension, Barnaby moved toward the self-opening door, peeking in.

He couldn't see much, nothing but an empty space looking back at him. Most of the room was obscured by a fluttering green curtain. A soft mechanic whirring further inside caught his attention. He glanced at the door next to him hesitantly. Perhaps he'd set off something automatic. He'd like to believe that, at the very least.

The voice caught him as he took a step back toward the staircase.

"No, please come in."

Barnaby froze, staring at the doorway.

"I believe you're looking for me," the voice continued.

Moving slowly, Barnaby stepped into the room, debating whether he should run back out as the door shut behind him.

"Please."

Catching the edge of the curtain, Barnaby stepped through.

A patchwork of monitors covered the walls, black-and-white images sticking to each for a few seconds before flipping to another. In the center, a white-haired man sat behind a desk. He swiveled as Barnaby paused, offering a smile. "Welcome. Barnaby, isn't it?"

Barnaby still didn't move from his spot by the curtain.

"Yes?" The man stood, short enough that it seemed he would barely reach the middle of Barnaby's chest.

"I'm just trying to decide if I should be surprised you know my name or not," Barnaby said, finally taking a step forward. In this far . . . what else could he really do?

"I've been watching you." The man motioned to the monitors. "You have been quite dedicated, from what I've seen."

Barnaby looked at the screens, then back at the man. "I'm sorry, but . . . who are you?"

"Oh, pardon my manners." The man moved forward, offering his hand. "Oz."

Barnaby shook it slowly. "As in Oz, the great and—?"

"Oh no." The man smiled. "Oscar Diggs retired years ago. I just thought I'd keep the name. After all, I am now the Man Behind the Curtain."

Barnaby glanced back at the cloth hung across the room and remained silent.

"I take it you're here about Miss Eloise?" Oz continued, turning back to his desk.

Barnaby's brow furrowed.

"*Very* dedicated, I suppose I should have said." Oz picked up a tablet of some kind. "You're the first to have made it this far."

"This far?" Barnaby finally asked.

"Most of the anchors get caught over at Assignment and Transportation. One didn't try much at all, quite disappointingly."

Barnaby just frowned.

"You were having your friend trying to break into the trial folders last night?" Oz continued to smile all the same. "You obviously figured out this isn't the first time we have tried this."

"Tried what?" Barnaby asked.

"To shut down the sets." Oz pressed something on his tablet, the screens behind him stopping their scrolling as they settled on their individual images. He motioned backward. "Hundreds of them. And hundreds still caught in dead sets. No way for us to bring them home."

"You can see the sets?" Barnaby took another step forward before he caught himself.

"You get the feed from somewhere, over at the Recording Office," Oz said, turning to look himself—everything from city to tundra stretching across the little screens.

"Can you see Eloise?" Barnaby looked back at the short man.

"I'm sure we'll find her soon." Oz turned to face him. "She keeps hopping sets too quickly to keep a steady feed. Also the most determined of our subjects, it seems."

"Subjects," Barnaby repeated. "She's some test case to you?"

Oz gave a sad smile. "We have been trying for years to find a way to break out of the authors' hold on our world. You must understand, we would not put our subjects through this if we had any other solution."

Barnaby released a breath that seemed caught between a scoff and a laugh. "And how is Eloise supposed to do that? Break their hold?"

"Eloise, and you." Oz tapped something else on the tablet before lowering it to look at Barnaby. "Since our first subject, Mr. Travis, went in and had a not-so-easy time of it, we have been keeping a close watch on the School, looking for students with high potential. Miss Eloise showed a particularly high amount of Genre Awareness compared to her classmates. As far as we can tell, she would have been slated for a prep school drama without our interference. A complete waste, if you ask me."

"So you transported her into a story she didn't belong in," Barnaby said, trying to keep his fists from clenching.

"It seems the only way to be able to break the lock authors have on their stories." Oz nodded. "Eloise has done just as well as we hoped. Without someone who has such a natural instinct for stories—well, we are far too aware of how easy it is to be thrown off by the sets. The unfortunate Miss Paula went mad from it. Then again, her anchor gave up much, much sooner than you as well."

Barnaby shook his head. "What do I have to do with this?"

"It's not an easy thing, placing someone in a story that doesn't want them, Mr. Fitzwilliam. We've found it requires both the potential energy behind someone who has not been storied, along with a tie to someone who has. You serve as both a key into the sets, and an anchor back from them."

Barnaby let the words soak in, and then had to ask it. "Why me?"

"I couldn't tell you, Mr. Fitzwilliam," Oz said. "Certain people just seem to find themselves drawn to our subjects. You have proven to be one of them."

Barnaby's eyes went back to the monitors, scanning them one by one, looking for any sign of where Eloise might now be.

"And it seems entirely fortuitous, between your perseverance and your wife."

Barnaby's eyes flicked back to the man.

"I'm sorry. Ex-wife." Oz smiled.

"What's Catherine got to do with this?"

"We do our best to figure out who our anchors are," Oz said. "And while looking into you and your ex-wife, it seems she feels her own connection to the authors. We aren't quite sure if we might be able to use that yet, but we are hoping, if Miss Eloise becomes too lost, that we might find that to be another connection to the sets."

"What do you mean 'connection to the authors'?" Barnaby asked. "We never talked to our author."

"No," Oz replied, pressing a few more buttons before the monitors flicked over, each one forming part of a bigger picture. "But going through your footage, we've seen that she did attempt to write her own story while on your set."

Barnaby studied the choppy picture: Catherine, still in period dress, bent over a desk, pen in hand. He looked at Oz. "There are plenty of people who were writers in their stories."

"Yes, but not many who take it upon themselves to be," Oz said. "If you recall, she was not a novelist in your story. All of you are really quite remarkable."

Barnaby swallowed and tried to work through the information, too much of it coming at once. "And Eloise? What is she supposed to do?"

"She's doing what she's supposed to do." Oz reset the monitors to their scrolling feed. "She is bringing our people out of their stories."

"She can't possibly cross *every* set looking for people."

"No, but the more that leave, the weaker the sets' holds become on us," Oz said. "Enough, and we might be able to break that hold altogether."

Barnaby took the information, didn't fight it. "And what happens then?"

Oz smiled. "I suppose we'll find out."

Chapter Twenty-Four

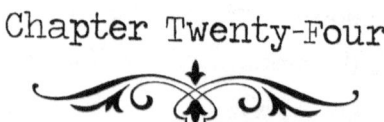

BARNABY SAT IN HIS CAR, NOT MOVING, NOT SO MUCH as bothering to put his key in the ignition as he filtered through everything in his head. Glad to know, angry at being tossed around his own life like he was still in-story, everything just left Barnaby feeling numb.

And knowing or not, there was still too much to do. Eloise was still out there, wandering God knew where.

The thought hit, and Barnaby dialed quickly before he started the car.

"You find anything?" Sven didn't wait for a hello.

"Yeah." Barnaby didn't bother to elaborate. "Can you take lunch or something and meet me?"

"Meet you where?" Sven asked.

"Corner of Latham and Bennet."

"What's there?"

"Catherine's house." Barnaby didn't wait for a response, ending the call and throwing the phone on the passenger's seat as he pulled out of the parking lot.

Twelve. Of course she had ended up with a little band of twelve following along. And Eloise had tried to be so careful too; she'd been secretly relieved when one of those wanting to go volunteered to travel with Owen instead, to help make sure they made it through the dunes.

But then, Echo had chosen to travel toward the border. Eloise released a breath, doing her best to stay on the camel she had been given. If one of the new travelers turned out to be a Fake Defector or something of the kind, she would have to stab herself. Of course, she wasn't exactly being persecuted by non-believers, so hopefully that would be her saving grace. But still, the sooner they could get off this damn set, the better she would feel.

"Is that it?" Echo called, pointing out in front of them—at least, Eloise assumed the smaller woman was pointing, as the desert-appropriate robe she had been given swallowed up her hand.

Eloise squinted into the distance, the telltale shimmer of black just barely visible on the horizon.

"It looks like a mirage," Ali answered before Eloise was able.

She glanced at him. "It looks like no-man's-land." Hopefully, she was right.

The black expanse stretched out in front of them, the sand slowly tapering off—as though some had blown onto the edges of the no-man's-land from the set.

Echo focused on the set across from them. "It looks like it's in color."

"What?" Sabeen frowned.

"The sets go gray when they aren't active." Eloise checked the compass, making sure they were on the western edge a final time before she looked across from them. Definitely still active, it seemed to be another city, though it looked run-down. Eloise was able to make out windows that had been boarded up even at the distance. With each of the sets next to it seeming gray, however, the city was likely their best hope at finding more people.

After agreeing to let Owen go into the thick of the narration behind them by himself, the very least she could do was look for more Lost of her own.

"All right." She clapped her hands together, looking at the apprehensive group behind her. "The trick is, you have to run—"

The wind picked up again, Eloise's new robe catching. She lifted her eyes, looking for any sign of a sandstorm. At least they would likely be able to outrun it this time.

"Eloise . . ."

Echo's voice broke Eloise out of her thoughts. Some of the characters doubled over, the remainder looking ill as words began to float in on the wind.

"The author's narrating." Eloise met Echo's scared eyes before looking at the others. "You need to get off the set. Run. Just run. Don't stop until you hit solid ground."

The group didn't argue, taking a few hesitant steps onto the no-man's-land before they began to sprint. The ground rumbled unhappily. Eloise didn't stay to see why.

Legs pumping, she ran for the derelict city over the unsettling ooze in the center. The ground turned solid again, and Eloise finally let herself slow, studying the city as she tried to catch her breath. If it had appeared a little run-down at a distance, it looked awful up close. Rust stains ran down many of the buildings; graffitied two-by-fours boarded up some of the windows, while others were simply open save for a few shards of broken glass.

Echo cautiously nudged some trash that had spilled onto the street with her foot. "Can't we just once end up in, like, Tahiti or something?"

Eloise fished the compass out, looking down the eerily empty street. "Well, that's still west. We'll walk quickly."

If anyone had any objections, they kept them to themselves, the entire group making their way through the abandoned streets.

"Where do you think we are?" one of the men—Hamid?—asked.

"This can't actually be somewhere *real*?" Sabeen's eyes scanned the buildings, bad only seeming to go to worse as they walked along.

"It looks . . ." Eloise didn't want to say it, but couldn't think of anything else it might be. "Post-apocalyptic."

Everyone turned to her.

"What does that mean for us?" Ali asked.

New group, same looking to her for answers. Eloise shook her head. "We keep moving, and try not to touch anything until we know what happened."

The other twelve nodded, continuing forward.

Deep into the streets of Scenery Gorn, a dog barked. Eloise jumped, the sound stark in the silence of the Ghost City.

It barked again.

The eyes turned back to Eloise.

"Post-Apocalyptic Dog," Eloise said, not sure if it was to herself or the others. "Let's see who's there?"

The group frowned, but again, they obeyed without comment, turning the corner.

What looked like a Jack Russell terrier stood in the street, off toward a boarded-up building at the end of the block. It barked once more, dropping its head slightly before taking a step backward.

Scanning the rest of the street, Eloise moved forward, finally crouching when she was a couple yards from the dog. "Hello there. Do you have anybody with you?"

A shotgun pump answered.

Turning her head slowly, Eloise looked down the barrel, sliding her eyes up to the blonde woman standing at the front door of the building. She lifted her hands slowly.

"Who are you?" the woman asked.

"Eloise," Eloise answered, just as slowly lifting herself to stand. "And you?"

The woman kept the shotgun leveled, but her eyes went down the street to the rest of the group, the lot seeming just as frozen a little further back. She looked back at Eloise. "You're human?"

Eloise frowned, glancing down over herself quickly. "Yes?"

The shotgun lowered, just an inch. "Are you mad? What are you doing on the street?"

"I'm sorry?"

"Get in." The woman waved back at the building, the Jack Russell running inside, tail wagging.

Eloise glanced back at the rest of her little group and motioned them forward.

The space inside the old building didn't look any better preserved than the city outside.

A man stood from his spot in the corner. "What is it?"

"I found this lot just wandering around outside." The woman motioned back at Eloise and the others with her thumb.

"What?" The man's forehead wrinkled as he looked at them. "Are you trying to get yourselves teared apart?"

The gun, the dog, "*teared apart.*" Something clicked in Eloise's head. "Is this a zombie novel?"

The woman scoffed. "You don't know?"

"We actually just got here." Eloise motioned to the entirely out-of-place desert clothing. "We're from the next set over."

The man and woman blinked, and then asked in unison, "What?"

Once again going into her spiel, Eloise caught them up in as few words as possible. "And so, we were trying to make it across this set to the next one."

Another beat of silence, and then the woman spoke again. "You're trying to *walk* across the sets?"

Eloise nodded. "And it's going passably well at this point. Is this an active set?"

"Unfortunately." The man looked them all over once again. "You didn't come across the zombies, I take it."

"Can't say we did," Eloise answered, as it seemed the rest of her group didn't feel the need to.

"You're lucky." The woman finally set her shotgun against the wall. "Ted's already been torn apart three times out there."

Eloise's eyes swung to the man. "You're—?"

He shook his head. "Josh. Ted's recovering upstairs."

"Can't die without the author, but still hell to come back from," the woman mumbled.

"Nat." Josh motioned to the woman as means of an introduction.

"You're welcome to come with us," Echo finally piped up. Everyone looked at her. "If you like."

"Come with you?" Nat asked.

"Doesn't seem like a fun place to hang around." Echo shrugged. "We just walked everyone else off their set."

Nat continued to look at Echo as though she were insane. At least it was someone else's turn to get a few of those stares.

Josh crossed his arms. "You're lucky as hell you weren't torn limb from limb coming into town. You'd never make it past the zombies out there going any further. They're mindless even in-story. Without the author, they just circle, destroying anyone they come across. Nat's the only one who hasn't been caught by them at this point."

"And I intend to keep it that way." Nat bent, petting the Jack Russell behind the ears as the dog reappeared at her ankles.

"We can't very well just sit here." Ali frowned, meeting Eloise's eyes.

She shook her head, looking back at Josh. "How many of you are there?"

"Started with seven," Nat answered before Josh could. "We're down to four."

"And things aren't looking so good for Sarah." Josh's face turned grim, glancing at the staircase against the far wall—the wood seeming a sickly green from the light coming in the mostly covered window.

Eloise read his face. "Your author's using Anyone Can Die here?"

"Seems that way." Nat leaned back against the wall.

Eloise looked at the rest of her group, turned back to Nat. "They can't kill you if you get off the set."

Her eyebrows creased.

"It's why we took them." Eloise motioned back to the group behind her. "Get off the set, and the author can't feed you to zombies."

From the look Nat and Josh gave each other, the offer was at least a little appealing. Eloise would certainly take that over more people questioning her sanity.

"How many zombies are there?" Ali asked at their silence.

"Enough." Nat's face turned hard again. "Even if we wanted to walk off into the sunset—*lack* of sunset—we'd never make it."

Eloise looked down, mind working. "How standard are your zombies?"

"What?" Nat asked.

"Slow, Zombie Gait, mindless corpses? Or can they actually run?"

"Zombie Gait," Josh said. "Pretty standard Flesh-Eaters."

"And Plague Zombies, based on the set?" Eloise glanced back at the door.

"Supposedly it's a virus, I think?" Nat watched her.

"Plague Zombie, Zombie Apocalypse," Eloise mumbled under her breath as she ticked off tropes, looking between Josh and Nat. "And you're fighting them? In-story?"

Nat made a face. "Trying to."

"Night of the Living Mooks, then," Eloise said, doing her best not to think about just who had been turned for this story. Already mindless, they had long been counted amongst the dead back home, more than likely. "If they aren't thinking, they aren't hunting you while the author's gone?"

Josh shook his head. "They circle the streets. They've never come inside without the narrative making them."

"They're likely on autopilot, then, in the lulls," Eloise stated, not allowing herself to consider it too closely. "Which would mean they'd follow some sort of pattern, contained in a certain area. If we could get around that . . ."

"And how, exactly, would we do that?" Nat asked.

"Eloise could manage it," Echo said. "She's the Queen of Genre Savvy."

Josh frowned. "This isn't even your story."

"I've never had a story." Eloise forced a tense smile. "I just studied them in school."

Chapter Twenty-Five

WHERE BARNABY HAD OPTED FOR AN EASY-UPKEEP townhouse after the divorce, Catherine had never moved out of the beautiful, six-bedroom colonial she had picked when they'd been freshly post-storied. Barnaby had to admit it fit her generally old-fashioned tastes—something she had never grown out of from their story. He also had to admit she more than likely would boot him from the front step the moment he rang the bell.

That was assuming she was even home.

Having fallen into an Internal Travel Planning job on their return, Catherine had worked from home for as long as Barnaby had lived there. But who knew what could have changed since then. He hadn't exactly been checking in.

The door opened on his second ring, surprise showing on Catherine's face for a split second before her eyes narrowed. "I'd ask if you were here to apologize for earlier, but that seems about as likely as a lightning strike."

"I came to ask for your help, actually," Barnaby said. For once, he didn't bother sparring with her.

"My help?" she repeated.

He nodded. "Could I come in?"

Another suspicious look, but Catherine took a step back. Likely, it was the best case scenario Barnaby could have hoped for.

The house was as neat as Catherine had ever kept it, though the pair of men's shoes by the door and large coat hanging on the rack showed she wasn't entirely living alone.

Barnaby caught his hands behind his back as he followed her to the kitchen. "Love what you've done with the place."

Catherine sent him an unamused look, leaning back against the kitchen island. "So, what is it?"

"You talked to Christophe after I left?"

Her jaw went hard as she spoke through clenched teeth. "He still wouldn't tell me anything."

Barnaby sighed. "Well—"

The front door opened, Catherine frowning as she leaned forward.

"Cat?" Christophe's voice came from the front entry.

"Chris?" she replied, taking a few steps toward the door.

Christophe appeared, Sven following close at heel.

Sven met Barnaby's eyes, motioning at Christophe quickly. "Sorry, he gave me a ride."

Catherine's dark eyes flicked between the men. She shook her head. "What the hell is going on?"

Barnaby opened his mouth, realized it would take too long to go through it all, especially to Catherine's standards, and truncated. "Long story short, Eloise was sucked into a story she wasn't meant to be in. And we've been trying to get her out."

Catherine looked at him, not speaking for a long moment. "What?"

"What happened?" Sven spoke over her, eyes on Barnaby.

Barnaby tried to think of a way to explain that didn't sound entirely insane—figured there wasn't really a way to. "I met with someone at the General Counsel, and they're trying to shut down the sets."

The other three in the room looked at him, seeming to have all been struck mute.

"They think that, if Eloise can lead people out of their sets, they'll be able to shut them down."

Another beat, and Catherine shook her head. "Are you drunk?"

Barnaby didn't bother to look at her. "That's what I found out."

"So, why are we here?" Sven asked, apparently already long past his disbelief as well.

"Because Catherine might be able to get in contact with her."

Catherine scoffed, looking between the men. "Me?"

"With Eloise?" Christophe finally spoke.

Barnaby nodded, taking a moment before turning to Catherine again. "The man I met with said you tried to author a story while we were in ours."

Catherine's mouth opened, no words emerging as she recovered. "How could they possibly know that?"

"They have all the feeds to the stories," Barnaby said. "And feeds around here. He knew what I'd been doing to try and find Eloise."

"Big Brother is Watching?" Sven frowned.

Barnaby just made a face, looking back at Catherine. "But that may have given you a connection to the sets. If so, you could try to contact Eloise."

Catherine shook her head, releasing another incredulous breath. "That's entirely absurd."

"Did you, Cat?" Christophe asked. "Write?"

Her shoulders pulled up, eyes going between the men once again, beginning to look like an animal that had been cornered. "It wasn't anything. Just hearing that narration day after day . . . I dabbled a little, trying to stay sane."

"Just try," Barnaby insisted. "Please."

"It's *absurd*." She crossed her arms.

"After everything I've gone through with this, Cat," Barnaby said, "believe me, I am more than willing to try absurd."

Catherine just frowned.

Christophe turned for the doorway. "I'll go get some paper."

"Chris!" Catherine looked at him.

"We might as well try." He gave her an apologetic shrug, heading for the stairs.

Catherine's nostrils flared as she looked back at Barnaby. "I may pull my hair out if you two become friends."

Barnaby actually smiled.

Hobbling, decaying, there was no denying these were standard zombies. Eloise could only hope that that meant her assumptions were correct. Having made it this far, only to end up eaten by Undead Mooks would have to be the worst ending she could think of for this journey.

What had to have been hours of watching, high in various buildings, said there was at least some sort of pattern to the zombic movements, like the author had set them all on a track and the zombies had nothing to do but shuffle along it, looking for things to kill.

"So," Nat finally spoke into the silence. "Are we going to try this?"

"We wait any longer, the author might come back," Josh answered, sending a glance back at Sarah.

Looking the youngest of the four survivors—perhaps fifteen or sixteen—with her arm already in a sling, Eloise had to admit that it did seem likely the girl was next on the chopping block. As awful a death as it would be to be eaten by zombies while trying to make it to the edge of the set, Eloise had to imagine it would be worse having it happen while author-frozen, helpless to stop it as narration carried on describing it. And, if the detail of the set said anything, this author wasn't the type to hold off on the gore.

Watching the last of the horde limp by, Eloise nodded, mostly to herself, steeling her nerves. "We should have ten minutes before they circle back up the next block. That should be enough time to find another building to wait out that wave."

Whether or not the other sixteen people in the space doubted the sincerity of her false confidence, they still moved, trekking down the wobbly staircase for the street.

Stopping in front of the door, Nat brought her arm up. Her wristwatch beeped. "T-minus ten minutes."

They moved as quickly as possible without entirely running, even Echo's short legs seeming to keep pace as heads swiveled, looking for any early signs of zombies.

The set skipped, leaving Eloise feeling as though they had somehow been thrown forward. Nat's watch went off, the beeping seeming to echo in the dead streets.

Nat looked at it. "That can't be right."

The sound of limbs dragging and low moaning started down one of the side streets ahead of them.

"We time jumped." The words came out of Eloise's mouth before she could properly think them. "We need to get off their track."

"If they see us, they'll follow," Sarah said, eyes wide.

"Then we better run." Sabeen took off down the street, the rest of them following at her heels.

The set gave the same low rumble as they moved off the zombie's track, as though it were angry they dared leave it. Or, perhaps more likely, as though it were angry *its characters* dared leave it. Eloise didn't risk slowing, pushing herself forward.

Another skip. The moans grew louder.

"They're there!" Josh called from near the front of the pack. "We need to get off the road."

"Scatter!" Nat turned sharply, heading for a row of buildings. The others followed suit.

Grabbing Echo's hand on instinct, Eloise did her best to judge the buildings ahead of them. She ran up to a door, found it locked. She rattled the handle and felt the set skip again. Zombies appeared.

"Really?" she shouted up at the sky.

Echo tried the next door over, the same locked rattle sounding as the zombies grew closer.

"At least try to be original!" Eloise finished, turning back to the streets.

Nat reappeared from a side street, looking confused as to how she got there. Her eyes hit Eloise's. "They've spotted me. All the doors are locked."

"Come on." Eloise started down the street again, heading for what she could only hope was no-man's-land.

`And then she started to write because her idiotic ex-husband told her to, and it was incredibly stupid.`

The sudden narration nearly made Eloise miss a step. She glanced up, then looked at Nat. The woman didn't look ill. Eloise checked behind her. Zombies started to appear around a corner, a safe distance away for now, but who knew with the time skips. Eloise tried all the same, the voice vaguely familiar. "Catherine?"

A pause and the set shook again, the color flickering to gray and then back.

`Holy crap, can you actually hear me?`

"Yeah," Eloise answered, the set color flickering once more.

The zombies froze, started again.

"We're kind of about to be eaten by zombies," Eloise shouted as she nodded Nat and Echo forward at a run. "Anything you can do about that?"

Nothing answered for a long moment, another skip bringing the horde too close for comfort.

And then all the zombies disappeared?

The mass froze, and then seemed to be cut out in a skip of their own. A hard shift, and a slow cracking began to echo in the sudden silence.

"Watch out!" Nat pointed.

The street cracked, a chasm opening as the set continued to quake. The color came and went, making Eloise's eyes ache as she grabbed a twisted railing for balance.

"Eloise!" A splinter seemed to chase Echo as the short woman ran.

"Oh jeez . . ." Eloise glanced at the sky once again, moved forward, and caught Echo's hand before she could tumble off the set all together.

Did that work? Catherine's voice came over the crashing as buildings came down along the split.

"Seems so," Eloise grunted, Nat moving beside her to help pull Echo back up.

A long pause, and then: I take it you didn't hear that.

"Hear what?" Eloise asked, looking at the large white space that had opened up opposite the crack—almost as though a blank sheet of paper had crashed headlong into a developed set.

Barnaby tried writing.

"Barnaby's there?" Eloise looked back at the sky.

"Who's Barnaby?" Nat asked.

"Eloise's boyfriend," Echo answered, still panting as she brushed chunks of asphalt and dirt off her clothes.

He's the one who told me to try writing. He's going to be entirely impossible to live with now that he's right, I hope you realize.

Another pause.

He asks if you're all right. The voice turned annoyed.

"As good as can be expected." Eloise stepped forward, chancing to touch the expanse of white coming out of the crack. Springy, like the no-man's-land, her fingers sinking in an inch before being pushed out again. "Are you doing that?"

Doing what?

"It's like . . ." Eloise shook her head. "You're writing, right now?"

Yeah.

"Can you . . . try writing, like, a set or something?"

Like what?

Eloise glanced at Echo. "Tropical island would be nice."

Catherine's voice continued, hesitant, while not entirely losing its displeased edge. Tan sand appeared out of the white, joined by calm blue water and palm trees as her voice mentioned each in turn, a full tropical island rising out of the post-apocalyptic city as though two sets had somehow crashed into each other.

"Holy crap," Echo murmured.

What? Catherine asked.

"You just created a set . . ." Eloise kept her eyes on it, finally forcing herself to look around just in case the magically gone zombies decided to reappear just as suddenly.

Echo looked at Eloise, as if for permission, before finally taking a few hesitant steps onto the sandy beach. She moved to the water, cupping a handful before letting it run through her fingers. She looked back at Eloise, eyes wide.

Eloise looked at Nat. "We should still probably get you guys out of here." She addressed the sky once again, "Could you try to write the rest of our people back here? There should be fourteen more people out there."

As Catherine wrote the words, bodies began appearing, some bruised, some bloody, but every single traveler there once again.

Eloise nodded Nat over to explain, then returned to staring at the sky. "I'd ask you to try writing us home, but the last time a set shut down, things didn't go so well for us."

The new arrivals began exploring, stepping cautiously onto the beach, a few chancing to step into the water.

Barnaby says to say he was at the General Counsel earlier and talked to someone who admitted to putting you in there.

"What?" Eloise's attention snapped away from the island set as she went to stand.

They've been trying to shut down the sets and needed someone to start getting people off of them to break the link or something?

"This was on purpose?" Eloise's voice turned shrill. A few of the nomads looked over, and Eloise tried to bring her voice back under control.

Barnaby says, if you can get enough people out of the sets, maybe you'll come home.

"Do you know how long it takes to get across these things?" Eloise shook her head, sitting on a cracked step. "I could be doing this for years if I'm just trying to get people to leave with me."

A pause. He says you can also keep walking west.

Curling her hands into fists, Eloise did her best not to snap. He was trying to help. Hell, he'd gotten Catherine to help, apparently. Yelling wouldn't accomplish anything.

A thought hit her. "What about the RO?"

What about it?

"Barnaby could talk to me in his story. Why couldn't others talk to people they're recording? Tell them to leave?"

No one answered.

"Hello?"

The men are discussing it.

"The men?"

Sven, Barnaby, and Christophe have all started a little "Save Eloise" gang, it seems.

"Well . . . tell them thank you for me?" Eloise released a long breath, taking out her compass. It still pointed north, as it always did—desert, forest, or zombies.

They say they'll try it. That you should keep walking though.

"Of course," Eloise mumbled, not sure if Catherine could hear, and not especially caring. She spoke up again. "We need to get the people here out anyway. I don't know if you shut down the set or not, but if you didn't, a few of them are likely going to be zombie chow once the author comes back."

Good luck, then.

Not bothering to answer, Eloise moved to the edge of Catherine's set, not quite willing to set foot in it. Because she was worried about its appearance, or because she was worried she'd never leave it—looking warm and safe and beautiful—she didn't know.

Barnaby looked at Catherine in the silent room as she nearly seemed to slump over the little kitchen table. "Well?"

"Well what?" Catherine pushed the stack of paper away from her as though she couldn't bear to look at it any longer. "Nothing else is happening."

"Is she off the horror set?" Barnaby did his best to keep his tone level, but wasn't quite sure how he was managing after the day he'd already had.

"You're really asking the wrong person, Barnaby dear." She stood with a jerk. "I will be a happy woman if I never have to do that again."

Christophe stepped forward, rubbing Catherine's arms as he spoke in low tones. She nodded, looking away.

Finally taking a moment to really look, Barnaby noticed Catherine's hands were shaking, the normally hard outer shell she always wore around him wavering.

"Was it that bad?" he asked.

She glanced at him, frown coming back at full force. "Just hope your girlfriend can make it the rest of the way by herself. I need to go lay down."

Catherine swept out of the room sharply, Christophe hesitating between following and staying with Sven and Barnaby.

"I'll go try to talk to her . . . ?" Christophe's voice slid up in a question.

"You go make sure she's all right." Barnaby shook his head. "Sven and I will head back to work."

Sven didn't speak again until they had reached Barnaby's car. He shut the door, looking at Barnaby in the driver's seat. "You know I basically destroyed your computer hacking into it, right?"

"Hopefully, second time will be the charm." Barnaby pulled away from the large house, hoping the General Counsel wouldn't have a reason to stop them this time.

Chapter Twenty-Six

Sven's head disappeared for another moment, popping back up as the computer sparked and hissed. He met Barnaby's eyes. "That should do it, more or less."

Barnaby simply nodded, staring at the computer monitor slowly blinking to life.

"Well?" Sven brushed himself off as he stepped back in front of the desk.

Barnaby released a breath and looked at Sven. "I'll try it out here; you go try to hook up the next one."

Sven frowned. "You want me to tell other people what's happening?"

"I'm sure they'll find out soon enough if this works." Barnaby sat at his desk, the entire experience seeming foreign after everything else he had done trying to reach Eloise.

Words slowly began to fill the screen:

The school was floating in darkness the stormy night Savannah Carew arrived at the Grier School for Girls.

Savannah walked up the stairs and looked at the marvelous stonework that cascaded down the ceiling like it was liquid, swirling and dripping like the water in the pond she had outside her window at home, where she had used to pull her delicate, white tapered fingers through the surface, watching the water shimmer and ripple . . .

Barnaby grimaced. At least he had a good chance of convincing anyone who was in-story to go, if only to get away from the Purple Prose.

The text finished filling the screen, stopping a few pages in, where Barnaby had to assume the author had left Savannah and her friends—in a dull, dark, overly poetic dormitory.

He typed hesitantly, the screen flashing unhappily, but not shutting down altogether. `Hello?`

The words came back up.

`"Hello?" Savannah answered, looking around.`

Barnaby forced himself forward. `This is going to sound very odd, but I'm Barnaby Fitzwilliam from the Recording Office, and I'm going to need you to do something for me, if you're willing ...`

The skips only seemed to get worse as Eloise continued to walk. What little sense of time she'd had shattered as entire sets seemed to shift under her—leaving them at the edge of a town one minute, and in the middle of a bridge the next.

Still, they all continued forward, gathering the few, confused people they could whenever a skip brought them to a group of Lost or equally confused mSCs who'd been suddenly thrown out of place.

"Are we going the right way still?" Echo asked, still dripping from when the last jump ended up with the poor woman waist-deep in a pond.

Eloise pulled out her compass, adjusted the needle, and nodded. "It still says—"

The set around them flickered.

"West," Eloise finished, eyeing the new buildings around them cautiously.

"Is it just me, or did everything go grayscale?" Sarah stopped where she was, off to Eloise's right.

"I think we entirely jumped sets this time." Eloise slipped her compass back away, taking in the dark buildings and classic cars—nothing like the meadow they had just been moving through.

"How is that even possible?" Sarah shook her head.

"How is any of this even possible?" Eloise returned, the sound of gunfire making her jump.

"No one should be here." Echo frowned. "If it's a closed set?"

Eloise heaved a sigh. "I suppose we should go see while we're here."

"If you insist." Nat pumped her shotgun, lifting her eyebrows when Eloise sent her a look. "Just in case."

Most of the gray set seemed to be in night; streetlamps cast little cones of light as they walked along, catching all of them oddly. Eloise paused as she stepped beneath one, the lighting nearly looking stylized.

"What is it?" Ali asked.

Eloise shook her head, picking up her pace again at the sound of shouting. Rounding the corner, a group of men in what seemed to be trench coats and fedoras held revolvers at a group of girls in school uniforms.

"Whatever it is you're doing, stop it, see?" One of the men motioned with the gun.

"We're not doing anything," the tallest schoolgirl answered. "We're just walking through."

Somewhere in the back of Eloise's mind, it clicked. She glanced at Echo before starting forward. "It's not closed. Someone was writing Film Noir."

Two of the revolvers swung toward Eloise as she approached. She put her hands up, looking at the pack of men. Even their skin was grayscale.

Definitely Film Noir.

"Sorry to interrupt." Eloise met the men's eyes before looking at the school girls—fully in color there. "We were just jumped to your set as well."

"What do you mean 'jumped'?" the first man spoke again, voice so stereotypically detective-story gangster it nearly made Eloise cringe.

"These time skips?" Eloise motioned around her, as though it would illustrate some point. She looked at the girls. "You're from a set nearby, I take it?"

The tallest girl nodded, finally seeming secure enough to lower her raised hands. "Savannah. Someone from the Recording Office told us to go. That the sets were going to shut down?"

A small smile broke free. So the guys *were* managing to do something. Eloise nodded, looking back at the gangsters. "People are walking off their sets and the sets don't seem to be taking it too well."

"How can you 'walk off' a set?" one of the men further into the pack asked, voice not quite as Bugsy Siegel as the other.

"By walking," Eloise said. "Though, with the time skips, we didn't actually walk onto this one."

"Should we keep walking?" one of the other school girls asked. "With the sets doing this?"

Eloise nodded. "We don't have much other choice."

The set you are attempting to contact is currently experiencing technical difficulties. We apologize for any inconvenience.

Barnaby sat back in his chair, staring at the words in the middle of the screen. He could only hope that meant something good.

Meghan appeared in the doorway, her voice a pitch too high. "Do you know where Sven is?"

"Wandering around." Barnaby swiveled to face her. "Why?"

"The computers are going crazy down the hall. All of them crashing." Meghan motioned. "Nobody knows what's happening."

Barnaby nearly smiled, but caught it at the last second as the phone on his desk rang.

Meghan just shook her head, moving off quickly.

Barnaby grabbed the phone. "This is Barnaby."

"Mr. Fitzwilliam," the familiar voice came over the line. "Would you be so kind as to join me down at the General Counsel."

Barnaby hesitated for just a moment before opening his mouth. "I—"

"You'll likely want to hurry," Oz finished. Professional, yet good-natured, the voice still made Barnaby's shoulders tighten.

"I—" Barnaby started again, but the line went dead before he could get anything out. He didn't bother to overthink it, patting his pockets as he stood to make sure he had everything before moving into the hall.

The growing chaos was evident in the halls—heads appearing out of offices, people questioning each other. Barnaby did his best to avoid them all while still checking the most obvious places he could think of for Sven.

The snap of electronics sparking led him to Caroline Drier's office.

"Sven," he said even before he could see the shape behind her desk.

Sven's head popped up. "I'm working as quickly as I can. Got John's and Aaliyah's computers—"

"I got a call from the General Counsel." Barnaby didn't bother to let him finish. "Want to come?"

Sven hesitated, just for a second, then nodded. He looked at Caroline. "We'll be back."

"Should I do anything?" Caroline frowned.

"See if you can reach anyone." Sven pointed at the computer, already half stumbling toward the door. "It should be connected."

Barnaby didn't wait to see what Caroline did, already heading for the elevator to the garage.

The door to the room in the sunken hallway already sat open, as though waiting for Barnaby and Sven's approach. Fighting down any apprehension, Barnaby forced himself forward, pushing through the curtain without invitation.

Oz's chair faced the screens, the earlier scrolling seeming sporadic, pictures coming and going in flashes, a few screens going black entirely before they picked up another shaky feed. The chair turned, and Oz looked at Barnaby with a small smile. "Mr. Fitzwilliam, it seems you have broken all the sets."

Barnaby felt Sven stop next to him, but didn't bother to look. "That's what you wanted us to do, isn't it?"

"It's quite remarkable." Oz just continued to smile. "All of it."

"All of what?"

"You, Miss Eloise, Mr. Sven." Oz's eyes turned to Sven. "I don't believe anyone has thought to rewire the feeds before."

Sven visibly swallowed, but didn't answer.

"Can you shut them down now?" Barnaby asked, motioning to the feeds. "People are leaving like you wanted."

"I can certainly try." Oz turned back around, watching as more and more of the monitors sputtered. "We have never gotten this far before. The sets were always too strong. But now, they've been weakened enough that it has a high likelihood of success."

"Well?" Barnaby clenched his fists, nervous energy nearly driving him forward.

Oz picked up his tablet, turning back to Barnaby. "Would you care to do the honors?"

Barnaby's brow furrowed before he quickly recovered. "Me?"

"This has been as much your effort as anyone's." Oz stood, as short as ever, offering the tablet. "And, after how many years as I have spent down here, I'm not sure I could do it myself. All my feeds will be shattered as soon as that button is pressed."

Barnaby looked down, a little, unassuming green button visible on the tablet's screen. Innocent as it seemed, a knot still formed deep in Barnaby's stomach. He glanced next to him. "Sven's the tech guy."

Sven blinked and finally found his voice. "You want me to?"

Barnaby nodded, crossing his arms as the energy in the room grew to the point he nearly felt he would break.

Watching Barnaby for one more moment, Oz turned to Sven, offering him the tablet.

Hesitantly, Sven reached out and took it, looking at the lone button on screen. "You just want me to . . . press this?"

Oz nodded, sadness leeching into the man's expression though the smile never left its place.

A last look at the malfunctioning monitors, and Sven released a breath, finger coming down on the screen.

The screens all flicked to black at once, the low mechanical whirring in the room winding down to nothing.

Barnaby waited a moment, looking around. "Did it work?"

"We will have to see," Oz answered. "All of our Lost should be returning to our side of the Wall right about now if it did."

Not waiting for any more explanation, Barnaby turned on his heel, heading for his car.

The set jumped again, again, and again, so bad Eloise didn't even have enough time to place herself before the next set slid into the last one's place. People appeared and disappeared—young, old, dressed to suit a million different stories. Ones she couldn't even begin to imagine. Echo tried to yell something, disappeared, reappeared a hundred feet away, and then disappeared again.

Eloise crouched down, curling into herself as her mind felt as though it would split from the sight, from the growing cacophony of sets moving and bodies trying to speak, not managing before the next voice took its place. She shut her eyes, squeezed them tightly, and tried to breathe, everything growing louder, the ground shifting, coming back, and shifting again.

And then it was silent.

Eloise remained where she was, her heart pounding in her ears too loudly in the sudden quiet. Slowly, she forced her eyes open, lifting her head.

Entirely gray, what once must have been a beautiful garden surrounded her, perfectly trimmed hedges filled with blooming gray roses lining a gravel path. Pushing herself up from her crouch, she looked around, turning slowly. Echo, the nomads, all of the others who had been flickering by were missing; it seemed as though she were entirely alone.

"Hello?" she called, taking in the large gray manor house sitting off to one side of the garden. What looked to be woods stretched out beyond it.

No one answered. Nothing so much as moved.

"Hello?" she tried again, taking a few steps toward the house. She couldn't even hear those, the gravel staying in place as she moved, not crunching, not a single piece sliding.

She frowned, trying to ignore the feeling that something was terribly wrong this time, even as her throat threatened to close up. No eyes on her, no one looking to her for answers; yet the weight of the past week, month, however long it had been began to press down on her, threatening to break whatever remaining strength she'd been pretending to have. She attempted to swallow. It didn't help. But her options were to continue forward and see what was waiting for her this time, or collapse.

Forcing her legs to move, she headed for the manor house.

Chapter Twenty-Seven

POLICE HAD SHOWN UP TO CLOSE OFF THE STREET, government officials came and went, and what seemed to be every single person from every single sector dropped by to see the absurdity that had unfolded. Barnaby finally sat on the Wall, watching the last, lingering set-refugees move off with people willing to help get them a place to stay for the night. At least until the OAT and General Counsel and whoever else could deal with the unprecedented onslaught.

Behind him, the sets all sat gray, dead, a few already seeming to crumble as the link between them and the real world was severed. Barnaby took out his phone, checking the missed calls. Coworkers, friends, but no sign of Eloise. He looked back at the last of the crowd. Perhaps he had missed her in the first wave. With everything she had done, it would make sense that someone from the General Counsel would have picked her up.

Some unhelpful sense of intuition told him, however, they hadn't.

"There you are." Christophe moved forward, a rather sour-looking Catherine behind him. "Everyone's looking for you."

"Me?" Barnaby frowned.

"Your name got leaked in association with everything happening." Christophe looked around. "We drove by your place. There's press basically camping out on the lawn, waiting for an interview."

Barnaby's jaw locked. He nodded, and simply looked back out to the sets.

"Everything all right?" Christophe asked.

"You haven't seen her yet?" Catherine supplied, still seeming better at reading him than Barnaby would especially like.

Barnaby shook his head.

"You probably missed her in the crowd," Christophe said. "We were watching back home, and it looked like a madhouse down here earlier."

"Maybe," Barnaby said.

"You can always find another girlfriend, you know, if she doesn't show up," Catherine continued.

Barnaby sent her a dark look. "Thanks, Cat."

Her dark eyes scanned his face quickly, looking confused for just a second before she recovered.

Christophe spoke before she could. "They're getting a list together of everyone who's appeared. You can keep your eye on that for when they find her."

Barnaby nodded again, scanning the rest of the crowd for a second before he turned back to the sets once more.

"Barnaby?" Catherine asked.

He turned back to her, lifting an eyebrow.

She frowned, then finally asked, "Are you going to be all right?"

The genuine concern in her voice nearly threw him. He met her eyes for a moment, and then finally shook his head. "I'll be fine. I'm just going to walk a bit."

Not waiting for an answer, he moved away, following the Wall as best he could without running into the police—or worse, press—lingering here and there. The phone in Barnaby's pocket began to vibrate. He jumped, hand already half pulling it free before he paused. It could be her, but it was just as likely that someone camped out in front of his house had found the number. He checked the number on the screen, then frowned and answered.

"Hi, Barney," Alice's voice came over the line. "Looks like you've been having an exciting time of it."

Barnaby sighed, looking out at the dead sets. "Look, thanks for all your help, but I'm really not—"

"I just thought you might be interested in getting over here," she cut him off.

He hesitated. "Over where?"

"The OAT. Where else?"

Barnaby checked behind him. The others still around didn't seem to be paying him any attention. He turned away anyway, curling in slightly. "I thought you weren't there anymore?"

"They apparently didn't deactivate my key card." The mischievous smile made it through Alice's tone. "And really, with everything on the news? Like I wasn't going to check out what was happening."

Barnaby dropped his voice. "Something's happening there?"

"Oh yeah," she said, something beeping in the background. "Something's happening here."

Barnaby stared at the round platform, feeling the static charging the air. He had vague memories of the transport room, when he had stood on top of one of the little circles, waiting to be sent into his story. He remembered the pit he'd felt in his stomach, climbing up there. But even as intimidating as that moment had been, the platform hadn't looked like that. He remained just inside the door with Alice, staring at the blue light arcing around the edges, crackling and hissing around the platform in the center.

"The rest of them are dead," Alice supplied after a moment. "I checked. All connection was lost. Except for that one. It's trying to connect to a set."

"Why?"

"As far as I can tell, it thinks someone's still there."

Barnaby's gaze snapped to her. "Someone who didn't transport back?"

Alice shrugged. "Seems that way."

Barnaby looked back at the platform as another arc whipped through the air. It didn't mean anything. Alice could have misread something—she had lost her job, after all. Or, if someone was there, it didn't mean it was Eloise. But then, didn't it? She had been chosen. She'd been their leader. Assigned or not, she'd become a Main Character, perhaps *the* Main Character. Of course she would be the last one there when the stakes reached their climax. He looked at Alice. "Could you send me in?"

Alice raised an eyebrow.

He wasn't sure how to explain himself. He just looked back.

"Step on that platform, it could kill you." Alice finally motioned across the room. "And even if it didn't, the sets are dying. There's no saying we'd keep connection long enough for you to make it back."

He let her words turn over in his mind, let everything that had happened play back. He made up his mind. "But you can try?"

Alice crossed her arms. "If you're sure?"

He nodded.

She didn't question him again, moving to the control panels by one wall. "I'll see if I can get a recall button set up for you. If you're lucky—and I mean inexplicably, improbably lucky—the connection will hold, and it will let you jump back out when you press it."

Barnaby continued to nod, eyes going back to the platform.

"You might want to put on some rubber boots or something, Barney." She paused in her typing to look at him. "I don't think this is going to be pleasant."

Nobody. There was absolutely no one on the set as far as Eloise had found. And with bits of it starting to crumble away, turning into the odd, blank white space she had seen before Catherine had made her set, Eloise had to admit it. The sets were dead. Disconnected, and already decaying.

She took a deep breath to try to calm herself as she looked around. Thick, leather-bound volumes lined the shelves of the room she'd wandered into, the thick spines still somehow regal, even in grayscale. As suiting a place to end up as any, after everything.

Surrounded by books.

She moved to the shelves, pulling one of the volumes free. The title, *Moby-Dick; or, The Whale*, stared up at her, the silvery letters seeming to glint. She shook her head. She hadn't particularly enjoyed the book in school—even if the Teachers loved whatever essay she had done about it. Going to crack the spine, she froze. Something nearly seemed to explode, the charge shooting through the air too active to be just another part of the decay. She moved to the window, her brow furrowing at the blue electricity circling a new crater in the gravel path. Glancing at the white slowly encroaching where the gray set flaked off, she moved for the back door, not bothering to set down the novel. At least that lightning was something new.

The gravel remained still as she stepped on it. Nothing moved save a spark or two of the lightning as it died off. Approaching carefully, she waited until the electricity was nothing more than a heady buzz in the otherwise discomforting silence. Perhaps four feet deep, the crater looked like the ground had merely dented from whatever had hit it, the gravel path stretched oblong to fit the new space, each individual pebble exactly where it had been, matching the new shape. And in the center . . .

Eloise's eyes widened, her feet moving down the slope before she could reconsider it. "Barnaby?"

The man winced, his face slightly blackened, as though he had been a cartoon character in the midst of the lightning.

"Barnaby," Eloise repeated, dropping to her knees next to him.

He finally got his eyes open, glancing up before they settled on her face. "I don't remember transporting being that painful."

"What . . . ?" Eloise's mind reeled. "What are you doing here?"

He slowly pushed himself up to sitting, almost experimentally. "I came looking for you. A friend at the OAT said one of the transporters was still trying to connect to a set, so I figured that had to be you—"

Before she could think about it, she was swatting him with the book in her hands. "Are you crazy? What the hell were you thinking? You could have been killed."

"Hey." He caught the cover. "You'd rather be trapped here forever?"

"You couldn't have even known it was me here." She released a breath as the fresh wave of panic passed.

"You were placed in here for a reason." Barnaby held her eyes. "You were chosen to make this happen. If that doesn't make you the protagonist around here . . ."

She dropped her hands, leaving him holding the novel.

"Who else would be singled out at the end, if not you?" he finished.

Eloise just looked at him, everything that had been her life slowly trying to take structure in her mind. Joining the RO: inciting incident. Losing Columbine: catastrophe one. Dan's set shutting down: catastrophe two. She'd assumed some sort of lingering structure would run through everything on this side of the Wall, but if her entire life, all of it, fit as a plot . . . "Are you saying this is supposed to be the climax?"

"We're still trying to get you home, aren't we?" Barnaby placed the book beside them, going for something in his pocket.

Eloise swallowed, her eyes flicking up as the gray sky above them started to fade to white. Something silver came out of Barnaby's pocket, the glint catching the corner of her eye. "What's that?"

"Recall button." He turned it over, brushing some dirt off the top. "For the transporter."

She shook her head. "It's not going to work."

Barnaby frowned, clicking the center. No electricity. No spark. Nothing.

"If this is supposed to be a climax, we're not getting out of it by pressing a button." Eloise stood, pressing her hands to the sides of her head as she tried to think. "It's got to be bigger than that."

"Bigger how?" Barnaby pushed himself up after her.

"Something that's been built up. Something all of this connects to." She began to pace. "Something I've missed."

"Like what?"

"I don't know." She curled her hands into fists, then dropped them, trying to remember everything that had happened, everyone she talked to, anything seemingly insignificant that wouldn't be in-story. She looked out over the edge of the crater. The whiteness continued to creep ever farther, the woods at the end of the garden now entirely gone. Something clicked. She mumbled, "He reversed the traditional symbolism of pure white, making it something threatening, conveying both a lack of meaning and an excess of meaning."

"What?" Barnaby shook his head.

"*Moby-Dick*." She looked at him.

He continued to frown.

"The book I picked up from that house" —she pointed behind them, the building so far standing— "was *Moby-Dick*."

"Yeah, you couldn't have tried hitting me with something shorter?" He nudged the book by his feet.

"It was a library full of books," Eloise went on, ignoring the comment. "I was surrounded by them. I could have picked up anything. But it was *Moby-Dick*."

Barnaby looked at her, brow furrowed, still plainly confused.

"The great white whale." Eloise motioned widely to the encroaching whiteness around them.

Barnaby nodded slowly, obviously much less enthusiastic about Eloise's epiphany. "Doesn't . . . everyone die in that story?"

"No—well, yes." Eloise waved it away, returning to pacing as her mind worked everything together. "But that's not the point. The whiteness conveyed a lack of understanding. The entire book is about people not being able to see the truth of things filtered through their own perspectives. And it all becomes vaguely religious if you dissect the symbolism, man not being able to understand God, the futility of believing one can fight against that. I wrote a paper about it years ago."

Barnaby continued to watch her, frowning. "You need to give me more than that, El."

"But the authors *are* the gods in the sets." She glanced around. "Were, at least." The whiteness opening up when Catherine had begun writing, the manuscript half stuck to the vault with the black goo. Eloise glanced down and saw similar black flecks where Barnaby had brushed off the useless recall button. Connections to their world as much as the no-man's-land was a connection between the sets and the Wall. She turned for the slope back out of the crater. "Come on."

"Come where?" Barnaby asked, following all the same.

"We need to find some paper." She didn't bother with more, pulling herself up to the flat, unmoving gravel path and running back to the crumbling manor house.

With more and more of the white claiming bits of the set, Eloise had to find a new path back to the library, ducking through a dining room with a missing far wall and claustrophobic hallway. The library remained as it had been, the books lining the walls stoically, as if the world around them weren't dissolving to nothing. Eloise didn't take the time to examine them, going to the desk at the far corner.

"Eloise." Barnaby's heavy footsteps stopped in the doorway. "You've got to tell me what you're doing."

"Catherine could connect to the sets." Eloise continued to fumble, half the drawers were false fronts, others held nothing useful. "Her *writing* connected to the sets." A few crumpled sheets of paper sat toward the back corner of the next drawer. Eloise pulled them out, along with a fountain pen, trying to flatten the pages out as best as she could on the desk. "Give me the button."

Barnaby didn't argue. "You're going to . . . write us out?"

"I'm going to try." Eloise set the button at the top of the flattest sheet she could manage. "I'm a good analyst. Not writer."

If Barnaby had any more questions, he kept them to himself.

Eloise began to scribble some sort of narrative down, eyes glancing between the words and the recall button. It didn't have to be pretty. Catherine had created an entire new set out of the white on her end. Eloise just had to reestablish a connection, just for this, just long enough to get out.

The room grew lighter, the outside wall crumbling.

The button started glowing blue again. The connection took. Eloise's writing was barely legible as she scratched out the words. Still, a faint blue started around the edge of the little silver disk. She took some heart in that, continuing forward, as awkward as the writing felt.

"Eloise?" Barnaby asked.

She kept writing, shaking her head. "People will have to forgive me for just calling the damn thing a Portal Network." She set the pen down, only half the library left behind her. She reached out for Barnaby's hand. "Are we willing to try it?"

Barnaby stepped up behind her. "Don't think we have much to lose."

Sending a last glance at the gaining whiteness, Eloise took Barnaby's hand, bringing both of their palms down on the button. The world shifted. Blue lightning—like

Eloise had seen outside—surrounded them, shooting them through a tube. Eloise suddenly wished she had taken the time to write something gentler than what she first pictured as a teleporter. It was too late now. She just closed her eyes, praying to any and everything that this would work.

A final twist, and she came down hard, the wind knocking out of her as Barnaby's weight came up behind her. She forced an inhale, blinking as her eyes tried to adjust.

"Holy shit," a female voice sounded from somewhere behind them. "You actually made it back."

Eloise shifted, grimacing at the sticky black keeping the recall button glued to her palm. Disgusting or not, she had to take that as a good sign.

Barnaby moved off her. "Are you all right?"

"I'll survive." Eloise let him help her up, her eyes falling on the tall blonde woman standing at some kind of control panel in the square, beige room. Whether beige was a better or worse sign than gray, Eloise wasn't entirely sure.

The woman moved forward. "You must be Eloise."

Eloise nodded.

"Alice," Barnaby explained quickly. "My contact with the OAT."

Eloise stopped trying to peel the button free from her palm and looked at him. "We made it, then?"

"Seems that way?" Barnaby looked at Alice.

"Last I checked, I hadn't spun off into oblivion." Alice smiled brightly. "Good to see you back, Barney."

Eloise raised an eyebrow at Barnaby.

He shook his head—not explaining the nickname use, at least for the time being—before looking back at Alice. "Are the sets all closed now? Do you know?"

Alice moved back to her control panel, scanning it quickly. "Certainly looks that way."

Eloise opened her mouth to speak, but a vibrating sound cut her off.

Barnaby fished for his phone, frowning at it quickly before he answered. A moment later, he held it out to Eloise. "It's for you."

"For me?" She frowned.

He shrugged.

Bringing the phone cautiously up to her ear, Eloise asked, "Hello?"

"Miss Eloise," a man's voice came over the line. "So glad to have you back with us."

Eloise stiffened, looking at Barnaby and Alice questioningly before she said, "Who is this?"

"I go by Oz," he answered. "I'd explain it, but something tells me you wouldn't need me to."

Eloise started to respond, but ended up mute as she realized she had nothing to say.

"If you'd like to join us, I think there are some people here you might like to see."

"Wh—?"

"Mr. Fitzwilliam knows where," Oz answered before Eloise could get the rest of the sentence out. "See you in a few minutes."

The line went dead.

Slowly lowering the phone, Eloise looked at Barnaby, her eyebrows raised. "An Oz would like us to join him?"

Understanding came over Barnaby's face. "Of course."

"Was there *literally* a Man Behind the Curtain?" Eloise asked.

"You have no idea." Barnaby shook his head, looking out the door of the little beige room.

Chapter Twenty-Eight

NEARLY SUNSET AND THE ROADS WERE STILL PACKED. Eloise did her best to remain out of sight, letting Barnaby lead her to a back door of the grand General Counsel building. Entering the relative privacy of the marble hallways, she finally spoke. "Should I be worried?"

"They can't send you back into the sets again," Barnaby said, face a little hard. "So I'm not sure what else Oz could do to you."

Eloise clenched her fists, then relaxed them again, following down to a lower hallway. Familiar heads came into view as she reached the bottom. "Echo! Owen!"

The group turned—everyone from the original set. Eloise ran up to hug each of them in turn, trepidation lost for at least a moment.

Releasing Owen, she looked behind her, Barnaby standing a little ways off.

Owen smiled, offering his hand. "You must be Barnaby?"

"Owen, good to meet you in person." Barnaby smiled back before looking at the rest of the group. "All of you."

Eloise found herself smiling along. Even Hebe looked genuinely pleasant where she stood.

"Miss Eloise." A voice came from the doorway behind her.

She turned, looking at the little man standing there.

"Oz," Barnaby supplied, moving just behind her once again.

"You'll accept my apologies for dragging you straight down here after all you've been through." Oz stepped forward. "I just wanted to meet the woman who finally managed to break the sets. You were truly remarkable." He looked at the rest of the group. "All of you."

Eloise found herself at a loss for words; relief, anger, joy, all swirled in her enough to keep her mute.

"What happens now?" Hebe finally asked.

"What else?" Oz smiled. "We take stock of all we have and try to live our Happily Ever After."

Eloise didn't move. Barnaby's hand went to her lower back. The support was enough to snap her out of her daze. "You think we'll be able to live a Happily Ever After?"

"You all made it back in one piece." Oz looked around the group before settling on Eloise. "It seems a good starting place, at the very least."

Unsure what else she could say, Eloise just nodded.

"Thank you," Oz continued.

"For what?"

"For putting me out of a job. It's been a long time coming." Oz turned back into the room behind him, picking up a manila envelope. He held it out to her. "I hope you'll forgive my presumptiveness, but I've given out my other gifts. This one is for you."

Eloise frowned, taking the envelope.

"I am Oz, after all." He just smiled.

Pulling the papers free, Eloise looked at the first page. *Eloise Ashe* sat at the top.

"It seemed only fitting for you to get a full name," Oz said after a beat. "I believe that was your choice?"

Eloise nodded, eyes still on the page.

"You should all be very proud of yourselves." Oz pulled the door shut behind him, brushing his hands off on his pants. "Now, I believe everyone has been assigned their homes. I suggest we all find our various ways there and have a well deserved night off. I know that is what I intend for myself."

The group watched the little man go before looking between each other.

Eloise offered a weak smile. "It does sound like a good start to a happy ending."

Everyone seemed to agree. Pan and Echo linked arms. Hebe went so far as to give Eloise a brief almost-hug. "We'll meet up sometime, maybe."

"Get some coffee?" Eloise suggested.

"Maybe after I sleep for a month." Hebe shook her head, stepping back.

Owen took her place, bending once again to hug Eloise. "We'll definitely get together. I'll even drag Hebe along."

Eloise laughed lightly, pulling back to look at Owen's face. "I really couldn't have done it without you."

"I think you would have managed," he said. "I was just a helpful SC."

Squeezing his arm a final time, Eloise let Owen step back to where Hebe was waiting. Some more hugs, promises for coffee, and a slightly inappropriate comment from Savitr, and the hallway emptied, leaving just Barnaby and Eloise.

She turned, looking up at him. "Should I assume I'm still welcome at your home?"

After a moment, he leaned down to kiss her, speaking against her lips. "It wouldn't be a very happy ending if you weren't."

Eloise smiled, touching his face as everything settled in. She was back. This was real. Somehow, they both had made it. "Then, let's go home. You can fill me in on everything I missed."

"I'll do my very best." Barnaby slipped his arm around her waist, turning with her toward the staircase. And home.

About Jessica

Jessica Dall finished her first novel at age 15 and has been writing ever since. She is the author of such novels as *Grey Areas* and *The Bleeding Crowd*, the *Broken Line Series*, and a number of short stories which have appeared in both literary magazines and anthologies. When not writing, she works as a freelance editor and creative writing teacher in Washington, DC.